A Hunter for the Suspicious Cowboy

STAND-ALONE NOVEL

A Western Historical Romance Book

by

Sally M. Ross

Copyright© 2022 by Sally M. Ross

All Rights Reserved.

This book may not be reproduced or transmitted in any form without the written permission of the publisher.

In no way is it legal to reproduce, duplicate, or transmit any part of this document in either electronic means or in printed format. Recording of this publication is strictly prohibited and any storage of this document is not allowed unless with written permission from the publisher

Table of Contents

A Hunted Bride for the Suspicious Cowboy 1
    Table of Contents 3
    Letter from Sally M. Ross 5
Prologue 6
Chapter One 11
Chapter Two 20
Chapter Three 28
Chapter Four 35
Chapter Five 42
Chapter Six 49
Chapter Seven 56
Chapter Eight 62
Chapter Nine 69
Chapter Ten 76
Chapter Eleven 83
Chapter Twelve 90
Chapter Thirteen 97
Chapter Fourteen 104
Chapter Fifteen 111
Chapter Sixteen 118
Chapter Seventeen 125
Chapter Eighteen 132
Chapter Nineteen 139
Chapter Twenty 146

Chapter Twenty-One...154
Chapter Twenty-Two..162
Chapter Twenty-Three 171
Chapter Twenty-Four 179
Chapter Twenty-Five..188
Chapter Twenty-Six 196
Chapter Twenty-Seven 205
Chapter Twenty-Eight..215
Chapter Twenty-Nine 226
Chapter Thirty...233
Chapter Thirty-One 240
Chapter Thirty-Two 250
Chapter Thirty-Three...262
Chapter Thirty-Four 274
Epilogue 288
   Also by Sally M. Ross..292

Letter from Sally M. Ross

"There are two kinds of people in the world those with guns and those that dig."

This iconic sentence from the *"Good the Bad and the Ugly"* was meant to change my life once and for all. I chose to be the one to hold the gun and, in my case…the pen!

I started writing as soon as I learned the alphabet. At first, it was some little fairytales, but I knew that this undimmed passion was my life's purpose.

I share the same love with my husband for the classic western movies, and we moved together to Texas to leave the dream on our little farm with Daisy, our lovely lab.

I'm a literary junkie reading everything that comes into my hands, with a bit of weakness on heartwarming romances and poetry.

If you choose to follow me on this journey, I can guarantee you characters that you would love to befriend, romances that will make your heart beat faster, and wholesome, genuine stories that will make you dream again!

Until next time,

Sally M. Ross

Prologue

Windy Reach, AZ, 1880

Pauline trembled, her face as white as the sheet that covered her husband's body as they hefted it onto the wooden stretcher. The undertaker and his assistant carried the corpse past them to the wagon waiting outside. She leaned against her father, Frank Mack, for support. Pauline had run to him first when she'd found Herschel Hogan dead. Just as she had a dozen times prior that week, she had come home from the general store with all the fixings to make his dinner. Instead, she'd found him with a bullet hole in his chest.

Terrified, in shock, and not knowing what to do, Pauline had rushed to her father's townhouse. The rotund man standing across from them cleared his throat, breaking the silence. It was Sheriff Bert Morrison. Though Pauline didn't think he was much of one. He had a reputation around town for doing the bare minimum to keep his badge. Anyone who didn't want to make an earnest living was questionable in her book. Yet now her fate rested in his polished hands.

It was little after midday by the time the Sheriff had gotten there. They were standing in the foyer as the coroner finished up. The house wasn't very old, and the yellow paint still looked new. Outside she could already hear the locals talking amongst themselves, not loud enough to hear inside, but loud enough to know there was a crowd.

"So, tell me again what happened, young lady." His voice was deep and slow.

Bert was a large man, clean-shaven with short blonde hair. He was in his thirties and had been the Sheriff for more than ten years. Yet he still seemed lost about his duties.

"I just got home from the general store," Pauline stammered. "I... I walked in, and he was just lying there, blood everywhere."

Her voice was soft and unsteady. The shaking in her hands wouldn't stop. Pauline's face was red and puffy from the crying that would come without warning. She kept wringing the handkerchief in her hands and wiping her eyes. Her large eyes began to dart back and forth around the house as if she were looking for the person accountable for the murder.

"So why did you run to your father's home and not straight to me?" he demanded.

"I wasn't sure if there was anyone still here. I was scared! I just ran to the closest place I knew," she whispered.

When she'd arrived at her father's townhouse and explained to him what had happened, he'd immediately sent his farmhand to fetch the law. It was only then that he went with Pauline to check on her husband.

The lawman produced a notepad and pencil from his pocket. "Looks like there was a bit of a struggle. Does it look like anything is missing or not in the right place?"

Pauline looked around the house, struggling to remember every detail. Nothing was out of place. Even Herschel's oak desk was just as she had seen it earlier. He was a meticulous man in every way. The slightest speck of dust or canister set ajar would send her husband into an angry rage. She'd learned to keep things perfect for him. That along with the ability to hide a bruise with a bit of cooking fat and clay dust had set the tone for their marriage.

"I don't rightly know..." she muttered. "Well now, come to think of it, did the coroner find Herschel's pocket watch?"

"I'll have to check with them."

"He never goes anywhere without it," she said. "It was a family heirloom and should be in his vest pocket."

He adjusted his belt and looked hard at Pauline. She could feel his eyes burning through her. She knew that Bert was aware of how her husband treated her. Heck, the whole town did, but no one ever talked about it. No matter how much she tried to do for Herschel, he would come home drunk from the saloon and always get rough with her. Leaving bruises and scars that she would have to try and hide time and time again.

Shame crept over her at the elated sensation she felt knowing he'd never strike her again. Pauline never loved Herschel. It was only out of obedience to her father, who had arranged the marriage, that she'd agreed to wed. Yet she was a faithful wife; she could never kill anyone. The Sheriff looked around the small space. Pauline wondered if she should have offered him a beverage, but this was no social gathering. Their home was modest, yet the space felt cramped every time the Sheriff rocked back on his heels. The floorboards creaked beneath his weight, echoing off the bare walls. Herschel always hated artwork; he called it useless clutter.

"You want to know what I think?" the Sheriff sneered. His breath stank of tobacco each time he opened his mouth. "I think you need to give me more to go on. You're hiding something; I can feel it in my gut."

The statement took her by surprise and caused a rush of fear to overtake her. At the same time, she was angry that the so-called Sheriff thought she might be hiding something, or worse, that he thought she killed her husband.

Pauline glared at him. She had a feeling the only thing going through the Sheriff's gut was that morning's grits. Bert wasn't known for being a great Sheriff. Pauline couldn't remember a time when he had solved anything. Every time she went to town, Pauline heard the people talking and the rumors going around about how careless he was with any investigation that fell in his lap.

Pauline crossed her arms, hugging herself tightly. "I told you everything I know. I'm not hiding anything."

"Herschel was well-known and liked 'round here," the Sheriff threatened. "I wouldn't venture too far away from town. I have a feeling I'm going to have some more questions."

The duo watched Bert walk away before turning for her father's home. A former military man himself, he had remained mostly quiet during the gentle interrogation. He trusted the law, or at the very least hoped they would do a good job. Despite his silence, Pauline had known he would intervene if needed. It was simply his stoic nature to let things run their course. Herschel was a popular businessman. Everyone in the community had drunk or gambled with her husband at least once.

They walked the path through the field leading back to Frank's house. Tall grass swayed on either side of her. The scent of the fresh flowers filled the evening air. She couldn't help but notice how quiet her father was. Despite it being a hot and sunny day, there was a chill when she looked at him. There was worry behind his kind eyes.

"Did you kill him, Pauline?" he asked. "I wouldn't blame you if you did it."

Pauline skidded to a stop, her jaw dropping in complete shock. She couldn't believe that her father had just asked her the question. For years she had done everything possible to prove to him that she was a good person. Yet one lazy Sheriff had called into question his entire view of her. Instantly she was overcome with rage that gave way to a deep sadness.

9

"No, I did not kill him!" she snapped. "How dare you ask me a question like that!"

Pauline was horrified. The thought of her father doubting her brought tears to her eyes. She scowled at him even as her blue eyes started to moisten. She looked down at the healing bruises on her arms and spun away from him, anger evident with each step as they walked back to her father's house. The clear blue sky laid a foundation for the storm she knew was coming.

"Listen," he growled.

Pauline stopped and her father continued, "It's my fault you were married to that monster. I think we need to start talking about getting you out of town. Whether or not you did it, I've got a bad feeling."

"You think I did it, don't you?"

She knew he was only trying to protect her, but it still hurt that he could ask. He had talked to her about his regret for arranging her marriage before, but it had been too late. She had been trapped, married to a man she didn't love, a choice she made for another man she loved, her father.

Her father didn't reply. Instead, he started walking again. This time, it felt like he was leaving her behind as well.

Chapter One

Windy Reach, AZ, 1880

Pauline could count on one hand the number of close friends she had. Of those, Lucy Long was her nearest and dearest. It was the spunky young woman who came to check on her later that evening. She adored everything about Lucy, from the woman's feisty nature to her innate ability to cheer Pauline up even on the darkest of days. She kept her petticoats brightly colored and snug, just for the gentleman callers that tried to court her.

They sat on her father's porch together, talking about the day's events. It was nice to have a moment of normalcy as they watched the wagons and horses bustle by. Each new wheel and rider brought with it a flurry of dust clouds. She loved to daydream about where the riders might be coming from or going. How she longed to listen to their stories. Lucy cleared her throat, tugging Pauline's attention back to the conversation.

"How are you getting along?" Lucy asked.

She sighed. "Part of me is happy that he's gone. I never have to go through the pain of his touch again. I know what people must think. I'm just torn, confused, and at this point, probably looking at getting hung for murder. Lucy, I can't eat, I can't sleep, I just spend my time going back and forth between being pleased and bawling my eyes out. What am I going to do?"

"I wasn't planning on saying anything, but folks are talking," Lucy admitted, touching Pauline's hand to comfort her. "Everyone has heard about Herschel's murder. Even Betty Cartwright at the general store was talking about it."

Pauline's heart started to race; a rush of panic moved through her. She already knew people would be talking. Her palms began to sweat and tremble all over again. The fact that the townspeople might already think she was the killer created an aura of fear around her. She knew the consequences for murder, and she was not ready to die for something she didn't do.

"What does she think happened, Lucy?" Pauline asked.

Lucy leaned forward, her tone hushed. "Well, I overheard her talking to Norma. She was saying you probably did it. She told her that he probably came home drunk, and you shot him before he could smack you around again and of course, old Nosey Norma just fed right into it."

"If she's talking about it like that, then that means everyone is likely thinking the same thing," Pauline said.

Lucy put her hand on her friend's shoulder. Her voice was caring and friendly. "Not everyone, honey. I know you better than that. Things will all work out for the best in the end."

It was getting late. The evening sky was beginning to darken as the sun slowly settled across the horizon. Pauline loved watching the sunset, the official end of each day. The two young women talked until the sun was gone. They said their goodbyes and Lucy promised to come back the next day to check on her. Pauline stayed on the porch just long enough to watch her friend disappear into the night.

She walked into the house and right to her old bedroom. She hadn't slept there since the night of her wedding, but Papa kept it the same for her anyways. Her father was still working late in his study. They still hadn't spoken since he'd asked if she was a murderer. Pauline was angry with him, there was no denying that. She always did as he asked, constantly doing all she could to earn his approval. Since her mother had died shortly after Pauline's birth, her father was the only real family she had. The rift between them ached.

She quietly readied herself for bed before blowing out the candle and climbing between the sheets. The old room, with its white walls, creaked with every gust of wind. Despite how hard she tried, Pauline didn't sleep at all that night. She kept thinking about her husband's body. Her thoughts were interrupted by a knock on the bedroom door. She hadn't realized until then that it was morning.

"Honey, I just wanted to tell you I'm sorry," he said through the door. "I really don't believe you killed your husband. I just... I had to ask."

"I know you didn't, Daddy," she said. "I don't think I could handle it if you believed that."

Pauline could sense the sincerity of her father's voice, but there was something else there as well. She could tell that part of him was unsure, a man questioning a woman's word. The thought saddened her, but she tried to hide it from him, not wanting to add to his burden.

"Daddy, what's the matter?" she asked.

Her father opened the door and stepped inside. She could see the worry in his eyes. Pauline sat up and looked at her father with concern. He looked away from her, his brow creasing with regret.

"I never should have agreed to that marriage. I just thought he was a better man. He was such a good businessman, after all. I thought we would make good business partners," he said sadly.

"You can't blame yourself for this."

He sighed. "I'm so sorry for doing that to you."

"I understand," she promised. "I forgive you, Daddy. I only wanted to make you happy."

She rose from the bed and closed the distance between them. Without her wardrobe at his home, she had slept in her dress and petticoat all night. He wrapped her into his arms and held her tightly. Pauline fought back tears as she silently reminded herself to be strong, if not for herself, then for her father.

"I'll go make us some breakfast," he said.

He walked out of the room and into the kitchen, leaving her to ready herself for the day. Pauline made the bed and brushed her hair. She wasn't ready for what the day might bring, but no sense in dwelling on it now. She had things to keep her busy, as she walked out of the bedroom.

***

Pauline spent the morning busying herself with household chores that would normally fall to one of the maids. She didn't mind the work but found it was more lonely than usual. Her father still had work to do, and she was left to herself for most of the day. She washed laundry in an old barrel with a washboard and hung them out to dry in the warm air. At least a slight breeze made her feel some peace.

It wasn't long before she was humming a hymn, her heart light for the first time in years. She was happy to be able to help her father with the house; it made her feel useful and a little less guilty for all the trouble she'd caused. It brought back memories of her childhood. Her father always put his business first, but she knew he loved her.

The pair didn't see each other again until later that evening when they shared a hearty stew. As her father retired to his study for a cigar, Pauline worked on cleaning up the kitchen.

She saw Lucy dart past the window a split second before she rushed the back door, out of breath and obviously flustered.

"Heavens! What's wrong?" Pauline asked.

"I came over as soon as I could. Mama was taking care of the twins today; they've got a cough, so I filled in over at the Sheriff's office."

Pauline's stomach dropped. There was a look in Lucy's eyes that couldn't be ignored. A look of concern and fearfulness.

"There was a man that came in to talk to the Sheriff. He told Bert that he had come over to your house to talk business with Herschel and overheard the two of you arguing," Lucy said, still catching her breath. "He said that he heard you threaten to kill your husband!"

Pauline was horrified. She knew it wasn't true, but that wouldn't stop the Sheriff from arresting and hanging her for murder.

"Oh my God, Lucy! They're going to hang me for something I didn't do simply because some man says he heard something! Did you get a look at the man he was talking to?" Pauline asked.

"He had his back to me the whole time," she answered. "I tried to see his face, but he never even glanced at me."

"I just don't know what I'm going to do," Pauline said.

Lucy hugged her friend. "It's all going to be all right, sweetie. If you need anything, please let me know. I have to go check on Mama and see if the twins are feeling any better. I just wanted to let you know what I heard before I had to get home."

They quickly said their goodbyes and Pauline watched her leave before turning back to the counter. She leaned against it, her heart beating as a wave of panic set in. Behind her, she heard the wood creak and spun around to find her father watching her, a worried expression on his face. She could sympathize—she was worried too.

"What am I going to do, Daddy?"

Her father was silent for a moment. "If the Sheriff believes that man, there is no reason to think he will look any further. He'll come for you and then you'll be hanged. We have to get you out of here."

She looked at him sadly. "I don't have anywhere to go. We've been here my whole life."

"Well now, I do have a brother over in Dodge City. If we can get you to him, you would be safe," he said.

Her father pursed his lips. She could tell from the tension in his shoulders that he hated the idea of sending her away. The weight of the decision had aged him overnight. Pauline wondered if he had slept at all. She hated how much pain she was causing him. If he was thinking of reaching out to his brother, she knew the situation was life and death. She desperately wanted to stay busy, but the house was already well-tended. Instead, she ran her fingers along the dining room table, looking down at it while her thoughts raced. She couldn't meet her father's eyes.

"We haven't talked in years, but family is family. I know he'll take you in."

Pauline remembered him talking about her Uncle John before. She was young the sole time she'd met him. Yet she could still see a glimpse of his face in her memories. Pauline had a photographic memory. It helped when she would draw or paint. Suddenly, the thought of being alone frightened her.

She knew there was no other choice for her but to flee. Despite how desperately she wanted to believe that people were good, she knew the Sheriff wasn't going to look any further than he already had.

"How will I get there? Are you going to come with me?" she asked.

"Honey, I can't go with you. There's too much at stake. I have a lot to do around here," he said.

Worry took over her thoughts as she took in what her father had just said. Going to Dodge City and living with an uncle she hadn't seen since she was a child was overwhelming. The thought of being on her own with strangers scared her. Especially while being on the run for murder.

"How will I get there?" she asked.

"I have a friend who is a merchant. He's always taking livestock and caravans to Dodge City," he said. "It will cost a little bit, but he'll take you to Dodge City, he owes me a favor or two. I just saw him a couple days ago. He told me he was getting ready to head out on another trip. If we leave tonight, we should be able to catch him."

She could hardly believe it. She knew she had no choice but to leave and go to her uncle's house. The Sheriff already had his mind set on her being the killer. If she didn't go now, she'd be hung for sure. At least she would have a chance to prove her innocence if she were alive, even if it was on the run. Pauline swallowed, her throat dry, as if she could feel the noose already tightening around it. She tried to study her breath to keep from having another bout of panic. Her world had been completely turned upside down.

"I know I haven't always done right by you, but I am going to make sure you are safe," her father promised. "This guy is an old friend from the war."

"Okay," she whispered. "I trust you."

"Good, now go pack a few things in my saddlebags and I'll go load up the horse."

She went to her bedroom and packed some of the few things she still had there, along with some clothes that were her mother's and pictures of her parents. They were old and tattered, but she still wanted them as a keepsake. Grabbing her pad and pencils off the nightstand and putting them in the bag, she glanced once more around the room, not knowing if she'd ever see it again.

Her father was waiting for her at the door. He handed her a delicately made silk scarf. It looked too elegant for her dusty wardrobe.

"It was your mother's," he said. "I thought you should have it now. You can cover your face on the way out of town, best not to be seen leaving."

"Of course," she whispered, fighting back tears.

"It's not a long ride," he said. "The horse is ready and if we leave now, we can still catch Henry. We'll get you on your way and you'll be safe. Chin up, sweetheart."

They walked out of her childhood home for what she hoped would not be the last time. Her father hopped up on his faithful mount, Chestnut, with ease before pulling her up behind him. Pauline could see a rider approaching from the west when her father suddenly spurred the horse. The gelding lunged forward and nearly knocked Pauline off. Luckily, she was holding tight to her father's waist.

As they rode out of town, Pauline couldn't help but think that this could be the start of many 'last times.' The last time she got to ride with her father, the last view of town... everything brought her sorrow.

She had little faith in the Sheriff, but she still believed that somehow, she would prove her innocence. Pauline was scared but determined to not let this be the last of anything.

Chapter Two

Windy Reach, AZ, 1880

Dan York stood in front of his foreman, Bill, and eight farmhands who had worked for him over the last couple of years. Dan's shoulder-length hair hung below his hat. They had been working hard in preparation for Dan's departure. He was about to leave on his first cattle run in months. Dan wasn't a rich man. His parents had left the ranch to him when they passed, three days before his fifteenth birthday.

Like so many other ranches in the area, his was a single-story house, with a barn and a hundred acres of land. The ranch foreman had worked for his parents, and Dan kept him on when he took over. He trusted his foreman more than he trusted anyone else on the planet. It had been Bill who had shown Dan the ins and outs of making the ranch run smoothly.

"It's been a good day, boys," Dan said. "I think this place will be in good hands while I'm gone."

Dan knew he could be a charming man, and he knew how to talk to people. He could talk on the same level as anyone he met. He was well-educated, thanks to his parents making him go to school.

The sun had been beating down on them throughout the day. He could tell the men were tired. With their help and hard work, they were able to get everything ready for his departure. Still, he could sense a little dissension among the ranks. They couldn't fathom why a rancher would drive for another cowboy. Dan left on many cattle drives throughout the year, but this one was different. He would be gone longer than normal and not with his own men. This drive would take him to Dodge City, Kansas, far from his home and the memories that haunted him.

He was waiting for all his men to circle around him, and his mind wandered. Dan had been heading up cattle runs since he was eighteen years old. He had been married just a few short months when the ranch started to struggle financially. Times were hard. But they had their ranch and little family. One day while in town, he'd caught wind of a man needing help with a long drive. The man, Henry McCall, had instantly showed enthusiasm over Dan's request to join the next run. A week later, Dan had joined up for a few local runs. Martha had been supportive until the first long drive came about. Only then had his beloved shown trepidation.

Yet he'd pressed forward until after their son had been born. Only then, when the ranch was finally making a profit, did he hang up his whip and stay closer to home. He shuddered at the memory of his wife and son. He'd built a wall around his heart. Yet with each memory of their passing, his stomach would clench with consuming guilt. They were dead because of him. Every night he'd wash his hands at the well, trying to wash away the memory of his son's blood on them.

"I'd like to thank you all for the hard work you have put in. I know I wouldn't have gotten all this done without you," Dan said. "No way this ranch would run as well as it does, either."

"Come on now, you know you're just stalling! You sure you're not too old to be doing long-runs?" Bill chimed in jokingly.

Bill was a tall, skinny man. Dan had known him for most of his life. When his father died, he leaned on Bill more than anyone.

Dan chuckled. "I'll give up drives when you give up whisky."

Bill cringed. "Well then, guess you'll be driving till the good lord calls you home, son."

"Y'all have a good night and I'll see you in a few months," Dan replied with a grin.

He shook each of their hands, thanking them again for their hard work before heading into the house. As the farmhands went on their way down to the barn, Dan started thinking back to the days when his wife and son were alive. He could almost hear his son's infectious laughter and smell the fresh bread Martha would make and set on the window's ledge. His jaw clenched as he slammed his fist on the barren table.

A single moment, one last drive to help them get through the winter. That's all it was supposed to be. A simple job had transformed into the worst day of his life. One of the drives he went out on was a little longer thanks to some lousy weather. When he came back home, he found that bandits had come to the ranch and robbed him. He saw his front door open, and his barn doors were broken. Several of his horses were missing. He'd immediately run toward the house.

That day, just two years ago, he ran through the front door and found his wife and son murdered. Their lifeless bodies lying side by side. Pools of blood had already started to dry as he dropped to his knees and held them in his arms. Tears had covered his face as he screamed out in agony. Around the room were several knocked-over chairs and their belongings thrown all around. Years had passed yet the memory still haunted him. Despite the bandits being caught and hung, Dan couldn't let the guilt go. He refused to forgive himself for being gone and not being home to protect his family. The nightmares hadn't stopped. The images in his mind of their blood on his hands and their lifeless bodies had become still frames in the dark spaces of his thoughts.

If anything, they had gotten worse and were much more vivid than when they had started. The images in his head had become clearer and more frequent. It felt like the longer he was home, the more they would take root and fester; growing like cancer until it consumed him. Dan used the cattle runs as an escape from the pain. He loved herding the cattle from state to state. Usually moving west to east, they could turn a higher profit selling further east. The open range and the bustle of the cattle he herded made some of the memories fade away for a while. Out there, he felt free.

There was a short knock on the door, and it opened without invitation. Dan glared at Bill.

The old foreman stepped inside, slowly approaching him. Dan knew he was being cautious. He couldn't count the times he had snapped in front of Bill. Sometimes, his emotions could get the best of him.

"You're thinking about Martha and Johnny again, aren't you?"

"You've known me long enough to know the answer to that, Bill," he growled. "Being here with all those memories... knowing I'm to blame for them not being here anymore. It's just too much to take after a while."

"You can stop that thinking right now, young man. No one is to blame but those bandits and they hung for it," Bill snapped back. "Saying you're the one to blame is akin to saying you're to blame for a draught... It just ain't true, friend."

The men were still standing just a few feet apart. Bill pulled out a chew, while Dan started packing his bag. Dan wasn't upset that he was trying to get him to stay, but he knew he needed to get away.

"I'm still leaving for this cattle drive," he said. "I've already made a commitment to Henry. Besides that, I gotta get away from here... Just make sure the farmhands keep up with the cattle, I need them strong and healthy when I get back."

"Do what you have to do, Dan," Bill said. "I'll make sure to keep all the men on task. When you get back home, this place will be just the same, like you were never gone."

"It does make it a whole lot easier to leave knowing you're here to take care of the ranch, Bill," he said. "You've been a good foreman, but an even better friend. I know you will take care of the place."

Bill grinned. "This has become my home too, son. I'll look after it while you're gone; as if it were my own."

They shook hands and Bill headed back down to the barn. Dan worked his way through the house to make sure he had packed all the things he'd need. The house felt empty without his family. Gone were the flowers Martha would pick every week; the house no longer smelled like them. It baffled Dan that a home he had been born in, the home he had grown up in, the one he had shared with his beautiful family, could now bring him so much pain.

He'd given up trying to make improvements on the small homestead. The driving motivator behind it had been Martha. Without her there, the property felt more like a prison than a home. Had it not been for the men he employed, Dan probably would have burned the place down and never looked back.

Eventually, he made it to the kitchen where Chuck was finishing the last of the day's chores. Dan assumed the reason he was such a big man was the way he could cook. He glanced at Dan, a friendly smile forming.

"Just about ready to head out, boss?" Chuck asked. "You look like you're really looking forward to this drive. I'd say a bit more than usual."

Dan glared at him. "I'm heading out soon. Just double-checking to make sure I didn't forget anything. I left a credit at the general store for all the food you should need. The owner knows you will be taking care of the meals here while I'm away."

Chuck was a good cook; he had taken over all of the meals since Martha's death. On top of that, he had a knack for keeping things spotless. In fact, he had done all the cooking and cleaning since that terrible day. Dan knew eventually he would lose the old man, but he'd hang on to him as long as possible.

"All right, boss," Chuck said. "I'll take care of all the things I normally do. No need to be worrying about that. Be safe out there."

"It's never safe, Chuck. But I'll make sure to get back alive so that I can pay ya," Dan said with a chuckle.

Chuck returned to finishing his chores as Dan headed down to the stable to pack his horse and head out. The sun was beginning to settle across the plains. It left the sky a mix of orange and red. The slight breeze rustled the line of trees next to the fence. There was almost a small forest on the property, and the flatland was green with new grass. The way the sun hit the grass made it look like a field of emeralds. The base of the hills, off in the distance, marked the end of his property. All the beauty that the ranch offered went unnoticed as Dan walked. His thoughts stuck on the memories of his family and the pain of his loss. He knew he

25

had to hang on just a little bit longer to the pain of being at home on the ranch with all those memories.

"Jesse!" he called out before giving a high whistle.

Jesse was his trusted steed and an old friend. Dan had taken him on every drive since he turned eighteen. The gelding's calm nature was only matched by his powerful size and loyalty. He was a majestic creature. Measuring at nearly seventeen hands, his bloodline could be traced for generations. The animal had been a gift from his father's brother when Dan took over ownership of the ranch. Since then, they had worked as a team flawlessly. The horse trotted to where Dan waited at the gate.

"There ya go, boy," Dan whispered. "Good boy."

Dan reached out and stroked his horse, calming Jesse's excitement and reassuring the majestic creature that he wasn't leaving him behind. Dan placed his saddle blanket saddle on the horses back before strapping on the bridle. He loaded Jesse up with all the gear for the ride ahead. Along with his own gear, he had to be sure to pack for his horse as well. He always brought with him a currycomb, a picket pin for staking out the horse, and some rations for the trip. He reached into his bag and pulled out a carrot for his best friend. Jesse knickered as he took the carrot from his owner's hand.

Placing one foot in the stirrup and his hand on the horn, Dan pulled himself onto Jesse's back. He rode him every day around the ranch and into town, but it always felt different when he was going on a long cattle drive. Dan was very skilled with horses; Bill showed him the ropes and trained him well over the years. He had a passion for riding and a craft for driving cattle.

They walked down the driveway leading from the ranch to the road. With every step, Dan's mind seemed a little more at ease. The weight of Martha and Johnny's deaths almost felt lighter. Dan would never be able to outrun the ghosts of his past but heading out on those cattle drives made it feel like one day he could. For now though, this was as close as he could get. There was no dream of the future. Just a lingering sense of self-doubt and hate.

As he rode off into the sunset, to a cattle drive that would free his soul, the freedom was already taking root in his spirit, and he was finally able to glance up to the sky. For the first time in months, he noticed how beautiful the sky looked in front of him. The dust kicking up from Jesse's hooves, he could feel fresh air forcing its way through his nose. The house he had lived in for his entire life now behind him, he felt more at home on the range. The emptiness of the house after they died was just too much to handle.

Chapter Three

Dan rode up to the meeting place early the next morning. The sun was rising, and the sky was clear. They'd only be at the meeting spot for a short time before hitting the open trail, but it was a beautiful location, and they had a perfect view of the sun rising. The vibrant colors of the fields and the crystal-clear creeks that ran through the area truly were an unbelievable sight.

He was mesmerized by the beauty the place always seemed to offer him. His worries now left behind, the excitement of the cattle drive began to take hold of him. It had been several months since he had seen his old pal Henry McCall, but he recognized him immediately about halfway through the camp.

He brought Jesse to a halt and hopped down from his saddle. After tying Jesse off to a nearby tree, Dan took off to greet his friend. The little bit of pep in his step was considerably noticeable. Dan couldn't help it; his happiness to be free from the confines of his home lifted a huge weight off his shoulders.

The camp was laid out with several tents, and Dan could smell the aroma of breakfast in the air. The mixture of dried beans, flour, ground corn, and lard was an unmistakable smell. Blending in with the smell of breakfast was also the smell of coffee beans being brewed over the fires nearby. Dan had missed all those smells—there was something about meals cooked over an open fire and fulfilling the natural desire to simply ride and drive all day. He missed the hard work and the friends he had grown to trust on the trail.

Henry was only seven years older than Dan. Yet the cattle drives made him seem older, maybe even wiser for his age. Dan took to Henry from the moment they'd met, and they had been friends ever since. He even took Dan under his wing, showed him how to drive cattle, and all about the trails along the way. He didn't always talk to Henry like he would with Bill, but Dan knew he would be there if he needed him.

Henry was deep in a conversation with his wife, Dorothy, when Dan arrived and hadn't noticed him sneak up. Dorothy looked behind Henry's shoulder and her eyes lit up. She smiled at Dan, and he felt instantly warm and happy that he had come. Her smile grew bigger as Dan approached and she reached out with both arms to give him a hug. At the same time, Henry turned around and saw him as well. A big tobacco pouch in his mouth didn't keep him from grinning ear to ear.

"Oh, my word," Dorothy said. "It is so good to see you! How are you doing, honey?"

Her voice was cheerful and soft. She hugged him tight, truly happy to see him. She was taller than most women, with long brown hair she hid in her bandana. Aside from Bill, Dorothy and Henry were the only other friends he had. They were practically family with as much time as they spent together on these drives. It always made him happy to be around the people he considered family, especially since the death of his beloved wife and son. He couldn't hide his happiness and smiled, hugging her back.

"I'm doing okay, Dorothy," he said. "I'm happy to be on the range with you guys again."

"Hot damn, boy! Glad to have you here again," Henry exclaimed.

Henry reached out his hand to him after they finished their hug. Dan reached out and shook his hand. He half-embraced him, surprising himself with this uncharacteristic showing of emotion. He couldn't help himself, though.

"I already feel better myself," he said. "I've been anxious to get back out."

The freedom of the trail had already started to ease his mind with the open fields and fresh crops. The challenging road ahead always kept him busy. He didn't have time to think about the past because there would always be something to do. Rounding up the herd of cattle was always an exciting challenge. There would always be a stray or two that didn't want to cooperate. Dan smiled at the thought. Chasing them down and turning them in the right direction was always his favorite part.

"You know you're welcome to come with us any time," Henry said, still smiling. "You're the best man I got out here."

Dan wasn't surprised by his friend's comment, but he was shy about his skill as a driver. He was one of the best herders around and everyone knew it.

"Aw, Henry," Dorothy said giggling. "You're embarrassing him. His cheeks are all red."

"I'm just teasing him, Dorothy. He knows I need him on the drive. Wouldn't be the same without him," he said in a playful tone.

Because of his past, Dan didn't really think that highly of himself. So anytime someone gave him a compliment, he wasn't sure how to react. They thought the world of him, and he thought the world of them. He just didn't believe he deserved their praise.

Dan remembered that Jesse was still loaded down after the long ride. "I need to get back to Jesse. I will catch up with you guys in a little bit, once I get him settled in."

"All right, dear," Dorothy said. "We can catch up on everything you've been doing after dinner tonight."

Dorothy always accompanied her husband on the drives. She helped in any way she could. She also took on the cooking responsibilities; she had always enjoyed preparing meals for everyone.

"Sounds good, Dorothy.'

"Meet me over by the main tent when you're settled," Henry called as Dan walked away.

"Will do, friend."

***

Dan had just finished unpacking Jesse and was feeding him carrots when he saw a rider come upon the camp. He didn't recognize them, which seemed strange since he thought he knew everyone who worked for Henry. As the rider approached the camp, Dan suddenly saw another figure on the back of the man's horse. He realized immediately that the figure was of a woman. She had her face covered with a scarf and the only thing Dan could see was her eyes.

Suddenly Dan's heart skipped a beat, and a near panic swooped over him. The woman's eyes looked so much like that of his wife's. The way they had rushed into camp, he couldn't help but wonder what they were running from. He wanted to know why they were here and planned on asking Henry.

He finished settling Jesse in and went to find his friend at the main tent. As he approached, he noticed Dorothy off to the side, speaking with the woman who had ridden up with the man. The older gentleman was nowhere to be seen. Dan saw Henry alone at the front of the tent and stormed over to him.

"Who was that rider, Henry?"

"Oh, the man is my old friend from the war. Frank Mack and his daughter, Pauline," Henry responded. "I owe him a favor for saving my life in the war. His daughter is trying to get to Dodge City to live with her uncle and I told him that she could accompany us."

"I don't know if that's a good idea, Henry," he said. "The way they rode in and how she had her face covered tells me they're hiding something or running from someone."

"I already gave him my word I would get her there safely. He's a good friend, Dan," Henry argued. "Plus, he already paid her way and left to go back home."

Dan didn't like the idea one bit. He knew there was more to the story. There was just no way a man would send his daughter along with a team of drivers by herself. The fact that her eyes reminded him so much of his wife's was almost too much to bear. He was trying to outrun Martha's memory, along with the memory of his sons. He didn't want a constant reminder while on the trail. Although, his initial thoughts were not those of her eyes. He could see that she was a beautiful woman, and she feared something. But he knew Henry was right—it wasn't his choice.

For a moment or two, Dan thought about heading back home, but he looked over and saw the herd out in the field. They were being watched over by another cowboy, and he couldn't help but feel like that was where he was meant to be.

"You're right as usual, Henry. But I still don't like it and I imagine there's more going on than you're letting on," he grumbled.

"That's fair enough," Henry said. "I reckoned you'd turn back around, and I didn't know what I was going to do."

"Not gonna lie, I thought about it," Dan said. "I know you need the help, and you know I need the escape. I'll stick it out, but I don't trust her."

"Thank you, Dan. I know you're not happy about this and I'll make it up to you. For now, though, we need to get the cattle rounded up and ready to go. We're leaving right after the men pack up camp."

Dan walked away to group up with the other drivers. He was ready to work and let that take over his thoughts instead of the ghosts of his past. He still couldn't help but wonder what Pauline was running from. Something was going on there. Dan didn't trust people to begin with. The way Martha and Johnny had been senselessly murdered left Dan questioning everyone's motives.

Ross Owens was the youngest cattle driver on the team. Dan had worked with him only a couple of times. He was young and outgoing. Ross was about twenty years old and slightly shorter than Dan, though he looked a lot thinner. As funny as he could be, Dan knew he was hardworking. He'd seen Ross in action and was a quick study. The only real problem Dan ever had with him was that he could be somewhat of a blabbermouth. Dan knew if he wanted to keep anything a secret, Ross would be the last person to tell.

Dan walked up to the group just in time to hear Ross telling a joke.

"So, I tell my ma that I got two holes in my trousers. She looks at me all worried and says she can sew them if I want her to. I tell her 'Nah, Ma, that's where I put my feet through!'"

A couple of the men in the group chuckled while a few of them shook their heads and walked away. Dan approached the young man and greeted him with a handshake.

"I guess not everybody appreciates a good clean joke these days," Dan chuckled. "You ready to get to work?"

"Heck yeah, I've been looking forward to this drive," Ross said. "Glad to have you with us again, Dan."

Ross had a squeaky voice and the excitement of a child. He wasn't the smartest guy on the trail, but he was funny enough and gave Dan someone to hand down his knowledge to.

"Well, I'm just happy to be on the trail again." Dan smiled. "Henry wants us to round the herd up and get ready to head out. I'm gonna get Jesse. See you out there."

Ross grinned as Dan walked away. "Last one out there rides drag!" he hollered.

Dan just shook his head and kept walking to Jesse. He smiled a bit to himself. He knew Ross was stuck as the drag rider. Ross was the youngest and newest to the team and that position was saved for the green cowboys. The drag rider rode behind the herd to push the slower animals moving forward. There'd be a lot of dust and exhausting work.

After mounting Jesse, Dan rode out to the field. A beautiful warm morning and blue skies as far as he could see. The freedom of the wide open was exciting to him. Suddenly his mind jerked to the woman's—Pauline's—eyes. Worry rushed over him. Dan had seen a look in those big sad eyes. There was hurt in them; she was hiding something too. Dan was determined to find out what.

Chapter Four

Concho, AZ, 1890

Pauline and her father reached the camp early in the morning. She could see the fires ahead and spotted the main tent along with a few smaller ones. There was a group of men off to one side. When she looked off to her right, her eyes made contact with a man unloading his horse. He was a tall, handsome man with a lightly-colored, well-kept beard. At first, his eyes seemed soft and kind. In an instant it was gone, replaced by what looked like sadness. For a moment, she wondered if he had recognized her.

She quickly pushed the thought from her mind. Her face was still covered with her mother's scarf. Pauline was certain she had never seen the man before. She was concerned about joining the group. She didn't know any of these people. Pauline still wasn't thrilled with the idea of being around strangers, but she knew she had no choice. The town was against her, and the Sheriff would be coming for her. No way she could go back now. Her thoughts were interrupted by her father's horse coming to a stop.

"Come on now," her father said as he helped her down off the horse.

"Thanks, Daddy."

The man and woman approaching them did have a kind look about them. They had a peaceful presence. Suddenly, she felt a little better about the prospect of riding along with them. The two men shook hands.

"Hey there, Henry," her father said. "This is my daughter, Pauline. Pauline, this is Henry and his wife. Sure glad I caught you here still."

"Hey Frank, it's good to see ya. What brings you out?" Henry asked.

Her daddy took his hat off. "Henry, Pauline's in some trouble and I need to call in that favor. I'll still pay you, but it's a bit of a big favor."

After a few minutes, her father had explained the situation and why she needed to get to Dodge City. While they discussed the schematics of getting Pauline there, Dorothy pulled her to the side of the tent and properly introduced herself.

"My name is Dorothy, honey. I do the cooking and help where I can. I've met your father a couple of times. Pauline, you have nothing to worry about here with us."

"I'm just worried; I'm not very good with strangers," Pauline said nervously.

"Well girl, we ain't strangers anymore," she interjected. "You just keep with me and help with what you can. Everything will be okay. We'll get you to Dodge City."

The smallest hint of a smile came out as Pauline thought about that. Learning now that her initial thought of this couple was accurate, they were great people. A feeling of being safe washed over her. She could sense that Dorothy meant what she said and that they were friends now. That was how it seemed to work out here on the trails. Daddy knew lots of people he met on the trails when he was gone for business. Anytime he had spoken of meeting new people, it always seemed like he talked as if he'd known them forever. Feeling safe didn't make her worry less, but it was a start.

By then, the smell of coffee and breakfast was lingering. The rays from the sun layered out a ripple effect of colors in the sky. Pauline was mesmerized by its beauty. Her artistic mind began to wander with the endless possibilities of drawing on the way. Just then her father interrupted her daydreaming.

"It's all been taken care of. You'll be safe with them, and they will get you to your uncle," he said. "I have to get back to the house."

"Daddy, I'm still scared. I'm going to miss you," she sobbed.

He wrapped Pauline in his arms. "It's all going to be all right. You'll see me when this is over. It will all work out, sweetheart."

He hugged her tightly. Pauline couldn't help but cry. She'd never been very far from her father. The thought of never seeing him again filled her with fear. He calmed her with the hug, and they said their goodbyes. Her father hopped on his horse and rode off back to his home, leaving her standing there next to Dorothy.

"Come on, honey," Dorothy said.

She put her arm around Pauline's waist and led her back to the tent. "Help me get the wagon loaded, we'll be leaving shortly."

Pauline helped pack up camp and load the wagon. When they had finished up, they all headed out toward the herd. Pauline had never ridden a horse on her own, so she got to ride along with Dorothy in the wagon. It was a bumpy ride, but the view was spectacular, and she'd get lost watching the cowboys tend to the herd and push them one way or another. She caught herself wondering about the man she had seen when they first rode into the meeting place.

Several times throughout the morning their eyes had met. He would be glaring at her. It wasn't for fear of the man; she had only worried about being recognized. She'd catch herself and look away. For a man with such soft eyes, he gave a harsh judgmental stare. Pauline felt herself sinking in the seat of the wagon, wishing to make herself disappear altogether.

"Who's the man with long hair and the beard?" Pauline asked. "He looks like he has a story to tell."

"That man right there is named Dan. We've known him for several years now," Dorothy said. "He's a good man, but he's been through a lot. His wife and son were murdered a few years back, he just hasn't recovered. He comes on the drives as an escape. I suppose he's still running from his ghosts."

"That's an awful thing to have to go through," she mused, her heart heavy with sadness.

As Dorothy told her the story of what happened to Dan, Pauline was taken aback. She understood the pain. Pauline remembered seeing the suffering in his eyes. Still, it made no sense why he was constantly glaring at her. Maybe he suspected something, though she'd come to be unsure of everyone's motives since the murder charges. The way Dorothy described him, it made sense for him to be leery of new people.

For the rest of the morning, the two talked, with Dorothy explaining the ins and outs of life on the trail. She explained the process of how she liked to prepare meals. The woman was a wealth of knowledge and even told Pauline a little bit about the other men on the drive. There was plenty to still learn but having a teacher like Dorothy was already a godsend.

From bad weather to wild animals, the cowboys would always be on alert. The wagon would always ride ahead of the herd and cowboys so they could stop and begin preparing meals before the drivers got there. That way they wouldn't lose as much time throughout each day. They came to a stop around midday for lunch. They didn't unpack everything, just the main tent and some cooking supplies. Dorothy oversaw breakfast, lunch, and dinner. That day's lunch was salt pork, bacon, potatoes, and biscuits. The drivers needed to stay fed and hydrated to work these long days.

The tree line they stopped near offered an open field on one side and a wooded area behind it. It also gave them cool shade for the cowboys to sit and eat. Pauline helped finish preparing lunch, but with the last two days' events, she was unable to bring herself to eat. She just didn't have an appetite.

"You gonna eat, Pauline?" Dorothy asked.

"Not right now. I'm just not hungry," Pauline answered.

"I understand that, honey. I see Dan hasn't gotten himself a plate yet. I was going to do it myself, but why don't you go ahead and prepare his plate and take it over to him? I'll start cleaning up," Dorothy said as she smiled.

"Yes ma'am," she said. "If it will make it easier on you."

Pauline was already starting to like Dorothy. She seemed almost motherly over Dan and although she never knew her mother, thought Dorothy could easily fit the role. She hurried over and got a plate and filled it with food. She walked over to where Dan was sitting and handed him his plate.

She had seen him notice her as she walked up, but when he grabbed the plate from her hands, he never even looked at her. He didn't even said thank you. Pauline felt the coldness in his attitude toward her. She was confused by the way he acted and wasn't sure what to think. Dorothy talked about how nice of a man he was, but his actions were totally opposite. Not knowing how to react, she walked back to Dorothy and helped finish cleaning up. She tried to push the emotions to the back of her mind and started asking Dorothy about the trail.

"How far and how long will it take to get to Dodge City?" she asked.

"Well dear, we left from Concho and it's just over two hundred and twenty-two miles to Dodge City," Dorothy stated. "Aside from bad weather we can make it twenty-five miles a day, so it shouldn't take more than nine days. Ten at the most if we get a day of bad weather."

"That's not as bad as I thought it would be. I guess I figured it would take longer. I've never been very far from Windy Reach before," Pauline stammered.

They continued to load the wagon as the cowboys prepped the cattle to hit the trail again.

"Don't worry, sweetheart," Dorothy insisted. "We'll follow them up the trail and get a bit ahead of them before we stop for the night and cook dinner. I believe your father said you were something of an artist?"

Pauline blushed a little. She didn't think her drawings were that good and couldn't believe that her daddy had bragged about them. She was, however, comfortable enough with Dorothy that she showed her some of her sketches while they traveled in the wagon.

"Those are gorgeous, honey. Your father was right for sure. You are talented," she exclaimed.

"Thank you, Dorothy," she chuckled. "I don't think they are that good. I'm glad you like them, though."

"If I had a talent like that, I'd be going places." She grinned.

The sky around them was still clear and the sun beating down on them, a calmness in the air. The birds chirped in the trees and the grass over the fields swayed slightly in the breeze. It was an all-around gorgeous day.

Around that time, Pauline looked over into the field and saw Dan. He rode tall on his horse. She could tell by the way he rode and how he could turn on his horse that he was a well-seasoned cattle driver. He looked up and caught her staring. As soon as their eyes met, Pauline turned away. She still couldn't bring herself to look the man in the eyes. Something about him was just off-putting. She didn't know why, but Dan did not like her.

Her mind slipped away. She began worrying about putting her new friends in danger. She knew the Sheriff would come looking for her, or some sort of law. She couldn't help but think that someone, even within this seemingly friendly group, would find out about her being on the run and somehow turn her in. The fear consumed her. She sat quietly for a while. The panic had taken root deep in her soul.

For no reason that she could recall, she looked up and caught Dan riding off after a stray. She wasn't sure she could trust that one. He looked over at Pauline and she instantly dropped her eyes to her feet. She felt like a fool having been caught staring again. They rode on through the afternoon, the open fields and trees all looking like the others. They blended so magically that it seemed as if the scene went on forever. She thought again of the beauty on this trail. She began to sketch to distract herself, while they continued their journey, determined to distract herself from the panic constantly threatening to drown her.

Chapter Five

Western Cattle Route, 1890

After the first day on the trail, they settled in for dinner. Each unpacking their tents, setting up mini camps within the main camp. Dan was exhausted. He was somewhat used to being on the trail, but after a few months of only being around the ranch, he hadn't ridden as much as he did on the drive. He watched the other men set their tents up and every now and then, would look over to see what Pauline was doing. He'd heard her name several times throughout the day. No details had been mentioned, only Ross and some of the other cowboys discussing how nice it was to be in the company of a beautiful woman. Henry had reminded him not to worry about her and focus on the job. He fed Jesse and gave him some water. He'd had a long day too. There was a lot to say about a man who could stay with the herd during a drive. More could be said about a good horse doing it, though, and Jesse was a good horse. He had never let Dan down.

Dan unpacked his tent and laid out on the ground while he waited for dinner to finish. He watched the other cowboys unpack. The rush to get relaxed after a long day was evident in them all, and the morale of the group was good. High spirits and laughter could be heard around the camp. The clear sky was slowly starting to darken, and the cool breeze was relaxing to the men. Dan didn't interact much with the other cowboys in the group; he liked to keep to himself. But that couldn't be said of the other men. They all seemed to be enjoying each other's company and would gather around the fire, singing songs and telling stories. Dan watched as the cowboys started to unwind. It was always a fun sight.

Dan trailed off in his thoughts to Pauline. He couldn't help but think about the woman's eyes. He had seen her many times throughout the day, caught her glancing or staring at him on a couple occasions. Her eyes would captivate him. He would get lost in those eyes at first glance. Then, all the memories of Martha would flood his heart. The exact thing he was trying to run from. It still upset him to think about the danger a woman like that could bring on the trail.

"Dinner's ready, boys!" Dorothy hollered out. "Come and get it."

Her voice snapped him back to reality and he slowly stood up and walked over to the fire to join everybody else. Gathering around the fire was the only time he felt comfortable around so many people. He felt better with his horse and the cattle than he did with people.

"It smells great, Miss Dorothy," Ross chuckled.

He wasn't the only one who loved Miss Dorothy's cooking. When she started coming along with Henry on the drives, it was almost life-altering. Now, the food itself wasn't any different than the food he'd had on any other drives, but something about the way she prepared it made it one of a kind. That night she had made her normal dried meat and beans, with a side of dried fruit. But she also made her special 'pan de campo.' It sounded fancy, but there wasn't much to it. Dorothy just had a secret way of making it that put it way above anyone else's he had tried. She would prepare it only a couple of times on the trail, but it was a treat every time.

"Everybody knows you will eat anything, Ross," she laughed. She had a soft laugh that reminded him of his mother's.

Dan watched the interaction in amusement. He enjoyed almost everything about being on the cattle drives. He grabbed his plate and sat down next to the fire. He thought back to one of the first times he had met Ross. They were getting dinner when Dorothy had been called away for something in town and had accidentally overcooked the food. She had apologized over and over, and he could tell she had felt horrible. Most of them had just slow-picked the better parts of the meal and didn't eat much. Not Ross—he finished his plate and had gotten more. Later that night Dan asked him if he really liked it. He had told him no, and that he'd only done it to make Dorothy feel better. It had worked, and he had gained Dan's respect from then on.

Everyone had circled around, either eating or enjoying conversation. He kept catching glimpses of Pauline here and there. He caught himself watching her many times. Suddenly, Ross plopped down next to him. He had a big grin on his face, but an even bigger plate of food.

"Nice to see you haven't lost your appetite. Did you save anything for anyone else?" Dan joked.

"It's good to see you smiling, friend. Looks like you're having as much fun as me for once," Ross blurted. "I may have left a few crumbs for the birds."

"Better than nothing," Dan chuckled.

He hadn't realized that his mood had been much lighter than all the other times he had been on the trails since his wife and son died. Something on this trail was almost making him feel normal. He was almost enjoying himself—something he hadn't done in a long time.

"I like it out here. The hard work and all the beauty the trail offers. Nowhere else I'd rather be right now," Dan said, smiling.

He loved being on the trail. The smells and sounds. Even the storms had a certain beauty to them. It was always nice to be around Henry and Dorothy. Especially with her cooking.

"The beauty and hard work I can handle," Ross said. "It's the long days and short rest that wears me down."

Ross was a bit of a goof-off, but he'd done a fine job so far. There was no harm in giving the younger man a pat on the back.

"You do a fine job of keeping up," he assured. "Just rest when you can and make sure to drink that water."

Some of the other cowboys had finished their dinner already and were laughing loudly at something. One of them pulled out their guitar and started playing and music filled the camp. Dan glanced around and noticed Pauline sitting with Henry and Dorothy, giggling and smiling. Her long hair was caramel in color and those soft doe eyes captivated him again. He was momentarily lost in them. She looked over at him and as soon as their eyes met, she looked away. Dan felt foolish.

He didn't mean to be so judgmental. He'd only started judging people that harshly after the murders. He didn't know how to trust people. Besides the people he already knew, it was almost impossible to get close to him. He had just given up on people, keeping to himself and judging from a distance.

Ross' voice pulled him out of his thoughts. "Pauline sure is nice to look at, ain't she? That pretty smile and those big, beautiful eyes. It's great to have a woman out here with us. Something to take our minds off the long days. You gonna go over and talk to her?"

He didn't respond to Ross. He did, however, become angry with himself. Even after promising himself that he wouldn't, he was staring at her again. The problem this time was that he had been caught doing it. Ross didn't know any better. He didn't know the whole story of what Dan had been through. It wasn't his fault. Dan was just angry with himself.

"I heard a rumor earlier that she killed someone and that's why she's trying to get to Dodge City. Just a few of the guys talking. Hard to tell if it's true or not, you just never know with these cowboys. If it is true, that makes her pretty *and* dangerous. That's a bonus in my book," Ross quipped.

Suddenly, Dan didn't feel like eating, his appetite completely gone. He stood up and tossed his food in the fire, then stormed away from the group and walked toward the herd. He decided it was better to check on the cattle than to sit there being flooded with memories caused by those eyes. He was trying to run from those memories. Her presence there consistently triggered him and the ghosts he couldn't outrun. The fact that she was so attractive just aggravated him more.

The night was calm, and the cattle had settled in for the night. It was quiet aside from the crickets chirping and the rustle of branches from the breeze. He was enjoying the quiet and peacefulness he had found out by the herd, lost in thought when a tree branch snapped behind him. The noise caused him to jump, and he spun around to find Henry walking up on him.

"Damn, Henry. You scared my feet right out of my boots. What are you doing out here?" Dan exclaimed.

"I didn't mean to startle you; I was just coming to check the cattle and make sure you were all right. I saw you storm off from the camp. You doing okay, friend?"

"I want to know why Pauline is here. What's she running from, Henry?" Dan replied.

"Dan, you're a good hand to have around here, but you just need to let that dog lay," he warned. "If it's bothering you that much, maybe you should just head on back home."

Dan was confused; Henry had never spoken to him that way before, almost like a protective father would of his daughter. But even with that, he knew he couldn't go back home. His ghosts chased him everywhere, but the feelings were worse there. The constant reminder that he had failed them. At least out here on the trail, his days would be filled with enough work that he didn't have time to think about much else.

Dan cleared his throat. "You know that's not the problem. You've also known me long enough to know I can't just go back home. I just don't like that she's putting us in danger with whatever her secret is, and that you guys are keeping me from knowing the truth."

"Son, I ain't keeping you from nothing. All I'm doing is taking her to her uncle's. That's what her father paid me for. The man saved my life, I owe him this favor at the least. I'm not going to discuss it anymore," Henry asserted. "I need you here, but I need your head here too. Don't worry about Pauline."

"You're right, Henry. I'll leave it alone. It's not my place to interfere with your friends or business," Dan conceded.

"That's all I can ask," Henry said.

"However, I will be keeping an eye on her. The situation makes it hard to trust her, but she looks scared too," Dan promised.

Henry just shook his head, turned around, and walked back toward the group, leaving him standing alone with the cattle. Dan stood there watching him walk away. The glow of the moon allowed him to see the silhouette of him all the way to the tents.

He still didn't know what to think. He wanted to know the truth about Pauline, but he had known Henry long enough to know not to push the topic. He didn't want whatever she was running from to catch up with them. Dan knew she was bringing trouble, and if Ross was right, they could all get in trouble because of her. A part of him was torn, though. Her eyes kept drawing him in; they were beautiful, but they were fearful, too. But after the loss of his wife, Dan had become a lot more protective of the people in his life. If finding out what she was hiding would protect his friends, then he needed to find out the truth.

Chapter Six

Great Western Route, 1890

After the cowboys were done with their dinner, the camp settled in. Music and laughter filled the cool night air. Pauline stared into the campfire, the flickering flames causing shadows to dance across the trees. She was lost in thought. She knew Dan didn't like her and, at first, it had made her angry that he was judging her so quickly. She was hurt because he didn't know anything about her, or the life she'd had. After Dorothy had told her about the murder of his wife and son, it made a little more sense to her. She was more sympathetic to his situation and couldn't imagine the pain that had caused him.

She had caught him watching her a few times during dinner. Every time, though, she would end up looking away first. She felt like he could see right into her soul, and it was more than she could handle. She had seen Dan and Ross talking, and she had also seen Dan storm off into the darkness. It didn't surprise her that Henry had gone to check on him. He seemed like somewhat of a father toward him.

Pauline and Dorothy were washing the dishes when all the emotions overtook her. The thoughts of her new friends getting in trouble for hiding her kept creeping in. She didn't want anything to happen to them.

"I don't think I should be here. It puts you and Henry in danger, and I can tell that Dan doesn't want me here," she cried.

"Aw honey, there's no place safer than here with us," Dorothy reassured her. "Nobody ever stops us while on the trail, they all know how important it is to keep moving. By the time we get to Dodge City, they'll probably have figured out the truth and it won't matter anyways."

Her optimism calmed Pauline. The softness with which she spoke had a way of easing her mind. The thoughts were still there, but the panic would disappear. Dorothy truly felt like the mother Pauline never had growing up. She felt like she could open up to her. It just felt natural.

"I do feel safe with you, I just don't know about the rest of them," Pauline said, looking at the group. "I feel them all watching me, well, mostly just Dan. He really doesn't like me."

"I told you what Dan has been through. Just give him some time and he'll come around. I promise you have nothing to be afraid of with him," she said. "Now, no more worrying tonight. Let's get these dishes done and get some rest. Got another long day tomorrow."

They finished the dishes and loaded what they wouldn't need for breakfast. Afterward, Pauline headed over to the spare tent Henry had set up for her. She was tired from the trail and the calmness of the night caused her to fall asleep almost immediately.

She woke up startled the next morning. She'd almost forgotten where she was, and a quick panic unsettled her. The sleepiness quickly faded and, along with it, the panic. She went through the morning routine with Dorothy—preparing breakfast and coffee for the cowboys, then packing up and hitting the trail. The sights and sounds along the way filled her with ideas and she sketched throughout the day while riding on the wagon.

"Your drawings are amazing, darling," Dorothy interrupted. "It sure is nice to have another woman out here to talk to."

"Tha-Thank you," she stumbled.

The comment took Pauline by surprise as she hadn't realized Dorothy was watching. It made her feel good that someone appreciated her art. Herschel always hated her drawings and felt art wasn't worth anything. That thought reminded her about his watch. She didn't understand why it was missing and nothing else. She didn't think it was a robbery but couldn't think of who had been to her home or why someone would have killed him and tried to make it look like she'd done it. She shook the thought from her mind for now and went back to drawing.

The sun was directly above them when they stopped for lunch. It was slightly hotter than the day before and the only shade they could get came from the main tent they had set up. The two ladies prepared lunch and served it to the cowboys. They finished up the dishes and cleanup, then packed up the gear and headed back out on the trail. Pauline avoided Dan in any way possible.

As they moved along the trail, Pauline couldn't help but go back to thinking about her husband's watch with the letters H.H. etched on the back, Herschel Hogan. She knew it was the missing link. It would prove her innocence. All she could do now was hope the Sheriff had checked into it.

The attraction to nature took her mind away from that. The sun moved across the sky, still pouring its high heat onto them. The trees in the distance swayed back and forth, almost dancing to a beat of their own. The sound of the herd trampling across the trail, the rumble, could be heard for quite a way. The beauty enchanted her and she floated away in its peacefulness. She closed her eyes and her thoughts floated back to her childhood and running through fields of flowers chasing butterflies. Not a concern in the world back then.

Something snapped Pauline out of her daydream. She felt like someone was staring at her, but as she looked around, no one even looked her direction. She just kept feeling like everyone's eyes were on her and every set was judging her. She imagined that the whole group was probably wondering what she was running from. No girl in their right mind would hit the open trail with a group of cattle drivers otherwise. She started thinking about whether anyone else knew why she was hiding. She shrank down in the seat of the wagon, hoping to stay away from all their burning stares. Just as she tried to make herself unseen, Ross rode up next to the wagon.

"Howdy, Pauline," he smiled. "How ya doing on this beautiful day?"

"I'm doing good, Ross. You seem to be in a good mood today. How are the cattle doing today?" she asked.

Pauline couldn't help but smile. Not in a flirtatious way, just a friendly smile in response to him not treating her like dirt. He talked to her like she was just like everyone else. He didn't seem to care about what she was running from. He was just a funny young man who seemed to be a little chatty at times.

"Well ma'am, days like today when the cattle are basically driving themselves makes for a good day," he answered. "Miss Dorothy, how's the wagon holding up?"

"It's holding up just fine, Ross. Shouldn't you be getting back out there? They aren't going to drive themselves all the way to Dodge City," she grinned.

"Yes ma'am, I reckon I should. I just wanted to check in with the prettiest ladies I know," Ross chuckled.

"We're the only ladies you know, young man," Dorothy quipped.

"You could be right about that," Ross joked. "Knowing two women is better than only knowing one, though."

He laughed, then kicked his spurs, and his horse took off toward the herd, leaving a trail of dust behind him. Pauline was fascinated with how easy the cowboys made riding a horse look. She had never been properly trained on how to ride one. The one time she'd attempted, she fell off just a few feet after the horse had lunged forward. She hadn't tried again since that day.

"Don't mind Ross," Dorothy declared. "He's harmless. He's just an excited young man who talks to everyone."

"I'm not too worried about him. It's just nice to be treated normal for a change."

"Darlin', your life is going to be full of people who look at you differently. They may be judging you or they may be wondering why you're looking at them. What matters is that you know who you are, and you know who you ain't," she insisted.

Pauline took her advice and kept her mind off what other people were thinking. She focused on the trees' leaves and the streams they crossed. She could see small fish swimming along the channels. Most of the trail looked the same, but those little things that an artist's mind would notice stood out to her. Her memory allowed her to remember images from her past and draw them with detail and accuracy. Earlier that day, they'd passed through an area of open fields. When she looked out at them, she saw two children chasing each other through the tall glass. It might have seemed like just an everyday thing to the average eye, but her artistic mind saw it as something beautiful. So, she sketched it and placed the drawing in a leather bag she had gotten from Dorothy.

The day was just about over, and the women had just finished preparing dinner when Henry came over and checked in with them. Dorothy gave him a hug and a kiss on the cheek. The two were wonderful together. Pauline wondered why she couldn't find a love like that. They looked like best friends.

"Everything all right, Pauline?" Henry asked.

"I'm doing a bit better today. It's such a beautiful ride and Dorothy has been so helpful. Thank you so much for helping me and making me feel safe. It means so much to me," she praised.

"That sounds like my Dorothy. Always willing to help someone in need. You're practically family now, Pauline. Anything you need, just ask."

"The both of you are just trying to make me blush," Dorothy giggled. "He is right, honey. You're family now, and it won't take long for everyone to feel the same way. Our whole group is like a family."

"I hope you're right," Pauline said. "I'm going to head to bed. I'm not as tired as yesterday, but I'm still beat."

Pauline stood up and they said their good nights. She quickly stood up and left to her tent. She kept her distance from Dan; she didn't want the attention or the way his glare made her feel. Their eyes still met a couple times during the ride. She'd quickly turned and shrank into whatever she could. After the day with Dorothy and the freedom nature brought to her mind, Pauline truly did feel better.

She laid on the blanket and closed her eyes, though she didn't fall asleep right away. She thought about the day and how nice people had been. She thought about Dan, but she was more sympathetic now. He had his ghosts and she had hers. As she slowly fell asleep, her thoughts skipped to

Herschel's watch again. That was the key to everything. She didn't know how much time she had left, but she knew she couldn't run and hide forever. She only hoped someone found it soon and she could be free of this nightmare. Whoever had that watch was the person who had killed her husband.

She'd never loved Herschel, but part of her knew he didn't deserve to die. She had tried in the beginning, and then he started abusing her more often. She wondered—if she had tried harder, would he have loved her more? Pauline thought she deserved better. She had even thought about leaving him a few times, but her devotion to her father and marriage made her stay. She couldn't help but think, if she had been a better wife somehow, Herschel would still be alive. She pushed the thought from her mind, hoping these were not her last days.

She fell asleep, dreaming of happiness she was still unsure she deserved.

Chapter Seven

Western Cattle Trail, 1890

Dan woke up slowly on the third morning of the drive. It wasn't because he was worn out; it was because he hadn't slept much on the trail. Usually, the drive was the only time he did sleep. But he had been conflicted with thoughts of Pauline, of looking into those eyes. He couldn't stop thinking about what Ross had told him. Was it possible the beautiful woman was really a murderer? The thought angered him. Her eyes reminded him of his wife's, but the possibility she had murdered someone brought back all the memories of his family's murders. He quickly jumped to his feet and shook the thoughts away.

Exiting his tent, he realized that he was the first one awake. Dan got into his bag and removed his pot and coffee. He started every morning with coffee. Before he had his morning cup, he was as grumpy as the ancient herders he had back on the ranch, three times his age. After heating his water on the embers of the campfire from the night before, he took his cup and headed off to check on the cattle. He enjoyed the mornings alone. The sunrise cast a rosy, red tinge across the sky's light blue backdrop. Dan was mesmerized with its beauty.

For a few blissful minutes as he sipped, he was able to find a little peace. It was always in the wee hours of the morning when it happened, as if the day hadn't yet woken enough to remind him of his suffering. He thought back to the day before. He had only seen Pauline a couple of times, but she seemed to keep her distance. That was fine with him. Dan heard the camp getting louder and knew everyone was waking up. Tossing the remaining grounds in the bottom of his mug, Dan left the herd and went back to the camp to feed Jesse some carrots before hitting the trail again.

Before long, the rest of the camp bustled with activity before the morning push. Dan meandered around Jesse, giving the faithful steed a good curry before saddling him up. It was going to be a hard push to get the herd moving, but he looked forward to the labor. The day was mostly uneventful. A stray calf here or there was the most exciting thing that happened. Dan found his mind wandering back to his wife, his son, and begrudgingly enough, to Pauline. He quickly became caught up in the thought of her beauty. He did his best to stay on the edge of the drive throughout the day, limiting his interactions with everyone because of how his mood had soured.

As the sun started to dip beneath the rolling landscape, he was left with no option but to mingle with the others. They had stopped for the night and set up their camp. The routine was familiar and comforting as he filled a bucket from the creek and started to wash down Jesse. It was cathartic to wipe the day's sweat, flies, and mud off the steed. Dan prided himself on how well he took care of the gelding. Before long, the rest of the team fed their horses and gathered around the fire for supper. There was a little talk amongst the group but once again, Dan sat by himself for the meal. He didn't talk to anyone, his head swimming with thoughts.

After supper, Pauline and Dorothy did the dishes like normal. He tried his best not to watch them, though the other men on the drive did so openly. The rest of the camp moseyed to bed shortly after, leaving Dan by himself, staring at the fire after his mount had been tended. Looking around to assure himself that everyone was gone, he pulled out a faded image and ran his fingers over it.

He never went anywhere without a picture of his wife and son. He found himself staring at it constantly when no one was around. He missed them quite a bit and found himself getting lost in the memories every night. Dan allowed himself to get lost in one thought, a memory of his wife and son out on a picnic. They had ridden to a small watering hole close to Windy Reach. The happy couple had watched Johnny run around trying to catch butterflies and frolic through the grass. He had just turned three only a few days before. He was such a happy kid; he never cried or tried to cause mischief. They'd always talked about having half a dozen more just like little Johnny.

They sat together and giggled just like they would when they were schoolchildren. The day was warm, like any other summer day, but the partial clouds added an unseen beauty. Martha laid on her back and marveled at the sky. She'd always seen things Dan wouldn't notice and never failed to let him know what he was missing. That was one of his favorite things about her. He could have stormed into their house, in a rut of a mood from a lousy day, but one smile from Martha would turn it all around. The image stuck in his head, his son running around while he and Martha watched and talked. It was one of the happiest moments he could remember.

Dan heard someone walking up behind him and quickly put the picture away. Despite others knowing about what had happened to his family, he didn't want to share or strike up a conversation about it. He was a man who liked his privacy and kept his emotions well under wrap. Dan turned around to find Pauline standing a few feet behind him. Her cheeks flushed as her eyes darted to his breast pocket. He glared at her, knowing she'd seen the image. He tried to storm away from her but the second she spoke, he froze.

"Is... is that a picture of your wife and son?" she stammered. "They were beautiful. I'm so sorry for your–"

"That's none of your business," Dan growled. "You shouldn't go sneaking up on men like that. You're lucky I didn't shoot you."

"I was just trying to be nice, you looked lonely and sad," she muttered, her cheeks red with anger. "When I saw the picture, I thought it would make a good conversation starter. I hate to see anyone suffering so much."

"Maybe I wanted to be alone. Did you think of that? Of course not, you just wanted to strike up a conversation, right?" he snapped.

Her jaw dropped but she straightened her shoulders in defiance. Dan was shocked by the rush of heat that moved through him. There was a spark inside of her that he liked despite himself. He wanted to hate her, to cast her away, but the wounded look behind her strong eyes gave him pause.

"I don't think anyone deserves to be alone, despite what you might think," she said.

"Well, maybe I'm not everyone," Dan scoffed. "Why don't you go back to your tent and leave me alone already?"

"Honestly, Dorothy has told me about you," she countered. "She said you were a nice guy. Heck, maybe you are to her, maybe it's all just an act. You sure haven't been nice at all to me... but that's okay. She also told me what happened to your family too, and I'm so sorry for your loss. I don't know, I guess you looked like you needed a friend."

"I'm not your friend and I don't want to be friends with someone like you," he hissed. "It wasn't her place to tell you anything. Now please leave me be."

The color drained from her face as she spun around and stormed back to her tent. For a split second, he considered chasing after her, but his stubborn pride wouldn't let him. Dan didn't know why he snapped the way he did; it wasn't like she had done anything to him. He sprang to his feet and walked to his tent. He felt angry, but there was part of him that wanted to know her story. How could he not? It wasn't every day he rode the trail with a wanted criminal.

Those eyes would draw him in and all he could think about was getting to know her. It infuriated him. Dan felt a twinge of guilt as his mind flittered back to his late wife. He didn't understand why he was so torn. He wanted to know what Pauline was hiding, was that so wrong? He wanted to know if what Ross had heard was true. He wondered if she could really be a murderer. The impression he had gotten from their small interactions was that she couldn't be a killer. Yet the idea that she could have was enough to keep Dan away.

Dan knew he needed to get some sleep with another long day on the drive tomorrow. He laid down under the tent, which was nothing more than blankets draped over a rope tied off to poles on either end. Just enough to keep them covered from the rain. The sky was clear, and he could see the stars for miles above. The calmness of the night helped him relax, but he was still upset with Henry and the fact he had allowed Pauline to accompany them. On the other hand, she continued to draw him in.

There was a kindness to her. He wondered if she could even be capable of such a horrible act. He closed his eyes and tried to rest, his mind kept racing as he tried to get to sleep. He continued going back and forth about Pauline. He knew it was possible he was overreacting to her presence. How could he react differently though? The only woman he'd ever truly trusted had been Martha and he'd lost her. Dan's heart ached with longing. Finally, out of sheer exhaustion, he eventually fell asleep.

Dan slept hard and his mind opened to a dream. He stood in a field of long grass; a light fog rose from the ground. The sky was clear, and the sun was just rising. It lit up the sky with a fiery red glare. He caught a glimpse of Martha running across the open field. She smiled and giggled, teasing him to chase her. Dan called out to her, but she just kept running. He chased after her, following the trail of her laughter. When she would turn to look at him, he noticed something was different about her. When they reached the trees, he lost her for a moment. Her laughter continued to echo all around him. Suddenly, directly ahead of him past a large tree, he saw her run into another field. He chased after her, but when he got to the field, the sky quickly turned dark. A storm had taken over and the sky was nearly black, except for the lightning that struck all around them. The wind whipped hard, and it made the rain blow sideways.

Martha had stopped running and now stood straight in front of him. Her back was to him, and they were both soaking wet as he approached her. He placed his hand on her shoulder. She spun around, her giggle so infectious, Dan couldn't help but to smile. The woman who he had missed for so long was right in front of him. A single strike of lightning flashed, and their eyes met in the light. Dan reeled; the woman in front of him was not his wife—it was Pauline.

He jerked awake, shaking and covered in sweat and confused about what the dream meant. He knew the woman was his wife in the dream, but he was unsure why she had turned into Pauline. He shook off the panic and prepared for the day ahead. He was even more conflicted about Pauline, but somehow, he felt more sympathy for her than he had before.

Chapter Eight

Western Cattle Route, 1890

Pauline woke up the next morning earlier than normal. After last night's argument with Dan, she was left feeling angry and upset at his behavior. She was only trying to get to know him; she didn't feel like she had done anything wrong, but it still made her wonder how kind of a man he could really be. She shook the morning fog from her mind and decided to get up and start preparing the coffee for the group. When she exited her tent, she noticed Dan sitting at the campfire alone. She forced herself to look away; she didn't want him to notice her and certainly didn't want him to see her watching him. He seemed angry enough with her that she didn't want a repeat of the night before. As she prepared the coffee and items needed to make breakfast, Dorothy joined her.

"Good mornin', honey," she said. "How are you this morning? Did you sleep okay?"

She was constantly checking on Pauline. She made sure she was sleeping and eating. Pauline felt closer every day to her, as close to Dorothy as she had with Lucy.

"Good morning, Dorothy. I slept okay. I just woke up early and figured I would get a start on the day."

"Well, ya know I'll never turn down the extra help," Dorothy grinned. "I'm glad you're getting some sleep. I just wanted to make sure you were doing okay this morning. You're not usually awake before me."

"The mornings out here are so beautiful, and I woke up so early anyways, I just didn't want to miss any of it," Pauline answered. "I'm going to get started on breakfast once everyone has their coffee."

"Thank you so much. It's so nice to have you around here. You're so good at helping me that there are times I just don't know what to do with myself and the extra time on my hands," she said. "I'm going to go wake Henry up and then we can talk more."

Dorothy got up and walked back to her tent. Pauline felt good about being able to help. After all, they were helping her escape her past. Doing nothing just wouldn't feel right. She continued making coffee. Smiling to herself, she didn't notice Ross approach her.

"Hey there, Pauline! It's nice to see another smiling face early in the morning. Is the coffee about ready?" Ross asked.

Pauline's face turned red as a rush of embarrassment fell over her. She hadn't noticed anyone else had been awake yet.

"Well, good morning to you too. Coffee will be ready in a few minutes," she answered.

"That gives me enough time to check on the cattle. Save me a cup! I'll be back in shortly."

Ross walked out of the camp and over toward the herd. It was another great morning. The view on the trail made her feel at ease. The sunrise brought a wonderful peacefulness with it that made Pauline feel happy. She loved the beauty nature offered while on the trail. She looked around the open fields and noticed how silent everything felt. She glanced around the camp to see who else was up and about, noticing Dan still sitting alone. Her thoughts crossed over to a feeling of mixed emotions about him. She couldn't help but wonder if all the things he had been through had made him hard. She still hadn't seen the man Dorothy had described him. She couldn't understand why he snapped the way he did the night before.

She reached out for the coffee without thinking and abruptly felt a stinging pain. Being as distracted as she was, she had accidentally grabbed the scalding hot kettle handle, burning her hands. She cried out in pain and dropped the kettle. Time seemed to stand still when she noticed Dan rushing to her. She looked around to see if anyone else had seen her burn herself, but it was just him. A fear washed over her the closer he got. She wasn't sure how to react after the events last night.

"Pauline, are you okay? Those look like some bad burns, let me look at them," he urged, his voice laced with concern. "You shouldn't let that go too long untreated."

"You don't have to do that, I can wait for Dorothy to come back over," she protested. "They look far worse than they feel. I'm sure it isn't that bad."

"Look, I have a first aid kit right over there. There isn't anybody else out here right now and it looks like you need to get those treated quickly. I've seen bad things happen when you don't treat burns quick enough. Please let me see them, I promise I won't hurt you," Dan pleaded.

Pauline looked around one more time to find Dorothy. She couldn't be found anywhere. She wasn't sure about letting him too close, the distrust she had felt from him still fresh in her mind. She couldn't believe he'd even come over to her, let alone wanted to help. But she knew she needed to let someone look at her hands, and he seemed willing.

"I guess that would be all right, as long as you're sure you don't mind."

"I don't mind at all," he said. "I've dealt with many burns and have just the thing for it."

Dan walked over to his tent and brought back a little bag. He pulled out a bottle and a few cloth wraps. She could tell that he had been prepared for this kind of injury.

"Now let me get you all fixed up," he said.

It was the first time she had seen any hint of kindness from the man. She was suddenly intrigued by his willingness to help, even when it seemed as if he didn't like her at all. She caved in and held her hands out for him to check over. He was very gentle when he took her hands and even though she was prepared for his touch, it still startled her. The only contact she'd felt from a man, besides her father, was the harsh hands of her husband. She flinched at Dan's touch, and it was obvious he noticed. He held her hands still in his and felt a calmness she hadn't felt before. Pauline looked up from her hands and met his gaze.

There was a softness in his eyes she hadn't noticed before. He was attentive and caring. It was a side she hadn't expected to see. All the anger washed away, and they stood there for a moment. When she relaxed, he went back to taking care of her hands. She watched as he spread a burn ointment on her skin and wrapped them in a fabric to hold the ointment in.

She studied his face while he took care of her hands. She realized how attractive he really was. It was the first time she had looked at him in that way. At the very least, it was the first time she saw him as handsome. He was a well-built man and his long hair hanging behind his ears added a frame around his rugged face. His beard looked thick and well-kept; she almost wanted to touch it. She wanted to know how his beard felt in her hands. Dan's voice interrupted her thoughts.

"Keep the fabric on until lunch. Then you should be able to take the wraps off and wash up," he said softly. "It doesn't look like you burned them too bad, but better safe than sorry."

His change in attitude and the kindness he had showed her created a warm feeling in her cheeks. She knew her face was turning red. She was mostly embarrassed that she had showed the clumsy side of herself to him. The moment she had felt his touch and the kindness in his eyes, she knew her first impression of Dan had been wrong. Maybe he wasn't as hard as he had been letting on.

"Why are you helping me, if you don't even like me?" she whispered.

"It just seemed to be the right thing to do," he assured. "I don't really know why I came over here to help you. I was just worried that you had really hurt yourself, and I knew I could help."

By that time the camp was starting to stir. Dorothy had already started making breakfast and the rest of the camp was up and moving around. Dan quickly released her hands and put away what was left of his first aid kit.

"Remember to keep those on until lunch, and please be more careful."

"Thank you for helping me, Dan," she said.

Dan walked off and met up with the other cowboys. They set off to take the herd to a nearby river, to allow them a morning drink. Pauline approached Dorothy; she knew she needed to get back to work and help her with breakfast. The smell of coffee had already filled the camp, and the aroma of bacon began to fill the air too.

"I'm here to help, Dorothy. I would have started that if I hadn't been careless and burned my hands."

"Oh darling, are you okay? Do you need me to look at them for you?" Dorothy said, looking down at Pauline's hands. "It looks like someone already did that for you."

"It hurt at first, but I wasn't sure where you were, and Dan saw it happen. He came right over and looked at them." Pauline smiled. "He put some ointment on them and helped me get them wrapped."

She told Dorothy about Dan's help and explained that he had told her to keep the bandages on until lunch and then she could take them off. During that time the two women made breakfast. Every time she talked to her about Dan, Dorothy would light up. She kept grinning and smirking. Pauline didn't understand why she acted that way, but figured she was just enjoying the story.

"I think at some point today you should have Dan check them again. He seems to be quite the healer." Dorothy smiled.

That's when it hit Pauline. She had been glowing all morning since her interaction with Dan. She hadn't realized how happy she was and that she had been smiling the whole time she talked to Dorothy. She suddenly knew that she had a soft spot for Dan. He was handsome, and now she knew he had a kind heart. Whatever trepidations he had about her, he had helped her anyways. There was something about the way he looked at her that made her feel safe. It was a feeling she had never felt with another man. She still noticed a hesitation in him, but she pushed the thought from her mind. She had work to do and didn't have time to sit and daydream.

They cleaned up after breakfast and packed up the wagon. While they rode along the trail, Pauline couldn't help but notice how calm she felt. There was something freeing about being out here and the more time she spent here, the more she loved being on the open range. The sky was clear as far as the eye could see. The cowboys herded behind them, a cloud of dust in their wake. The smell of the fresh water from the river took over the air. Everything just appeared to be perfect that day. Pauline felt lighter and more in control of herself. She hadn't felt this kind of freedom in a long time. Herschel had always kept her on a short leash, and she never had the chance to make her own decisions. It was hard to trust what Dan's motives were, especially with her past and his sudden change of heart. But he wasn't as cold-hearted as she'd first thought.

A thought crossed her mind and while Dorothy drove the wagon, Pauline started sketching a new portrait. It was something from her memory, but she wanted it to be perfect.

Chapter Nine

Western Cattle Route, 1890

Dan, along with the other cowboys, had gotten the cattle down to the river. As he watched the cattle drink, he found himself wondering why he had been so quick to help Pauline. He still didn't want her here yet jumped to her aid as soon as he had heard her cries. Everything about her drew him in and he fought that urge more every day. When he'd looked deep into her eyes that morning, he'd seen nothing but kindness in them. He found himself thinking more about her and the likely possibility that she was innocent.

The hills cast a backdrop for the open fields on the other side of the river. A soft breeze pushed around the tall grass. The forest, not too far off in the distance, offered home to many birds. They chirped in a peaceful song-like rhythm.

After pushing the herd back on the trail and away from the river, Henry joined the group and rode up next to Dan. They hadn't talked much since their last conversation about Pauline. They had been friends a long time and he felt that with his feelings changing so quickly, now would be as good a time as ever to move past their dispute.

"Henry, I just want to apologize for the way I acted the other day," he said. "I don't rightly know what's gotten into me lately."

"There's no reason to apologize, son. You've been through so much. I know you didn't mean anything by it. Listen, I don't want you to think I am hiding anything. Let me tell you what I know about Pauline's situation."

Henry went on to tell him about her husband's murder, and how the town was instantly against her without knowing all the facts. He told Dan about the lazy Sheriff who just wanted to make the town happy.

"There's just no way she could have done that to him. I know her father raised her better than that," Henry concluded. "I don't claim to know the truth, but I trust her father."

Dan took a minute to process everything. It was all becoming a little clearer now.

"You have been so good to me, and I might have misjudged Pauline," he said with a half-smile. "Leave it to me to overreact."

Henry just laughed. "Well, of course you'd overreact to a beautiful young woman. What man wouldn't?"

Dan thought about how pretty Pauline was and how soft her hands had felt in his. He felt something warm when they had touched. Almost like something filling him with hope. Dan knew she was beautiful, but there was more to her than just a pretty face.

"I don't know if I trust her, but there is something about her that I can't shake," Dan admitted.

"The only way to find out what that is, is to spend more time with her. Don't be afraid to let your heart lead the way," Henry said, grinning. "There's nothing wrong with just getting to know somebody. You never know what kind of friendship you'd miss out on."

"I don't know what you mean by all that, but you've never steered me in the wrong direction before."

Dan knew Henry was right. They talked about the morning and how Pauline had burned her hands. Dan told him how he had taken care of her wounds and how he bandaged them for her. Excitement flickered within him when he talked about her.

"I'm very proud of you Dan, you did the right thing. Regardless of how you felt about her at the time, you still helped her because she was in need. You're a good man, Dan. Don't let your ghosts tell you any different. Let that man back out, you deserve to be free of them."

"Maybe you're right," Dan whispered. "I'm going to check on the stragglers back there, thanks again."

"Anytime, Dan."

He rode off to the back of the herd and checked on the slower cattle. None of them seemed to be too far off course, so Dan rustled up the few strays and moved them back into the rest of the herd. He pushed the cattle further on down the trail, enjoying his work. There were few clouds in the sky and the sun continued to warm the air around them. The flatland around them offered a long view of the surrounding area.

The day went on uneventfully. When they stopped for lunch, he couldn't help but watch Pauline interact with the rest of the group. She was kind and smiled at everyone. He was starting to see the good in her, and he became more fascinated. How could a woman as kind as her kill anyone? He didn't speak to her, but watched her throughout the day. He noticed her sketching several times. She looked so happy when she was sketching, and he found himself wondering what she could be drawing in that pad of hers.

The sun looked as though it was floating across the sky that day. A cool breeze kept them from being too hot and made the day fly by. They came to stop around dinner time and Dan helped settle in the cattle before joining the camp and setting up his tent. He was in a better mood than he had been since the first day and found himself enjoying the ongoing conversations around the campfire that night. Everyone was riding high on happiness, and they all told stories and carried on. He didn't catch much of what was said with everything going on, but he caught part of a cowboy's story, about a flood that had happened on one his drives. Dan was enjoying all the chatter when he paused to listen to Ross.

"Why do so many cowboys like to gamble?" he asked. Nobody answered. "Because they always liked raising steaks!"

It was quiet until Ross laughed so hard that everybody was laughing. Even Dan found himself chuckling, happy to see Ross enjoying himself, and his jokes weren't really that bad. Dan realized he was letting more joy into his life, and though he didn't understand what had changed, he had noticed the new way he saw Pauline. He was beginning to see her as a much kinder person. At the thought, he noticed Pauline was not anywhere near the group. He saw Dorothy on the other side of the fire and walked over to speak with her. He didn't know what he was going to say, he just felt a sudden urge to check on her.

"Hey Dorothy, have you seen Pauline?" He cleared his throat. "I wanted to check on her hands and make sure they were healing."

She smiled. "I think she went out to the cattle. Maybe you should go down there and make sure she's all right."

Immediately, Dorothy turned to Henry and whispered something he couldn't make out. They both smiled at each other, and Henry looked up at Dan with a grin.

"You don't forget what I told you earlier," Henry said. "Let yourself go and just follow your heart."

"Thank you, Miss Dorothy," he replied. "I guess thank you too, Henry."

He smiled at them and without really thinking about it, headed toward where Dorothy said he would find her. He walked easily through the cool night's air on his way to find her. The moon lit up the sky, pouring a hazy glow on all it touched. He spotted Pauline standing next to the cattle. As he approached her, he noticed she was talking to the animals. The same way he would talk to Jesse. He stopped and watched her for a spell. She was gentle with the cattle and talked sweet to them. Like she would talk to a family member, calming their nerves. The cattle were beginning to respond to her. He could tell she liked animals; the care she gave to the cattle made that clear.

He started to walk toward her again when she jumped and held back a screech. He clearly took her by surprise with her reaction.

"What are you doing here?" she snapped.

It wasn't an angry tone, but Dan could tell that she wasn't prepared for him to walk up on her. He instantly felt bad for interrupting her alone time.

"I'm sorry, I didn't mean to startle you," Dan assured her. "I was just coming to check on your hands. How're they doing?"

She looked to be more at ease after that. Her eyebrows relaxed and her shoulders dropped. He got lost in how gorgeous she really was. The moonlight brought a glimmer to her eyes and made her hair almost shine. The glow that the dim light provided made him see a beauty in her he hadn't noticed before.

"They're doing good, that ointment really did the trick," she said. "I took the wraps off at lunch like you said, they feel much better. Thank you so much for coming to my rescue this morning."

"It's an old family mixture. My grandfather gave it to my father, then he left it to me. It always seems to do a good job whenever I use it to treat burns. It was no problem at all. I'm glad they feel better. Let me look at them."

She took a step closer to Dan and he reached out to take her hands. The touch sent a jolt through him; something inside of him relaxed. He looked down at her hands. The moonlight was enough to make out the burns and how well they were healing. He couldn't help but let his hands linger, wrapped around hers. Her touch was warm and soft, and he found himself staring into those big blue eyes. He was lost in them, for the first time noticing how beautiful they were. Not just because they looked like his wife's, but with a beauty that was all her own.

He felt a freedom from his past, like a weight taken from his shoulders. The burden he had carried for so long began to feel lighter. The more he was around Pauline, the more everything became more unclear to him. Before that first touch, he hadn't trusted her. Now, he wanted to know more about her.

He must have left his hands on her for too long because Pauline blushed, and quickly pulled her hands away.

"I'm sorry, I didn't realize I was still holding your hands."

"It's not that, it's just..." Pauline hesitated. "It's been so long since I've been touched by anyone. It seems my cheeks betray me."

Dan grinned. "I rather enjoy the color. I can imagine how it must frustrate you to wear your emotions so openly though. It can't have served you well in the past."

Pauline cocked her head in confusion. "I've never had anything to hide, so I wouldn't know."

"I just meant–"

"Thank you for your help," she whispered. "I should get back to the others, no need to stir up the rumor mill."

He watched her walk all the way to the group. The moon cast an outline of her body as she moved. He was shocked. He didn't know what these feelings were that crept up on him. He suddenly found himself wanting to talk to Pauline more. He wanted to look into her eyes while she told him the story of her life. How could she make him feel a way he hadn't felt in years?

Dan sat down in the grass and stared up at the stars. They had a little more sparkle tonight than they had the past nights. His emotions confused him. Before they'd touched, everything had been so clear. His love for his family, his dedication to the land and nothing else, the driving force that kept him away from his home. Yet somehow, Pauline constantly fluttered through his mind. Each time he thought of her beautiful smile, his heart raced a little faster.

There was something about her determination to stay positive that drew him like a moth to a flame. What a curious woman she was, rugged yet soft. She didn't have the hardened heart of a killer, not like the ones he'd seen before. Women were fickle creatures, though. It had been so long since anyone had softened him so.

Dan finally got up and walked back to his tent. He had waited for the noise of the group to die down before going back. He was confused enough and didn't need another awkward situation to confuse him more. That night, he fell asleep quickly. Not because he had less on his mind. He fell asleep because he felt lighter. Something inside him was changing—he could feel it. He didn't know when he had found hope again, but now it rushed through him like a windy day. Even in the short time since they met, Pauline was somehow giving him this feeling of hope. The possibilities excited him.

Chapter Ten

Western Cattle Route, 1890

Pauline woke well-rested the next morning. Dan's touch had startled her at first, but there was something reassuring behind it. She thought about his rough skin and how it didn't feel so tough while touching hers. There was a slight smile on her face when she thought back to the look in his eyes when he touched her. Something inside her stirred. She didn't know what she was feeling. Could it be love? The thought frightened her; she didn't know what love was, not in the romantic sense. She'd never loved Herschel. Although, she still felt guilty over the possibility of happiness.

She joined Dorothy at the fire and helped her with the morning chores. More coffee and breakfast. It wasn't a bad routine to fall into; she enjoyed Dorothy's company and the work wasn't hard at all. They had really become great friends.

Dorothy wasn't the only one she had become close with. Henry had been there for her too. In a way, he'd taken on the role of her father on this trip, and she was grateful. He was kind, with a warmness about him, and made her feel comfortably safe. Everybody was becoming like a family to her. Ross fit in as the little brother she never had. He was the first one to treat her like a real person. He was funny and loud, but she was happy to have him around. He knew how to lighten the mood and she wasn't sure that he realized it. The other cowboys had all started talking to her and keeping tabs on her. They made sure to ask how she was doing and had a real sweetness to them.

Then there was Dan. She was still worried about what the future might hold for her. She wasn't sure what the outcome would be from her husband's murder. She felt insecure about herself and what she was worth as a woman. The only attention she had ever received from her husband was painful. Dan's touch erased all of that. The softness to his touch made all her pain disappear. When she was near him, she wasn't afraid of the future. Time stood still when they were together. She just didn't know what to do about it and she was still worried about his behavior before that first touch. He had been so cold and mean to her. She also knew that was a direct reflection of everything he had been through. She found him attractive yet had no idea how she could feel that way.

They had finished packing up after breakfast and were loading the wagon when Henry rode up to them. He jumped down from his horse and walked up to Dorothy, gave her a kiss on the cheek, and walked toward Pauline.

"Morning honey, how're you feeling today?" he asked.

"Oh, the hands, they feel great," she answered. "I already forgot I burned them."

"That's good to hear. Just be more careful, those hands are important around here."

"No need to worry about that, I'll be paying a good amount of attention to what I'm doing from now on." Pauline giggled.

"That's a good idea," Henry laughed. "Well, back out to the herd, you ladies have a nice ride."

The women finished packing and hit the trail. They rode along the trail all morning. They didn't really talk much, just enjoyed the views and listened to the cowboys move the cattle along. The morning had been as pretty as all the other mornings so far. The land would sometimes change quickly from one setting to another. Other times it would seem like you were in the same field all day. Either way, nature amazed Pauline.

Out of nowhere the wagon came to a stop. She had been so lost in thought she hadn't noticed a man standing on the side of the road and a horse lying dead on the ground next to him.

The man standing there dressed like a businessman. He was clean-shaven and looked as though he hadn't done any hard work in his life. As the women approached him, he looked at Dorothy and smiled. He seemed harmless standing there, tapping his left breast pocket. Something about the man looked familiar to Pauline. She wasn't sure where she knew him from, but she knew she had seen him before. Her photographic memory was helpful in seeing things from her past, but not always remembering where they happened.

"Good morning, ladies," he said. "The name's Charley O'Conner."

He spoke to both of them, but when he looked at Pauline, she felt a chill run up her spine. He did a double take when he saw her. Pauline swore he recognized her, too. There was something about Charley that caused her to be overly cautious.

"Morning, Charley. I'm Dorothy McCall and this is Pauline. We're part of Henry McCall's group and we're herding a group of cattle to Dodge City. What happened to your horse?"

"We were getting along just fine when something startled her. She reared up and knocked me off. Before I got the chance to calm her, she bolted and somewhere on this road broke her leg. I found her here groaning. There wasn't anything I could do, I had to put her down," he grumbled.

Life on the trail wasn't always sunshine and rainbows. There were times where it could feel challenging. It wasn't uncommon for a horse to be put down while on the road, but something about the way he said it made Pauline feel uncomfortable. She noticed there wasn't a sadness in it. She wasn't sure about the man; he acted strange, but he had a way of talking that seemed to win Dorothy over.

"That's just awful, are you okay? I know there are many injuries that can happen when you get thrown off a horse," Dorothy said.

"I'm actually just fine, ma'am. Just a torn suit and bruised ego," Charley chuckled. "Hey, did I hear you right? Did you say you were headed to Dodge City?"

"Yes, we are, Charley," she said. "If it's all right with Henry, you can ride along with the group."

About that time, Henry rode up to the wagon. He stopped and dismounted his horse. He must have seen the wagon had come to a stop and come to check on them.

"Howdy sir, my name is Henry," he said. "Looks like you got yourself a big problem."

Charley repeated what he had just told them. The two men discussed the dead horse and the possibility of Charley riding along with them to Dodge City. Some of the conversation was soft and Pauline couldn't pick up what was being said. While they were talking, Dan and Ross rode up to check on them as well. After a short time, Henry turned and walked back to the group.

"Ladies, I'm sure you've all had your introductions. Dan and Ross, that man over there is Charley O'Conner. He has a dead horse and needs a ride to Dodge City. Now we have some extra room and he's offering a good amount of money to take him the rest of the way, but we're a team and I'll leave it up to everyone."

Dorothy immediately said yes, but she was always willing to help someone in need. Ross seemed to like everyone and said yes almost as fast. Dan hesitated slightly but knew it was a good offer and agreed to it. Pauline didn't trust the man, but she had been wrong about people before. She hated seeing people suffer and her good nature came out.

"I don't think it's a good idea, but I hate to see anyone stranded out here like this," Pauline whispered.

"Then it's settled," Henry said. He turned back to the man. "Charley, welcome to the group. We need to get a move on if we're going to keep pace for the day."

Henry and the rest of the cowboys mounted their horses and headed back out to the herd, leaving the two women with Charley. Dorothy climbed back up into the wagon while Pauline climbed up next to her. Charley pulled himself up into the back of the wagon and situated himself into a position to be able to talk to both of them. Pauline still had a nervousness about the man, unsure how to feel about him. After all, she had been wrong about Dan it seemed. So maybe she was wrong about Charley too. Out of politeness and curiosity, she tried to start a conversation with him.

"Where are you coming from, Charley?" Pauline asked.

He shifted in his seat and tapped his left breast pocket when she looked at him. He was acting strange, but when he spoke, he had a certain cockiness about him.

"I was just doing some business out west; I was riding back to Dodge City to do some business there when my horse broke her leg. Talk about bad luck," Charley laughed.

Pauline knew then he was hiding something; she just couldn't pick up on what. She rode in silence the rest of the morning, thinking about Charley and trying to remember why he looked so familiar. She was quiet, but Charley and Dorothy talked until they stopped for lunch. The man seemed to be full of stories that were hard to believe. He talked about places he had been and business he had been doing. Nothing stood out to Pauline. He told his tall tales to Dorothy and Pauline just listened.

They stopped for lunch around midday. Charley walked off to see Henry while the women went about their duty of preparing lunch.

"You're pretty quiet, everything all right, honey?" Dorothy asked.

"Everything is fine. I'm not too sure about that Charley character, though. His stories are unbelievable and for some reason, he looks familiar, but I can't place him."

"Could be just a lack of trust with everything you've been through," Dorothy assured. "I wouldn't worry too much about him."

"Maybe you're right, I could be just overthinking everything."

"Of course, I'm right, honey! Now let's get these boys something to eat."

In only a few days, Pauline had become close to everyone on the drive. It truly had become like the family she never had. She suddenly became worried and wondered what would happen when they found out why she had left Arizona and why she was running to Dodge City. She was already worried about losing her new family—or worse, if they wouldn't believe her. Her thoughts trailed off as she gazed across the field.

The cowboys were herding the cattle to an open field; the sun hid behind clouds, and off in the distance, dark clouds rolled by. It looked peaceful but was eerily quiet. Pauline understood that a storm could be devastating on a drive like this. Dorothy had told her all about how the cattle reacted to storms and how difficult it was to move them during floods.

She worried for a moment about the possibilities, but let the worry fade away, hoping the storm would go right past them.

She couldn't help but think about Dan. She hadn't talked to him since the night before and hoped the way she walked away hadn't hurt him. She had been so lost in his touch that she had panicked and left him standing in the field by himself. She still didn't understand the feelings she had toward him, but she was happy he had showed her some kindness. The tension between them was dwindling and she knew he still had doubts about her, but she felt like they were getting closer.

Pauline cleared her mind and went back to helping Dorothy with lunch. Their routine felt natural and the two worked perfectly together. They prepared lunch like every other day and sat around the front of the tent. All were listening to the new man in the group, Charley. For her, there was no trust for the man, and she couldn't believe how easily they all were falling for his façade.

Chapter Eleven

Great Western Route, 1890

Dan quickly helped round up the herd and rode to the main tent. He thought about Pauline and the way she acted with the man on the road. He had to admit to himself that he did not trust the man, either. He didn't trust many people anyway, but his distrust of Charley was immediate; there was an oddness about him Dan hadn't figured out. He wanted to see the man up close before he decided on whether to trust him. By the time he reached the tent, lunch was ready and many of the others had already gathered around. Charley was going on about something.

"I couldn't believe he was standing right there in front of me, and the president himself shook my hand," he went on. "Can you imagine what that's like, shaking the hand of the president of the free world?"

Dan looked around the camp—everyone appeared fascinated by the man's story. Most of them had never met someone who had met a president before. He looked over and caught Pauline rolling her eyes. He could tell she didn't trust Charley and she certainly didn't believe the stories he told.

"So, you're telling me that you met the president, and he shook your hand? I don't believe it," Ross interjected.

Dan could only smile to himself. It wasn't the first story Charley had told that seemed a little too farfetched to be real. It was nice to see he and Pauline, who had objected to him staying on the trail with them from the very beginning, weren't the only ones who didn't believe him.

Charley moved his hand to his left breast pocket, patting it a couple times before he went on with his story. He acted nervous to his story being questioned, another thing Dan had noticed. He seemed to be overly anxious about something, changing the subject to some trip to England where he also met the King. The stories sounded like he was showing off or telling lies to gain the people's trust. Either way, a man like that made Dan worry.

Dan's eyes moved back toward Pauline; she was sketching in her book again. He thought about all the times he had seen her without her noticing him. She was always drawing in that book when she wasn't helping Dorothy. Pauline looked happy every time he had seen her sketching. For him, his happiness came from being out there on the trail. He assumed her happy place must be in those drawings. The rest of the group faded away as he watched her. She looked up and met his gaze. She blushed and went back to her drawing.

Dan finished eating and walked back to Jesse. Pulling a carrot from his bag, he fed it to the horse, who showed his appreciation by putting his head in Dan's face. He mounted Jesse and rode back out to the herd. It was time to get back on the trail.

The day slowly darkened as clouds covered the sun. Dan could smell the rain in the air as they pushed the cattle further down the trail. As the dark clouds moved toward them, he became concerned about the safety of the cattle. He had mentioned the storm a few times to Henry and was talking to Ross when the rain had begun to fall.

"I told you the rain was coming, Henry!" Dan hollered.

"I know," he grumbled. "I see an area of trees up ahead. If it gets worse, we'll move the herd over there and keep them out of the mud."

Almost instantly the sky opened and dumped more rain. The ground quickly became muddy with the flood of water and Dan noticed Jesse's hooves sticking more with each step. He knew they needed to get the herd to the tree line, where they'd at least have some coverage. When he looked over at Henry, he gave Dan a nod toward the trees and the group went to work pushing the cattle to safety.

He quickly maneuvered Jesse into position behind the herd. Ross was the drag rider, but Dan knew it was the hardest position to work. The downpour would make moving the cattle tricky. They weren't the most intelligent of creatures. Still, with good teamwork Dan knew they would get the job done. He positioned himself about fifteen feet away from Ross.

"Keep an eye to the left over there, I'll watch the right and we can both work the middle!" Dan hollered.

The heavy drops of the rain pelted the dry earth. Billions of tiny thuds chorused into a deafening crescendo that made it near impossible to hear each other. Ross nodded in understanding as they started. They worked back and forth, Ross pushing the left while he pushed the right, meeting back in the middle to push the herd up the center. With the help of the others, the technique worked in pushing the flanks of the herd on.

Dan could feel the deepening mud each time Jesse struggled to lift his hooves. Before long, he knew the cattle would panic. The simple herd creatures knew very little beyond danger, eating, and breeding. Their instincts to flee to higher ground would settle in if they didn't get them rounded and settled fast. With each clap of thunder, the lightening illuminated the herd. Dan, a seasoned cattleman, used Mother Nature to their advantage, scanning the horizon for any wayward livestock.

They had pushed most of the herd to the tree line when a huge strike of lightning hit not far behind them. The loud booming sound that followed sent a few of the cows into a fearful canter. They bolted straight to the right and slightly downhill. Dan swung Jesse around, using a delicate touch on the horse's flanks with his spurs to guide him. It wasn't much, but Jesse knew what he was doing almost as well as Dan did. He could hear other riders following him but didn't turn back.

All it took was a split-second distraction for disaster to follow. The heavy rain had soaked through his clothing, drenching and chilling him to the bone as he wiped sweat-laced rain from his eyes. The storm didn't seem to be letting up. He could barely see the cattle running in front of him, but he trudged forward anyways, confident in Jesse's footing. He heard the voices of the pair of men behind him—Ross and Henry coming to help. Throwing caution to the wind, he grabbed his lasso and began to whirl it around above his head.

The duo managed to wrangle two of the three heifers. The calf he now chased was obviously terrified. Dan could tell from the way the small creature moved, its gait exhausted and erratic as it bellowed out for its mother. He lined up the calf and timed the gallop of Jesse perfectly. When he released the lasso, it flew eloquently through the air before dipping down inches in front of the calf. Seconds later, Dan tightened the braided rope around his horn and slowed Jesse as the calves' rear legs lifted, jerking him to a stop in mud that nearly reached the creature's shanks.

Dan leapt from Jesse and jogged over to the calf. There was no time to try and lead the creature back as a brutal gust of wind nearly toppled him. Dan ignored the pain in his left knee as he hoisted the calf onto his shoulders, slinging it onto Jesse's withers before climbing back into the saddle. The calf called out for its mother, but they were too far from the herd for it to receive any reply. Another bolt illuminated the sky and Dan's heart sank. He could see flyaway bits of cloth and canvas dappling the air as the women struggled to secure everything again in the wagon.

There was no time to stop and help them. Most of the herd had taken shelter in the trees but half a dozen had taken their time and were now stuck in the foothills, their legs covered in mud as they struggled to free themselves. He quickly dropped the calf near the others and trotted back down, careful to take his time. A cow with a broken leg was a loss but not the end of the world. If something happened to Jesse though, Dan would never forgive himself. As the winds drowned out everything, He pulled the cattle free one by one, watching as they trotted to the rest of the herd.

Only one heifer now remained, buried to the point he wasn't sure he'd be able to free the poor thing, but he wasn't giving up. Through a lull in the downpour, he could hear the others calling after him but ignored them as a gust knocked him over. Jesse nickered his disproval of the situation but stayed where Dan had left him ten feet away as he lined up the heifer's neck with his lasso and threw the rope. It wrapped around the beast as Dan scrambled back onto Jesse, gently tugging on the reins as he pressed his heels down. Though slight, the horse instantly picked up on his commands and started to back away from the growing mud pit.

He felt the wind grab his jacket. It nearly ripped him from the saddle as he struggled to stay upright. The photograph Dan kept tucked in the breast pocket tumbled out. Suddenly the cow carried little importance as he shoved his hand into the now-empty pocket. As a burst of lightning sparked the skies, he saw the photo of his wife and son flittering through the air, landing a dozen yards from him. Ross and Henry were already galloping down the hillside to help him.

"Ross, grab that picture!" he screamed. "Please..."

In the moment he'd been distracted, Jesse had backed the cow out of the pit. It jerked when the thunder boomed, the rope unraveling from the saddle horn as the creature bolted for Ross and Henry. He gave chase in the same direction but not for the cow. As a final strike lit up the gully, his heart plummeted. The picture was barely visible. He knew it was ruined. Sliding off Jesse, Dan reached into the mud and pulled out the image.

Had the skies not been mourning, the rest of the team would have seen Dan's own tears. Besides the few memories still vivid in his mind, he felt the only connection he still had to his wife and son were lost with that picture. He stood silent for a moment, lost in thought. Ross and Henry had caught the last cow and Henry was leading it to the rest of the herd. Ross reached out and touched his shoulder, snapping him back.

"I really tried to get to your picture. I'm sorry Dan, I know what it meant to you," he apologized.

"Nothing could be done about it; I appreciate you trying. All the cows back together now?" Dan asked, wiping his face.

"It looks that way. Won't know for sure until we get up there and count, but we got the ones that bolted from the back, and it sure looked like we corralled the rest," Ross answered.

"Well, let's get over there to the trees, looks like the storm is about finished with us."

Dan grabbed Jesse's reins and the two men walked slowly back to the rest of the group. Henry was checking in on the women and the other cowboys were still settling the cattle when they reached camp. The newcomer, Charley, looked like he hadn't moved from the wagon. Pauline and Dorothy were still picking up the mess the wind had made of the wagon. Dan tied Jesse off to a tree and checked him for injuries.

All the while he couldn't stop thinking about the picture. He sat down next to Jesse on the wet ground, soaked and covered in mud; sitting in more mud didn't cross his mind. He pulled out what was left of the picture and just stared at it. He could make out parts of the picture but overall, it was ruined. All he had was the memory of it now. It saddened him, but he knew there were still things to do and mourning over a picture wouldn't help anyone. He got up and headed toward Henry. He needed to distract his mind and see what else he could do.

Chapter Twelve

Great Western Route, 1890

After a few hours, the rain finally subsided. When the storm first hit, Dorothy had guided the wagon to the line of trees she had seen the men head toward. She had explained to Pauline that they needed to get the cattle to the safety of the trees because of lightning and muddy fields. The storm hit so fast that by the time they had reached the trees, the wind had blown away several items off the back of the wagon. When the wagon stopped, she had hopped down and chased down the things that had blown away. A spare tent and a bit of clothing were among the items she had recovered.

She was still trying to catch her breath when she looked around the camp. When the rain had let up, they decided that even though it was early, they would set up for the night. It would be a good chance for everyone to rest and clean up after the storm, she had been told. Pauline watched the cowboys go through the motions of drying off and putting up their tents. She glanced over at Dan, sitting by the fire with what looked like a small piece of paper in his hand. There was a sadness in his face Pauline didn't understand. Hadn't they all just done a great job of saving the cattle and getting them all to safety?

As she watched Dan, she saw Ross walk over to him. He smiled and joked with Dan, but it didn't seem to be of any help. His mood still seemed to be soured. She began to feel anxious, wondering what had happened to make him so upset.

The rain had completely stopped, and she was hanging up her wet clothes when she noticed Ross walking her way. He always seemed to have a smile on his face. His personality always cheered up the people around him.

"Hey there, Pauline. That was a nasty storm, you doing okay?"

"I'm doing good, just a little wore out. I noticed Dan looks upset, is he okay?"

"He hurt his leg a bit, but I don't think that's what's bothering him. His picture of his wife and son was destroyed."

Pauline couldn't help but think about all the times she had caught him staring at it. She knew it meant a lot to him. Losing something that important had to take its toll.

"Oh no, that explains why he is so sad," she said.

"Yeah, as long as I have known him, he's carried around that picture. Why don't you go over there and check on him? I'm sure it would mean a lot to him," Ross smiled.

Pauline grinned. "It looks like you already tried that. Why do you think I'd make a difference?"

"Well Pauline, I don't have the womanly touch you have," he joked.

It made her feel good to know she might be able to make a difference. A quick thought crossed her mind. She had already been sketching the portrait for him. She had seen how tattered it had become and was going to give it to him as a sort of peace offering. She jumped up and grabbed her bag.

"Thanks for checking on me, Ross. I have a few things to do, but I will check on him after dinner," she said.

"That ain't no problem. Always have to make sure family is okay. I'll catch up with you later, too. Have a few things to check over myself."

She watched as he walked away; he was always cheerful, and it surprised her to see someone so happy all the time. She wanted that kind of happiness for herself. She pushed the thought from her mind and went to work sketching the rest of the picture for Dan. She had only seen the image a couple of times, but it was more than enough for her memory to recreate.

The smell of the fresh rain and the mud beneath it filled the air. The sun came out and lit up the sky. It was refreshing and calming to Pauline. She was growing attracted to the outdoors and to nature in a way she never had.

While the rest of the camp was still prepping the camp and drying off, she worked vigorously to try and finish the sketch. By the time dinner needed to be started, she was nearly finished with it. Pauline stopped working on the sketch and went to find Dorothy. She walked up on her, just as she was getting the last of the pots they needed out of the wagon.

"Hello, Dorothy. About ready to start supper?" she asked.

"Getting it started now, my dear. How are you feeling? I haven't seen you in a few hours."

Pauline told her about what Ross had told her about Dan's picture. She explained that she had been working to finish the sketch so that she could give it to him. She was hoping it would make him feel better.

"You're really a sweet girl. Well, if that's the case, help me get dinner started and I'll finish the rest. That way you can get back to finishing the drawing. How's that sound?" Dorothy asked.

"Oh, Miss Dorothy, that would be great! Are you sure you don't need more help than that?"

"Honey, I've been doing this alone for so long that it's absolutely not a problem. That sketch is going to make him feel so much better. It's far more important you get that done."

"Thank you! I hope it does," she cheered.

Pauline helped Dorothy get supper started. She seasoned the dried meat and beans with garlic, pepper, and chives. She then chopped several onions and added it to the mix. The aroma soon took over the smell of fresh rain. She couldn't help but to think back to her childhood and all the times she helped her father cook. A good meal could bring up images and memories that took her back in time. She smiled to herself as she finished helping Dorothy. It always made her feel cheerful when she could help others.

"Okay Dorothy, I'm going to go finish up the sketch. Thank you again for giving me the time to do so."

"It's no problem, honey. I can take care of the rest," she responded.

Pauline headed toward her tent. As she walked, she glanced over to the campfire and saw Dan sitting by himself again, picture in hand. She only had a few more things for the drawing and it would be ready. She could only hope it would help with his sadness.

She made it to her tent and pulled out her notebook. Pauline flipped to the image of Dan's wife and son. She was a beautiful woman, and the boy was gleaming from ear to ear. By far this had been one of her favorite sketches to recreate. Not just because of the beauty in it, but because she knew her sketch would mean something to Dan.

***

A couple hours slipped by before Pauline had finished her sketch. As she stretched and looked around the camp, she noticed everyone had finished their dinner and was enjoying the cooler-than-normal air. Everyone seemed to be in a joyful mood—except Dan, still sitting alone by the fire with a sad expression on his face. She was nervous, but she got up and headed his direction anyway. As she approached him, he spotted her and put the remains of his picture into his pocket again.

"Hey Dan," she said as she sat next to him. "Ross told me what happened to your picture. I don't know if this will help at all, but I did the best I could to recreate it for you."

She nervously handed him the sketch. She couldn't be sure, but she thought she saw a small smile build around the corners of his mouth. She could hear the ongoings of the group around them talking about the day's events, but all she could focus on was Dan, the handsome man right in front of her. He cleared his throat, obviously holding back some emotions.

"It really looks like the real thing." His voice cracked a bit. "You did this from memory?"

"I can take almost any memory and draw it back to life, it's something I've always been able to do."

"It's amazing, truly it is," he said softly. "There's only a couple of things that are off slightly, but it's so good. Thank you."

Pauline grabbed her bag and took out her pencil and pad. She smiled at Dan as she reached out and gently took the sketch from his hands.

"Tell me what's missing and I will fix it."

He explained to her a few missing minor details. He spoke to her about Johnny's shirt being slightly different. Some of the other clothing was off too. Martha's hair was a little different. As Pauline started to correct the mistakes, she took the opportunity to get to know him better.

"Tell me about your family, please," she insisted.

Dan hesitated. "I haven't really talked to anyone about them for a while."

"Tell me what your son was like. How did you meet your wife?"

"Johnny was such a happy boy. He was a good kid and, as young as he was, already enjoyed fishing. He'd tag along with me everywhere." He paused to keep from getting too choked up. "He just wanted to be with me all the time. I met my wife in school. We both seemed to know we were meant to be together. She had the most beautiful smile, captured my heart immediately."

Pauline was surprised he talked to her so openly. She could tell by the way he spoke of them that he had loved them very much. Her heart felt full as he listened to him explain who his family was; describing them brought a bit of happiness to him that she hadn't seen before. He continued as he pulled out what was left of the original picture. She could hardly make out even an outline of their faces. She finished the corrections he had mentioned and showed Dan the sketch again.

"Is this better?"

"Oh my, that's almost perfect." His faced turned red. "But... her eyes are still off some."

"What can I do to fix them?"

Dan seemed to pause before responding. He seemed to be deep in thought, like he was trying to decide if he should say what was on his mind.

"Ca... can you make them look more like yours?" he stammered. "I don't know why I'm telling you this, but your eyes remind me of hers. My son had her eyes, too."

Pauline paused momentarily; his statement took her off-guard. She thought back to the first time she had seen Dan, when they first reached the camp. The way he had looked sad when their eyes met. She must have been lost in thought while she was trying to think of a response, because Dan continued on before she had a chance to say anything.

"Not saying there is a physical resemblance, just that there's a... joy I see in them. Aside from whatever you are dealing with, you seem to be a happy person inside. I hope you don't take this wrong, but you have a happiness that lights up your eyes too." He smiled.

Pauline blushed. She didn't understand why she felt the way she did toward Dan; she hadn't even known him long. She quickly finished the adjustments to the eyes and handed the picture to him. A smile grew across his handsome face.

"That's perfect, thank you so much."

"You're welcome, Dan," she stumbled. "Uh, I haven't eaten dinner yet, I'm going to grab a plate before Dorothy puts everything away."

As Pauline stood up to walk away, Dan reached out and grabbed her hand. She jumped a little, not expecting his touch. He quickly withdrew his hand and apologized. The abuse she had dealt with had made her jumpy, and she knew he had noticed. She gave Dan an apologetic look, and then walked away.

His touch had startled her but was still soft. She thought about Dan as she walked back to her tent. Pauline was confused by her changing feelings toward him, but she also felt joy in making him so happy with her sketch. She slept peacefully that night, for the first time on the drive.

Chapter Thirteen

Dan awoke the next morning sore. His leg hurt from falling off Jesse, but he wasn't too concerned with the pain. He was still able to move it and there didn't seem to be any excessive damage. He sat up and couldn't help but grab the drawing Pauline had given to him the night before. She had surprised him with such a thoughtful act. The more he watched her, and got to know her, the more he knew she couldn't hurt anyone. The care she had taken to make sure everything was just right with the sketch showed him there was more to her than he understood. If he had been on the fence about her before, he was far more on the side of her innocence now.

He thought back to their conversation while she was adjusting the portrait. The fact he had been so upfront with her about her eyes took him by surprise. The sheer fact he had talked to her at all about Johnny and Martha shocked him. He hadn't talked to anyone, other than Henry and Bill, about them since they had died. She just had such a kindness in her eyes that he felt comfortable talking to her. It had felt nice for him to be able to let it out like that. Pauline was really growing on him. He smiled at the thought.

Since the rain a day earlier, the ground was still wet and muddy. He went through his daily routine of prepping Jesse and checking in on the cattle, but not before his morning coffee. It was a gorgeous morning, and the wet ground provided a foggy haze over the valley as the sun began to rise.

Trying to make up some time after losing half a day to the storm, they headed out early that morning. Dan felt happier than he had in years. He could only assume it was because of his newfound friendship in Pauline. As he rode alongside the herd, he began to think of how she jumped when he touched her the night before. Changing from his normal routine, he decided to ride ahead to the wagon. He hadn't spoken to

Dorothy since the day before, and figured it would make for the perfect excuse to check on Pauline as well.

He rode up alongside the wagon. "Morning, ladies! How are you two feeling this fine morning?"

"Good morning, Dan! I'm feeling great! Still think my boots are waterlogged, but other than that, I have no complaints." Dorothy smiled.

Pauline sat there quietly. When Dan first rode up, he noticed her put her sketch book away. She was listening and had a smile on her face, but there was a hesitation to her and he wasn't sure why.

"I think my boots are still soaked, too!" He paused. "How about you, Pauline? How are you feeling? Thank you again for the portrait."

"I feel fine, Dan," she said softly. "I'm really glad you like it!"

He noticed a glow in her when she spoke, a glow he had noticed in her the night before, too. He couldn't help but smile when he answered.

"Of course I like it, you did an amazing job! You really are a talented artist." He grinned.

Pauline just smiled, seeming at a loss for words. He glanced over and caught Dorothy's eye; she was smiling too.

"Dan, can you believe Pauline has never successfully ridden a horse?" Dorothy asked.

He almost couldn't believe it. "Are you messing with me? I think we're just going to have to change that!"

"Oh no, that's okay," she stammered. "That isn't necessary. I'm just fine riding in the wagon."

"Pauline, I know you're probably afraid to get on a horse, but there is no reason to be. If you are willing, when we stop for lunch, I'll give you a lesson. We'll have you riding like a pro in no time!"

He could tell by the look on her face that she wasn't thrilled, but she agreed to it anyway. He told the women he would talk to them later and rode back to his place in the herd, still smiling without realizing it. Ross was the only one to notice and came riding up to him with a grin on his face.

"Told ya she was pretty!" He chuckled. "I knew you'd take a liking to her."

Dan shrugged. "Don't you have something you should be doing?"

"Well, it seems to me I should be right here giving you advice about women. Can't you tell that girl likes you?"

Dan's faced turned red and he looked away to remove his hat. Dan ran his fingers through his hair and replaced his hat, hoping Ross hadn't noticed the color in his face change. He knew his feelings for Pauline were changing, but he wasn't sure how she felt about him.

"You know, they say I talk too much, but I don't mean no harm. Everyone can tell she likes you, that's all I'm saying," Ross said. "I may be young, but I've known you long enough to know you deserve happiness. Just think about it, she's a sweet girl."

With that, Ross rode off to the other side of the herd, leaving Dan alone in his thoughts as they continued to push forward. Ross wasn't the first person to tell him he deserved to be happy; he'd heard it several times before. Maybe they were right. Suddenly, he couldn't wait for the lunch break. His thoughts wandered back to Pauline. He was still torn about her, but the more time he got to be around her, the more he wanted to get to know her.

The morning seemed to drag by for him, but it was finally time to stop for lunch. After getting the herd settled into a nearby field, Dan went to find Pauline for their lesson. As he rode up to the wagon, he spotted her helping Dorothy unload their lunch supplies.

"You mind if I borrow Pauline for a little while, Dorothy?"

"If it gets that girl on a horse, you go right ahead!" She smiled.

"I don't know, I'm scared of falling off again," Pauline interjected.

He lowered himself off the horse and held Jesse's reins. He approached her slowly as he continued to speak.

"Jesse is one of the most mild-mannered horses I have ever ridden. I promise he will be easy to learn on. There's a spot over there in the field where no one will see, so you don't have to worry about people watching either."

"All right, I guess it can't hurt to try," she stammered.

"You kids have fun," Dorothy hollered as they walked away.

The two walked to an open spot in the field not far from the camp. It was flat, and the grass wasn't as tall as it was in other places. He knew it was a perfect spot to teach her how to ride. The sky was a gorgeous mix of blue and white. The sun was hanging high in the sky, as if someone hung it there especially for them. The gentle breeze brought along an aroma of fresh water from a stream past the trees. He thought that there couldn't be a more perfect day to be riding a horse. He took his rope and tied it around Jesse's harness.

"Now, I know you're scared, but I will be right here. There's nothing to worry about. Jesse will do most of the work for you," he said.

She smiled a nervous smile but didn't say anything. She walked up to Jesse's side, next to where Dan stood. Placing her hand on Jesse's neck and petting his mane, she spoke softly to the beautiful creature she was about to mount.

"Now don't you get all scared and throw me off, okay?" she whispered.

She grabbed ahold of the saddle horn, and with Dan's help, she mounted Jesse. Dan kept his hand on the rope, just for her peace of mind. He knew Jesse wouldn't bolt but reassuring her was important in the learning process.

"Now, when you are ready, I will lead Jesse around so you can get a feel for how a horse moves. You're in charge," he said. "You have the reins, but I will keep ahold of the rope so I can keep him in the circle."

He watched her settle into the saddle a few times before she looked comfortable. The sun touching her face gave her an angelic glow. He almost lost focus because he was staring and when she looked down at him, he felt something ignite inside of himself.

"I think I'm ready, Dan. Just take it slow, please," she said in a gentle voice.

"Okay, here we go."

He started walking and gave Jesse's reins a little tug. The horse began to walk alongside of him. It was only a slow walk, but he wanted her to adjust to the horse's movements. He kept Jesse moving in a circle, the easiest way to not wear him out more, and keep her from getting scared.

"When you're ready, give him a slight push with the heels of your feet on both of his sides. He'll pick up his pace to a trot and you'll understand the differences in the way he moves at different speeds," he instructed.

After a few minutes at a walking pace, he watched as she dug her heels in and the horse began to trot. He released a portion of the rope to keep up with the horse's pace. Pauline's face lit up with joy. Her smile captivated him. He continued to watch her as she trotted along on Jesse's back. It was the first time he had really seen her this happy.

"See, I told you it would all be okay. How do you feel about it now?" he asked.

"Oh, this is exciting! I can't believe I was so scared of riding. I feel like I've been missing out," she said.

Dan still didn't know everything about this woman. They had only known each other for that short time, but there was so much more to her than he had realized when he initially misjudged her. He thought about this as he watched her for a little longer. He kept Jesse circling around him as she enjoyed the first ride. Her happiness was rubbing off on him as he smiled like a fool.

He led Jesse around for a while longer, giving Pauline pointers for how to control the direction of the horse by leading the reins one way or the other and leaning into the turns. She took to the lesson well and he could tell she wasn't scared anymore. He then explained to her how to bring Jesse to a stop.

"Just pull back and say 'whoa' when you are comfortable. He'll respond to you; he can tell you aren't scared, and he'll take his cues from you now."

"Okay, let me try," she said. "Whoa, boy. Whoa."

Jesse came to a full stop. Dan smiled as he walked up to help her down off the horse. She lifted one leg over the saddle and sat sideways on him. Dan reached up as she slid down, his hands on either side of her tiny waist. When she made it all the way to the ground, they were face to face, closer than they had ever been before. They both stood silent for a moment, staring intently into each other's eyes. The spark ignited inside of Dan again. He cleared his throat before he spoke.

"I hope you'll keep riding, it's a freeing feeling."

"Oh, uh, yeah. I mean, now that I'm not so scared, I think I will enjoy riding," she stammered. "I... I think I'm going to go grab some food before we head out. I'm famished. Thank you so much for the lesson."

She turned and started to walk away from him. The glow from the sun still encased her small frame. He was absorbed in her beauty for several seconds before he realized he hadn't responded to her.

"You're welcome, Pauline!" he shouted out to her.

She just turned and smiled. She ducked her head down and turned back to the direction she was walking. Dan could feel something new building inside of him. The extra time he had spent with her had opened him up in a way he hadn't expected. Could he be falling for this woman? He thought back to her smile, lost in thought and smiling himself. As he led Jesse back up to the group, he couldn't imagine a better way to spend a break—and already couldn't wait for the next one with her.

Chapter Fourteen

Pauline was riding in the wagon after lunch, excited after her lesson with Dan. Her fear of riding was gone and almost couldn't wait to ride a horse again. Her thoughts trailed off to the moment she slid off the horse and into Dan's arms. For a split second, she could almost feel his lips on hers. She still didn't know what to do about the emotions coursing through her. She didn't know why, but he made her feel excited about life again. He had made her feel brave when she got up on the horse. One thing she did know for sure was that she intended on spending more time with him.

When they stopped for the day, Pauline realized she had just spent most of the time daydreaming about riding horses on the plains. It surprised her to find she enjoyed it as much as she did. She helped Dorothy unload the wagon and prepare for dinner.

"Do you mind if I go find Dan? I have some questions about riding," she said.

"By all means, honey. Feel free to do as you please. I don't actually need help; I just enjoy your company."

The sun was low in the sky as she headed off to find him. Her first stop would be down by the cattle. If she didn't find him there, she would check down by the trees. The breeze blew her hair into her face and when she swiped it back into place, she saw Dan riding up toward her. He smiled at her as he brought Jesse to a halt and hopped down off his back.

"What brings you out here, Pauline?" he asked.

"I was just coming to find you, actually. Do you think you could give me another lesson?"

His smile brought a smile to her face. The way his eyes relaxed when he smiled made her blush. She brushed the hair away from her face again before meeting his gaze.

"I think that would be great, but why don't we give Jesse some time to rest? We can do a lesson after dinner if you're up for it."

Disappointment swept across her. "Oh, okay. That would be all right."

"Hey now, I got an idea," he grinned. "How would you like to learn more about the outdoors and cattle? If you're willing to learn, I would love to teach you."

"That sounds perfect. I've never been out on the range before. It would be nice to have a basic knowledge at the very least."

"Great! Let me get Jesse settled in. I'll be right back!"

She watched as he walked his horse to the camp. He tied Jesse off to a tree branch and took what looked like a carrot from his bag and fed it to him. She marveled at how much care he took of his horse. He turned and started his way back toward her. She glanced over the rest of the camp and noticed Charley in the center of the rest of the group. He glanced over and noticed her, almost pausing his story mid-sentence. He looked like he was center stage, and everyone was cheering him on. Everyone else in the group had seemed to be won over by the man's charm and stories. She couldn't help but shiver at the sight. Something wasn't right about that man. He lifted his arms and touched his left breast pocket, then looked back at the group and continued.

"You look upset, everything okay?" Dan asked.

She had been watching Charley so long that she hadn't realized he had made it back to her. She nudged her head in Charley's direction.

"I just don't trust that man, something about him gives me chills."

"Charley? Yeah, I don't like him being here, either. I get the same feeling," he agreed. "Forget about him, let's go down to the cattle and I'll show you some things to keep an eye on during cattle drives."

"Okay, I'd like to learn as much as I can."

They walked side by side to the edge of the herd. She had been to visit them on her own on a couple of nights already, but that was only because of her love for animals. Being here with Dan made everything feel different. Just being around him lifted her spirits. They took their time as they walked through the herd, and she watched as he checked each one for ticks.

"So, why is checking for ticks so important anyways? They are so small, and the cattle are so much bigger. I guess I don't understand."

"Well, the ticks carry diseases that are dangerous for the cattle, and if they go untreated can actually kill them," Dan answered. "They show signs of fever and can get disoriented. Within a few days, they will lose their appetite. Basically, they will starve to death."

"It's amazing how something so small can completely destroy something so big and tough," she smiled.

"Life can be unpredictable like that," he said.

The pair finished checking the cattle together. They continued to talk about the cattle and what to look for. She soaked in all the information he shared, fascinated by the lifestyle. The sky had begun to darken as the sun drifted down below the horizon. The last glow from the sun beamed across the plains. They walked back to the group, watching the sun fade as the last bits of sunshine lit up the mountains to the north of them.

"It's such a beautiful evening," Pauline said.

"Yes, it is," he agreed. "Just wondering, do you know how to start a fire?"

"No," she said, dropping her chin. "Nobody has ever shown me any of the skills I would need to be out here."

"I can show you how to do that, too. That's unless you need to get back to Dorothy and help her with anything."

She thought back to her childhood and couldn't remember a single time anyone had taken this much time to teach her anything. They all just assumed she wasn't worth the time or hassle of teaching. She grinned when she looked back up at Dan.

"That would be amazing. I absolutely love it out here on the trail."

"Great! Let's go over to my tent and I will show you how to start a fire. I'll even show you how to tie a few knots that would be helpful for you."

Over the next few hours, she listened and watched Dan as he explained the Hondo knot, which was used to create the lasso needed to allow the rope slide and was best used to rope livestock. He showed her how to start a fire using a tinderbox. She marveled at how he would strike his knife against the flint, and the spark would ignite the fire. After a few tries, she was able to produce the same outcome.

"I've never done these things before. Thank you so much for taking the time to teach me."

"You're welcome, Pauline. I've really enjoyed spending time with you. I love being out here on the trail. I feel so free and nature itself is beautiful, as well."

Pauline blushed. She couldn't remember a time when anyone had said they were happy spending time with her. It made her heart beat faster. Guilt began to creep in when she realized she was still on the run, and that her husband was dead. She doubted she deserved the happiness that had taken hold inside of her. She wasn't sure what to do, but she needed to get away. This time, it wasn't Dan causing her anxiety—it was her fear of being truly happy.

"It's getting late," she said as she stood. "We should probably get some rest for tomorrow."

"You're right. I need to check on Jesse and head to bed myself."

"Good night, Dan."

"Night, Pauline."

She walked back to her tent. The night had become dark with the moon covered by clouds. The main campfire was the only source of light and lit the way. She thought about the day and how happy she felt knowing someone cared enough to teach her new things. Dan was patient with her, even though it took so many tries before she had gotten the knot right. She smiled to herself as she laid down for the night. The rest of the camp was asleep. The quiet night and the cool air helped to ease the tension in her mind. She wasn't sure about her new feelings toward Dan, or what the future would hold. She just knew she was content and that for the moment, she felt safe. She closed her eyes and quickly fell asleep.

The next morning, she awoke to the sound of Dorothy making the morning preparations for breakfast. A few of the others were well on their way to starting the day. She quickly prepped herself and scurried over to help.

"Well, good morning there, Pauline! It's not often I wake up before you," she laughed. "Did you have a good evening?"

"Oh Dorothy, it was such a nice night. I have really enjoyed spending time with Dan. He's nothing like I mistook him for at first."

"I did try to tell you, we're like a little family out here. I knew he would come 'round to you at some point."

Dan made her feel brave, and the fact he took the time to teach her anything astonished her still. She wanted to get to know him better. She wanted to be around him more.

"His whole attitude seems to have changed toward me. It was a really fun day," Pauline said.

"I've known Dan for a while, I knew he'd take to you. He looks so much happier too. You've definitely had a hand in changing him. By the way, I don't think he is the only one who has taken a liking to you. Charley was asking about you yesterday too," she teased.

"What did he want to know?"

"Oh, it was harmless questions," she promised. "He just wanted to know your name again and asked about where you from. I think he likes you."

Pauline frowned. "Well, I definitely do not like him. He's always telling those outlandish stories. Like he's someone all important."

The thought of that man, who she already had doubts about, was asking questions about her made her uncomfortable. She didn't like that he was trying to find out more about her but wasn't coming to her. Not like she would want to talk to him to begin with, but there was something dark about Charley and she couldn't put her finger on it.

"If it makes you feel any better, I didn't tell him anything about you. Just your name since we had already told him that," Dorothy assured.

"I appreciate that, I just don't want him to know anything about me. I'll keep my distance from him until the drive is over."

"I understand, darling," she said. "I won't give him anything you don't want me to."

"Thank you, Dorothy."

The smells of coffee and bacon filled the campsite. The morning brought a sunny haze across the fields and Pauline gazed at its beauty. The mountains off in the distance had a layer of snow on its peaks. The morning sun shined off them like a spotlight.

The two women finished cleaning up after breakfast and packed up the wagon to start the day. Pauline was filled with a new hope, thanks to her time with Dan. She knew there was something starting to develop in her relationship with him, but until they got to know each other a little better, she wasn't sure what that might be. The dread that hung over her because of the murder of her husband was heavy. The confusion left her feeling unsettled. As they jumped up into the wagon, she pulled out her notebook and started a new sketch. This was her escape from overthinking.

Dorothy whipped the reins and the horses lurched forward. The start of a new day filled Pauline with excitement.

Chapter Fifteen

Dan found the morning to be a beautiful gift. The sky was a light blue, without a cloud in sight. He was easily lost in thought after yesterday with Pauline. It made him happy to hand his knowledge on to someone else. She had such a gentle soul and was willing to learn. He still couldn't believe he was opening up to her. After his wife and son died, he'd built this tough exterior he thought no one could get through. Yet here he was opening up to a complete stranger. The thought brought him a smile, though. It had been so long since he had felt comfortable with anyone new that it felt like a new chapter in his life could be opening.

"How's it going, Dan?" Henry's voice broke his thoughts.

"It's a gorgeous day and I feel good about the day ahead," he said. "Been a while since I could honestly say that."

"Could it be because of the time you have been spending with Pauline?" Henry snickered.

"You sneaky little devils." He smiled as it all came together. "You and Dorothy both want me to get closer to her, don't you?"

Henry just grinned. "You both need new friends, which is all we want for you. I'm glad you took my advice. It's nice to see you smiling again, Dan."

"It's just feels good to have someone to teach. Most of these boys come in and think they know everything. Nobody has taken the time to teach her any of this."

"As long as it helps and makes you happy. There can't be anything wrong with that, can there?" Henry asked.

"No." Dan grinned. "I suppose you're right."

"There ya go, then. You need to enjoy life. Bad things happen and there isn't a lick of anything you can do about it. It's more than just surviving. You have to live it. I'm going to go check in with the girls."

"I don't know if I've told either of you how much I appreciate all the things you've done for me. I probably would have been driven crazy without these drives. Thank you, Henry."

"You're welcome, Dan. You're a good man, just remember that and everything will come together the way it should be. I'll catch up with you later, keep these guys in line for me," he smiled.

With that, Henry rode off to the wagon. Dan thought about what Henry had said. Maybe he was holding on too tight to the memories of his family. Was it time to let go and try to move on? He wasn't sure, but he spent the morning considering it.

While he would normally dive into his work and not think of anything else, that morning he kept thinking about Pauline. He was excited to spend more time with her and was already planning on new things to teach her. Dan and Ross had just finished getting the cattle settled in so they could stop for lunch. The sun was at its highest point, and the temperature continued to rise. There was no breeze to cool them off, so they had to stop at a small group of trees that supplied a well-shaded area for them.

"It's hot as blazes out here today," Ross said. "You ready to go get some lunch?"

"This heat has me hungry, I could definitely eat."

"Let's get over there into the shade and grab some grub then," Ross said as he wiped his brow. "I'm sweatin' like a pig on the fire."

Dan laughed at him, and they headed over to the camp. The shade was nice. Although it was still hot, at least they weren't out in the open fields cooking in the sun. Dan ate some dried fruits and drank water. It wasn't a big lunch, but it provided the nourishment he needed to get through the rest of the day.

The sun was still beaming when they headed back out to the trail. Besides the heat, it was a normal day. The cattle trudged along without a care in the world. The afternoon flew by and before long, it was time to stop for the day. After Dan and the boys finished getting the cattle down to the river to drink, they led them to an open field where they could graze. While the rest of the cowboys finished settling the herd in, Dan went to look for Pauline. He had been looking forward to spending time with her all day. The excitement he felt was a new sensation for him.

On the way through the camp, he saw everyone else setting up and starting the fire for the night. Whistling and conversations took place all around. Above everyone else, he heard Charley being loud and obnoxious, telling some story about wrestling a bear. His stories were so much larger than life that Dan was beginning to think he was trying to distract everyone from something else. Dan's gut told him that something was off. Knowing Pauline wasn't Charley's biggest fan, he figured she would love to get away for a bit.

Dan found her helping Dorothy unload the wagon. He watched her for a few moments, mesmerized by her movements. Suddenly, the girls started laughing, offering a moment of pure joy for him. This was the first time he'd heard her truly laugh and it made him smile. He was still smiling when he approached them.

"Hey Dorothy, mind if I steal her away for a bit?" he asked.

"Absolutely!" she blurted. "If you get a chance, could you look for some herbs for me? I've run out of a few things."

"Sure thing. Is there anything more specific you need?" Dan asked.

Dorothy grinned. "You know me well enough to figure it out. Find something to go into a nice stew."

"No problem. I'll see what I can find around here. Do you mind walking around with me, Pauline?"

"I could go for a walk. Need to stretch these legs out a little, anyway," Pauline said.

They had stopped not far from a wooded area. The temperature hadn't dropped much, but the sun was beginning to settle in the west, and it wouldn't be long before the night's cool air would push its way in. As they walked away from the direct area of the camp, they could still hear Charley telling his stories.

"I really don't trust him. Something in my gut tells me he's bad news," Pauline muttered.

"I agree with you. I get that same feeling every time I hear him talking."

"So, what exactly are we looking for out here, anyway?"

Dan smiled. "Well, we're looking for a plant called Lamb's Quarters. They'll add some great flavor to the stew Dorothy is likely making. Although, we might find some others that would blend well, too."

"Why do they call it Lamb's Quarters?"

"No idea, but it does taste good in her stew," he laughed.

They walked around for a few minutes before Dan spotted a few plants that would fit the meal.

"See this plant right here? These are called Cattails. This isn't what we're trying to find, but it has a sweet flavor. I think it would go good with the stew, what do you think?"

He pulled a handful of stems from the ground and broke one at its base. He handed the broken piece to Pauline, smiling as she took it. He watched for her reaction after she put the piece of plant into her mouth. She paused for a moment, and then smiled.

"I think that will be great," she agreed.

By the time he had finished pulling a few more Cattails, Pauline had walked about twenty feet away. As he walked to catch up to her, he couldn't help but once again notice how pretty she was. Her smile came to light in the soft glow of the sun going down. He was definitely growing a soft spot for her. He was almost to her when he watched her lean down, looking at something.

"What did you find, Pauline?"

"I'm not sure, what are these things? I can't tell if you even can eat them," she said as she laughed.

He smiled at her laugh. "Let's see what you found there."

He approached her and leaned over right beside her. Being this close made his heart skip a beat. He looked down to her hands still touching the plant. He almost couldn't believe his eyes.

"Would you look at that! You, my dear, have found exactly what we were trying to find. That plant you're looking at is Lamb's Quarters. You can tell by the grayish-green coloring on the leaves. See how it is shaped? That's an easy giveaway, too."

"So, these are the ones that we need? Still don't see why they call it that, it looks nothing like a lamb," she giggled.

Dan laughed a little, too. "I'd have to say you're right. No resemblance at all. If you kneel down here with me, I'll show you how to pull it out. That way you don't lose any of the flavor."

Dan kneeled to the ground and put his hand around the base of the plant. He looked at her as she kneeled beside him. When she did, a piece of hair fell into her face. Without thinking about it, he reached his hand out to brush it back behind her ear. As soon as his hand moved close to her face, her smile faded, and a fear washed over her face. She flinched. It all happened so fast, Dan didn't have a chance to react. Pauline looked away and began to stand.

"I'm sorry, Pauline. I was only trying to reach for the hair in your face. I didn't mean to frighten you," he pleaded.

He could tell she was upset, but she didn't say a word, instead rushing back to the camp. Dan was confused. He wasn't sure why she had reacted that way. He thought maybe she just didn't want him to touch her. That didn't seem right, though. They hadn't interacted much at first, but over the last few days, it felt like she wanted to be closer to him. He knew he wanted to be closer to her. Was it possible that he completely misread the signs he thought she was giving? He didn't know.

He stood along the tree line looking out over the field. The sun was gone. The moon lit up the field, and he could make out the outlines of the cattle. The subtle glow across the grass made the fields look like a sheet of emeralds. The beauty of the night was lost on Dan. He was still going over the possibilities of why she flinched. He eventually remembered that she had flinched once before, when he helped her with her hands. He was suddenly filled with anger.

The only way she would be that edgy was if someone had put hands on her. Dan hated the thought of any woman being abused. The thought crept into his mind that her husband had been the one to hit her before. He had only seen her father for a moment, but the fact he had gotten her to the group and was willing to send her away to protect her proved it couldn't have been him.

Dan didn't understand how anyone could lay hands on a woman. The thought continued to anger him. The night had cooled the air and as he walked back to the camp, he couldn't help but feel more protective of Pauline. She was a nice girl. He hadn't been there to protect his wife, but he'd be damned if he was going to let anything more happen to Pauline. He laid his head at one of the open ends of his tent, looking up at the night sky. He closed his eyes and pictured Pauline, with her big smile and bright eyes. Her kindness and the simple things she took joy in eased his mind. Things were changing inside of him, and he knew it was because of her. As he drifted off, his last thoughts were about protecting Pauline.

Chapter Sixteen

Pauline woke up early the next morning. She was sore and worn out from her time on the trail, unused to this much time on a wagon or the amount of manual labor that went into being on the trail. It had cooled overnight but was still much warmer than previous mornings. She stretched out from beneath the makeshift tent, and slowly stood up. The sun had just made its break over the horizon.

As she stood there watching the gorgeous sunrise, she couldn't help but think of the previous night's events. She enjoyed her time with Dan and knew she wanted to spend more of it with him, but her violent past kept him at arm's length. Every time he got close to her, Pauline would flinch and turn away. She knew it was because of the way her husband had treated her. She didn't mean to, but it had become second nature to her after living with Herschel. It wasn't anything that Dan had done wrong, but she still felt embarrassed and ashamed of her reaction.

She looked over to Dorothy's tent and noticed the older woman was already awake as well. She walked past the campfire to where Dorothy was preparing coffee. The aroma of freshly-crushed coffee beans filled her nose.

"I think I am going to need a cup of that today," Pauline joked. "I need that extra jolt to get me going."

Dorothy smiled. "I'll get you a cup, dear. How are you feeling aside from that?"

"I feel all right, just wore out. I'm not used to all this physical work. Plus, with everything else going on, I'm not really sure how to feel."

Dorothy poured them both a cup of coffee. They were quiet for several minutes, enjoying the fresh coffee and watching the sunrise. Dorothy broke the silence first.

"I can only assume you're talking about your growing feelings for Dan?"

"There is that, but also with all I went through with Herschel. I don't know if I deserve to be happy, Dorothy," she confessed.

"Oh sweetheart, let me tell you the story of how me and Henry came to be: I was engaged to a man before I met Henry. His name was Tom. At first, he seemed to be everything you would look for in a partner. Nice and caring. He went out of his way to be with me. Shortly after our engagement, and not long before our marriage, Tom became more aggressive. When we would go out to the saloon, he would get drunk and start arguments with me. Over the next few months before the wedding, he became physically violent with me…"

Dorothy became emotional while she was talking, her eyes watering. Pauline handed her a handkerchief to wipe her eyes and waited patiently for Dorothy to collect herself. It was only a short few moments before she continued on.

Dorothy cleared her throat. "Anyway, eventually he started hitting me. Sometimes once, but most of the time, he would hit me over and over. He always made sure never to hit my face and would come up with excuses as to ways I had hurt myself. I'm sure everyone thought I was the clumsiest person in the world. Eventually, I met Henry while in town at the general store. I had my arms full and dropped a bag of flour. He picked it up and carried it to the wagon for me."

"That's how you met Henry?" Pauline asked. "You guys are so good together, I just assumed you were school sweethearts who had spent their whole lives together."

"Not quite." Dorothy smiled. "To make a long story short, he noticed the bruises on my arms and began asking questions. In my depressed state, I ended up telling him everything. He eventually, like a knight in shining armor, chased Tom out of town. We've been together ever since. I struggled at first, wondering if I truly deserved happiness. There were so many habits I had to break. Tom and I were only together for a year, but the damage he left me with had me debating my own worth. Pauline, I understand more than most how you feel. You doubt you deserve to be happy and feel like every man is going to hit you, but you are a young woman. You didn't deserve the husband you had, and you surely don't deserve to be on the run now. It's just going to take time for you to believe that. All those habits you've created will slowly fade. Just have faith."

Pauline let that sink in for several minutes. They were both up earlier than the men, so the camp was still quiet. She couldn't believe Dorothy had been through much of the same thing she had. She understood now why she had such a fast connection with her. The woman was a saint, even after going through hell.

"I know you're right. It's just so hard to break the habits. I flinch every time someone gets too close. I'm afraid everyone wants to hurt me," she said, worried.

"Darlin', the feeling will pass in time. Just take it slow, the people who care will understand. I promise," Dorothy assured her.

"Thank you, Dorothy. For sharing that story and for the coffee," she said with a soft smile. "I think I saw a good place down by that creek to take a bath. I'm going to get in there before all of the camp wakes up."

"You're welcome, Pauline. I have to get breakfast started anyway. I hope my story helped. You deserve to be happy, don't forget that."

Dorothy grinned as she stood up and poured the rest of her coffee on the ground. Pauline stood and headed down toward the creek, not far from the camp. There were trees on either side of the water, giving her enough coverage that she felt comfortable stripping down. Even with the warm of the morning sun, the water was cold on her feet. The chill moved all through her body.

She flashed back to one late night, a short time after she was married. It was one of the first times she realized Herschel wasn't the man she thought. She had fallen asleep while waiting for him to come home from a late night at the saloon. Dinner had been finished hours beforehand, but she was tired from the day's work and had dozed off. Pauline had been ripped from her peaceful slumber by a bucket of cold water Herschel threw on her. He was drunk and angry that his food was cold. They had argued for hours, and it was the first time he had ever hit her. The memory made her shiver. She became more aware of the scars on her back, which she had received at the hands of her drunk husband.

Pauline stepped all the way into the water. It was just deep enough to reach her shoulders. She was scrubbing her body down when the feeling of being watched took over. Her head spun around quickly as she looked all around her. There was nobody there. She quickly dismissed the notion and assumed it was past trauma causing her to make things up. She continued to bathe and started whistling an old tune from the church she went to as a child. After a few more minutes, Pauline got the feeling she was being watched again.

Although she looked around and didn't see anyone, she decided to cut her bath short and got out.

She was trying to dress herself quickly and was about halfway dressed when she heard a crack behind her. When she spun her head around to find the sound, she saw Dan coming down the small hill toward her, his gaze filled with dismay. Anger rose inside of her. Had he been watching her this whole time? She quickly finished dressing herself and tried to rush past him, heading back to the camp.

"Where did those scars on your back come from? Was it your husband's doing?"

His question stopped her in her tracks. She hadn't realized he might have seen the marks on her body. It sent another chill down her spine.

"What are you doing down here? Were you spying on me or–"

"What are you talking about, Pauline? I just came down here to take a quick swim in the creek before starting the day. I wasn't spying on you, I just got here," he objected.

"You just thought you could watch me take a bath?" she hissed.

He looked confused and hurt by the accusation, but by then her anger and fear had already taken over. She quickly rushed past him and up the hill toward the camp, confused and embarrassed. Her heart raced as she thought about what had just happened. She couldn't even be sure that it was Dan who had been watching her, but it was clear someone had been, and he'd been the only person she saw.

By the time she made it back to the camp, her anger subsided a little. She knew she had overreacted but couldn't be sure Dan was telling her the truth. She was embarrassed for the way she acted, and now that he had seen her scars, she was ashamed. To her, each one of those scars was another way she had failed her husband. It made her feel unattractive and humiliated. Herschel had first broken her mind and then her body. Those scars were proof she wasn't good enough. She remembered Dorothy had been awake before her bath and quickly walked over to her.

"Hey Dorothy…"

"How did the bath go, honey?" she asked before looking up. "Would you do me a favor and grab that cup of coffee right there?"

Without thinking about it and before continuing on, she grabbed the cup and held it out for Dorothy to take. It was still hot in her hands. Dorothy was busy finishing breakfast and wasn't paying attention to her yet.

"Where would you like me to put this?"

"Oh, just set it over here by me. Dan left it here a few minutes ago. He said he was going for a quick swim, but I know he'll be back for it. He always finishes his morning cup," Dorothy laughed.

"So… so Dan was just here?" she stammered in disbelief.

"Yes, he just left," she said as she looked up at Pauline. "What's the matter, dear?"

"I just finished my bath and felt like I was being watched. I heard a noise and when I turned around, Dan was the only person I saw. I thought he was watching me."

"Well, I assure you, it couldn't have been Dan. He was here up until a few moments ago," Dorothy assured her.

Pauline's anger washed away, except now she was even more embarrassed for overreacting. She thanked Dorothy and headed back over to her tent. She needed to brush her hair. She couldn't help but wonder, if it wasn't Dan who had been watching her, then who? She knew she felt someone's presence out there, even before she saw Dan. She wasn't sure what to say to him now, so she decided to try and steer clear from him. Pauline figured because of the way she had acted toward him and the accusations she had made, he wouldn't want to talk to her anyway.

As she brushed her hair and prepared for the day, she couldn't help but think about the feeling she had in her gut when she was bathing. She was confused and upset that someone would spy on her but hadn't seen anyone out there with her. Her mind raced, but she tried to push the thoughts away. Pauline finished with her hair and packed up her belongings and tent. They'd be headed out soon and she wanted to help Dorothy pack up the wagon.

She muddled through the thoughts in her head as she carried her things to the wagon. She knew Dorothy was right—it would take some time to break old habits. The way she had accused Dan was a testament to that. She didn't want it to be that way with him. Pauline felt safe with Dan around; it was nothing like how the other men had treated her. She only hoped he'd forgive her for snapping at him, and not give up on her right away.

Chapter Seventeen

Dan stood by the creek, still stunned at Pauline's unusual outburst. He had no idea she was there and would have waited for her to come back up to the camp if he had. There was a beauty to her, for sure, but he hadn't come to spy on her bathing. The marks on her back still angered him. He wanted to know who had caused them, but it was obvious he wasn't going to get an answer from her anytime soon. He wanted to talk to her though, so he headed back up to the camp.

The early morning sun was peeking out from beyond the horizon, and nature had begun to awaken as well. The birds chirped and sang their songs, while the trees rustled in the breeze. When arrived back at the camp, he saw Pauline brushing her hair near her tent. He started her way but was quickly interrupted by Ross.

"I know it's still early Dan, but there are a few cattle that have gotten away from the group. Mind helping me wrangle them up?" Ross asked.

Dan hesitated. He could still see Pauline and had questions for her, but also knew his main task was to keep the livestock safe.

"Sure thing," he answered. "I'll get Jesse saddled up and meet you out by the main herd."

"Thanks. I didn't want to bother Henry with it this early," he grinned. "Old man needs his sleep."

Dan smiled and tipped his hat. He walked over to his horse and prepped him for the day's work. Never one to forget to give his powerful steed a treat, he fed him a carrot and mounted Jesse. Off he went to meet up with Ross. It wasn't uncommon for a few of the beasts to trickle away at night. Sometimes, they would graze and just keep walking. Really, the only problems with them getting away too far were them falling and breaking a limb or being attacked by wild animals. As he rode up to the herd, he saw Ross already waiting for him.

"I made a quick sweep, looks like they are over by that tree line out over there. Shouldn't be much work for the two of us," Ross said.

Taking a quick head count, Dan could see only three that had taken off. The good news was that it looked like all the calves were accounted for. The older and larger cattle were a bit easier to move without spooking easily. They had gotten used to being pushed around and, barring a storm or predator, would likely come back to the herd with no problems.

"Let's get to it," Dan nodded.

They headed toward the wooded area not too far off. When they got close, he spotted the three cows grazing. He instructed Ross to go around one side of them, as he maneuvered around to the other. The goal was to not scare them, and get behind them to push them back toward the group. They both moved into position behind them and called out to the cattle. Using their horses as guides, they hooted and hollered until the cattle headed back into the right direction. It wasn't hard work; within a short time they had led the trio back to the other cattle.

"That's a good job, Ross," Dan praised. "My only question is, weren't you on watch this morning?"

"I was, but honestly, after the heat yesterday, I was so exhausted I fell asleep. I'm sorry, Dan," he apologized. "It won't happen again."

"Ah, kid. It's all right. It happens to the best of us," Dan laughed. "I'm not upset, and we'll keep this between us, but I've done the same thing myself a time or two."

Ross smiled. "Thank you. Like I said, it won't happen again."

"I know it won't. Now go get yourself some coffee and get ready to go. I'll take over keeping an eye on the herd until someone comes down."

"Coffee sounds good. I'll see if Dorothy has any left. Maybe grab some breakfast while I'm up there. You know I'm never any good without a full stomach," he joked.

Dan laughed. "You're not very good with a full stomach, either."

Ross grinned, then turned and walked away. Dan watched the young man ride back to the camp. He was happy the kid had a good head on his shoulders and didn't try to wrangle the cattle up himself. Many things could have gone wrong. He looked over the cattle as he waited for one of the other cowboys to relieve his post, thinking back to the events from that morning. He was still concerned about Pauline but didn't know when he would get an opportunity to talk to her again.

The morning sunrise gave him a chill. The natural beauty of the world had been lost to him for so long, and he was just beginning to see life the way he did before the passing of his wife and son. Pauline was a big part of that. He wanted to find out more about this woman changing his outlook, but he felt like he kept messing it up. Just then, one of the other men took his spot with the herd, and he was able to get back to the camp.

He looked for Pauline when he got there, but she was already helping Dorothy pack the chuck wagon. He didn't want to pull her away from her work, so he decided to try and talk to her at lunch. Dan packed his gear and they all headed out for the day.

The morning went on uneventful. They had hit a stretch on the drive that was mostly flatland, and they could still hear the rush of the river not too far away. The sky was blue and even with light cloud coverage, it was still a warm day. He spent the morning driving the cattle along the edge of the fields; he didn't speak to anyone, still anxious to talk to Pauline. By lunch, his thoughts of her had completely taken over. After leading the cows to the drink, he returned and went looking for her. He found Dorothy first instead.

"Hey, Dorothy. How are you doing today?"

"I'm doing good today. Though, it's a little warm for my liking," she said. "You never came back for your coffee this morning. I was almost worried about you."

Dan paused. "Uh, yeah, I had to check in on Ross and the herd. Nothing to worry about. Do you know where Pauline is?"

"She said she was going to go for a walk, but I'm not sure where she headed off to," she answered.

"Thank you, Dorothy," he sighed. "I'll try to find her later."

With that, he grabbed a plate of food and sat on the ground by Jesse and ate quietly. The movement of the camp went unnoticed as he finished his plate. He mounted Jesse while the rest of the group finished up and prepared to leave for the second half of the day.

He noticed Pauline several times throughout the afternoon. She rode in the wagon and any time their eyes met, she looked away or went back to her sketches. He couldn't help but wonder if she was still avoiding him. He continued to think about how skittish she was at times and the fear in her eyes when she turned and saw him that morning. He also remembered the marks on her back and the thought of her being abused angered him.

Finally, they stopped for dinner. With Pauline avoiding him all throughout the day, he knew he could go to Dorothy or Henry for answers. Dorothy was still prepping dinner, so he headed out to the herd to find Henry. Dan hoped he would be able to clear some things up . He walked out to the herd and found Henry checking the cattle's hooves for cracks. It was a common thing, on the longer drives, for their hooves to take damage. If they were cracked though, it could lead to pain and possible lameness. Henry looked up just as Dan reached him.

"They're all looking good, Dan. What can I do for you this evening? Are you looking for Pauline?" Henry asked.

It's good that the cattle are doing so well," he said. "I know she left on a walk, but I had a few questions for you."

"Well, ask away," he said.

"I know you've known her father for many years, but what do you know about Pauline?" Dan asked with concern. "Do you know about the scars she has?"

Henry's grin faded. "Why do you want to know, son?"

He explained the events that took place earlier that day. He was quick to assure Henry that he wasn't watching Pauline, but her reaction had boggled him.

"To be honest with you, I only know the bit her father told me. Dorothy did tell me about some of their conversations as well. She told me Pauline thought you had been watching her this morning, but I didn't think much of it. I know better," he said. "What I've been told is that her husband would get drunk, then come home and pick a fight with her over the smallest of things. He beat her pretty bad a couple times. Or so her father told me."

The information didn't surprise Dan. Still, the thought angered him again and he felt sick to his stomach. The idea of a man beating on a woman disgusted him. The two men headed back to the camp together as they continued to talk.

"That explains why she flinches whenever I get close to her," Dan replied and shook his head. "Why would any man do that to a woman?"

"I don't know, Dan. I've never understood it myself, but I think it would do you some good to talk to her about it. That way you can hear it yourself straight from her."

"I've been hoping to have time with her all day, but she's avoiding me like a diseased animal," Dan muttered.

"Just keep trying, she'll open up eventually. The abuse she suffered at the hands of that man are bound to have more than a physical effect on her; it can take some time. Last time I saw her, she was walking back toward the camp herself. Maybe you could find her by the wagon there, or even where she hung her tent."

"Thanks for telling me, Henry. I need to find her and talk to her; hopefully she's willing. Between her husband's murder and the abuse, I want to help in any way I can."

"Anytime." Henry smiled. "I'm glad you're coming back around."

"Me too, Henry," Dan said. "I haven't felt like this in a long time. I feel like she's started to pull me out of the daze I've been in for the last few years."

They parted ways, with Henry heading toward the fire and Dan walking the other way to the wagon. He had to find

Pauline to try and work things out. He wanted her to know she could talk to him and that he would never hurt her. The thought made Dan wish he could have laid a beating on her husband himself.

Just as Dan rounded the corner of the wagon, he almost ran headfirst into Charley O'Conner. The man looked startled as he dropped his hand from his chest. He wore a guilty look on his face but said nothing. Dan was sure he had been listening in to his conversation with Henry. It felt strange to him that the man was right there, like he was purposely staying out of sight. But he didn't have time to think about that right now—he had to find Pauline.

Chapter Eighteen

Pauline continued to keep her distance from Dan. She didn't believe he was the one watching her bathe earlier, but she was still embarrassed by the way she had reacted. She couldn't help but to think he would want nothing to do with her after seeing the scars on her body. What man could want that? She sketched in her book, trying to clear her mind. The stress was too much for her, and art had always been her escape.

She had been sketching the scene of cattle on the move. It was from a memory earlier in the day. She knew Lucy's twin siblings loved animals and was drawing the picture in hopes of seeing them again. Many of her sketches went to other people. She enjoyed the smiles her art gave to those whom she cared about. She was uncertain she would see any of those people ever again but continued to draw for them anyway.

The sun had begun to go down. The cool evening air was a special treat with the hot days they'd had. She was shading part of the picture when she noticed pencil markings all over her hands. Absentmindedly, she wiped them on her dress as she'd done a thousand times before and looked up to survey the camp. It startled her to see Dan walking in her direction. Instantly a flush of heat raced through her body. She quickly tried to collect her things and stand up, but his voice stopped her.

Hands buried in his pockets, he kicked at the dirt as he spoke. "Hey, Pauline. I'm... I'm really sorry about this morning. I swear I didn't go down to the creek to spy on you, I honestly–"

"I know it wasn't you watching me, but someone was, and it scared me. When I turned and saw you, I got angry and overreacted. I'm sorry for that," she apologized.

He still had a bewildered look on his face. She wasn't sure what he would say next, but she was nervous, and didn't know why. Even on her wedding day, when she first met her betrothed, she hadn't had butterflies like the ones Dan gave her. Whenever he was around, her heart raced with such speed she thought she might faint. Pauline watched him. He seemed to be gathering courage. Finally, his eyes locked on hers.

"Look, we both know I've seen the scars on your back. Will you tell me where they came from? What happened to you?" he blurted out.

Pauline froze. The familiar flush of embarrassment mingled with shame coursed through her body. It had been fairly obvious from the moment she'd rushed past him that morning that he'd seen her scars. She didn't understand why he wanted to know about them. After all, nobody had cared about her before. She stayed silent for several minutes while he stared at her, silently waiting for a response until finally, he spoke again.

Dan cleared his throat. "It's clear those marks were made by a belt–"

"If you already knew, why bother asking?" she snapped, instantly regretting her tone.

He grimaced, as if he realized he'd misspoken. "I'm sorry. I already talked to Henry. He told me your husband liked to beat you. Is that true?"

Pauline cringed. "I want to tell you the truth, but aside from Dorothy and my old friend Lucy, I haven't ever spoken about it. I'm not happy Henry told you either, but it's only fair since Dorothy told me about your past, I guess."

"You can talk to me. I'll listen, and I promise I won't judge you."

Pauline wanted to trust him. Part of her wanted to break down and tell him everything. There was something about the man standing in front of her that made her feel like opening up. She was torn between keeping it all to herself and releasing everything she had been keeping from him. She struggled to find the words and didn't know where to begin. Eventually, she decided it was safer to just not say anything. As she often did, she looked to the sky and landscape to center herself.

All around them, the rest of the team carried on. The smell of the smoke from the fire filled the air, along with the dinner Dorothy prepared. The sun had settled, and the moon was out. As she looked around the camp, she noticed how joyful everyone was—sounds, stories, and laughter filled the camp. She longed to be as happy as the people who now surrounded her. Pauline sat back down and looked back at Dorothy.

Henry walked up behind her and wrapped his arms around her. He gave her a peck on the cheek and her face lit up with a smile. That was the feeling she wanted more than anything else in the world. The feeling of being loved and appreciated. It was a dream for Pauline. How she wanted to find a bond as her friends had. Her heart longed for it.

Dan waited patiently for her to speak. Even his simple act of waiting was foreign to her. There was no yelling or cursing as it was with her dead husband. Not once had she seen Dan raise his hand in drink or anger.

"Dan, I don't understand why I'm telling you this, but my marriage was arranged. I didn't choose to marry Herschel because I loved him; I chose to marry him because my father wanted me to."

He paused, seemingly contemplating her words. "Did you ever love him?"

"No. I don't think so. When we first married, I thought maybe I could learn to. I dreamed of having a family of my own. I guess you could say I wanted to love him. I tried. But in the end, I never could."

Pauline felt like a weight had been lifted from her shoulders, but she knew she couldn't tell him everything yet. He couldn't know she was on the run. No man would sympathize with her when he realized she was wanted for murder. Pauline was no fool. Part of her wanted to keep Dan safe from that knowledge. Perhaps it was selfish of her, keeping the full story to herself, but in that moment, all she wanted to do was protect Dan from the dark truth. When she looked up at Dan, he was giving her his full attention. He sat on the log next to her as she continued on with the answer to his question.

"My husband used to beat me several times a week. Every time he would come back from the saloon drunk, he'd find another thing to start a fight about. Sometimes over dinner being cold and other times he'd just haul off and smack me for no reason."

"Why didn't you leave or try to get away from him?" he asked.

She took a deep breath and then sighed. She didn't know how much to tell Dan. She hadn't opened up to many people about her past, and especially not to a man. The only men she had known on a personal level had been her father and Herschel. Her father never took the time to understand or listen to her, and Herschel was exactly what he was. Part of her still felt guilty for having any type of feelings toward another man. However, another part of her, down deep inside, knew she wasn't doing anything wrong.

"If it's too hard to talk about, we don't have to. I really want to know you better and if there is anything I can do to help, I want to," Dan said softly.

Pauline had only just begun to see the softer side of Dan. His harsh words when they first met were becoming a distant memory. This side of him was completely new. He made her feel safe in a way that she never had before, but she still couldn't help but keep her guard up. After years of her husband charming the world around him only to come home and beat her mercilessly, she was wary of any man's intentions.

"It's not that I don't want to talk to you, I just don't know how to talk about it. I thought about leaving several times, but the timing was always off, and I really didn't have any place to go. I was raised by my father. My mother died shortly after my birth. I had no idea what I was getting myself into with an arranged marriage. I just wanted to make my father proud. I don't even really know my uncle, yet he's taking me in now."

"That's who you're meeting in Dodge City?'

"Yes," she whispered, looking down at the ground.

"So, what about the scars on your back? When did that happen?"

"About six months after we were married. I still remember that night like it was yesterday. I prepared dinner for him as I always did. Of course, he was out getting drunk at the saloon and came home late. We'd argued earlier in the day. Looking back, it was my own fault. I wanted a dress I saw at the general store. He liked his games though and told me I would need to 'earn' it. When he came home, he was even worse than when he had left."

Pauline kept fidgeting with her hands and couldn't sit still. She looked down at the ground as she tried to keep herself from crying.

"He walked in the door and started in on me almost immediately. Next thing I know he threw me to the floor and started smacking me with his belt. One of the cuts was so deep, Lucy had to be fetched to stitch me closed. It was so bad I caught an infection and was in bed for over a week. I had to hide the marks for almost two months. Thankfully, after that, he only used his hands."

Her body betrayed her. Tears filled her eyes. She didn't know whether it was from the sadness of enduring the suffering again or the anger for having to the first time. Dan handed her his handkerchief. She thanked him softly and wiped her eyes. The truth had spilled from her just like her tears.

"You've been through hell, Pauline. No woman should have to go through what you have. I can't change the past, but for you I wish I could. I have to make a confession, though. I wasn't happy when you first got here. I could tell you were running from something. I didn't like the idea you could be putting us in danger, but I didn't know what that danger was. A couple of nights ago I asked Henry to tell me why you were here. He told me about the murder of your husband."

Pauline gasped.

"Now, I don't believe you are capable of murder, but... well hell, I'd have killed the bastard myself if I knew you. No woman deserves to be struck, no matter what. That's just a simple fact. He was a coward of a man for that. Honestly, I just want you to know I am here for you. As a friend, if you need anything, you can come to me. Same goes for Henry and Dorothy, as well. We're family here."

Tears covered Pauline's face. She tried to turn her head and hide them from Dan, but it was too late. When she looked back at him, his eyes were filled with compassion. Everything inside of her wanted to run to his arms, but that wasn't what she was used to. She wiped her eyes again with his handkerchief.

The overwhelming emotions inside of her had taken root. The ups and downs of the last few days were wearing on her, and it was too much to take.

"Thank you, Dan," she stammered. "I... I have to go. I can't do this right now. I need time to think and I'm not sure what to say but thank you."

Dan reached for her as she pushed past, but her emotion kept her walking past him. She needed some time alone to think.

Chapter Nineteen

Dan didn't sleep at all that night. His concern for Pauline grew with each minute he spent around her. It was still dark when he got up that morning. Nobody was awake yet, and he was still reeling from the previous night's events.

Stretching, he looked out toward the field where the cattle laid. He was ready for this drive to be over, but he knew he may never see Pauline again. Once this drive was over, she'd go on her way, and he'd go his. The thought worried him.. All he wanted to do now was to help her in any way he could. Suddenly, he knew just who he should talk to. Dorothy was the one who had spent the most time with Pauline. Maybe she would have the answers he needed.

Dan reached into his sack and pulled out his mug and coffee. The embers in the fire were still burning, and he needed his morning cup. Dorothy wasn't awake yet. He poured some water into his cup and set it on the rack just above the hot embers. He added his crushed coffee beans and waited. Soon the smell of fresh coffee filled his nose. It wasn't long until he had his first sip for the day.

The sun wasn't visible yet, but already he could see the effects. A small hint of blue began to fill the sky. He watched as the tips of the sun slowly became visible in the east. He was about halfway through his first cup of coffee when Dorothy joined him.

"How you doin', cowboy?" she asked.

"I'm doing okay. How are you this beautiful morning?"

"Well, I'm feeling great, but I can see something is bothering you." She smiled. "What is it?"

"You've always been able to read me like a book." He smiled halfheartedly. "What is it about Pauline? I mean... I don't know what I mean. I just know I haven't felt this way about a woman in a long time."

"Dan," she said softly. "You've been through a lot in your life. You're never going to understand why, but it's added to the man you are today. You care about people, and you have a need to help. She's not only a beautiful woman. She has a great big heart in there, too."

"Why does she always run from me, though? It feels like I can't do anything right when it comes to talking to her. I just want to know her story."

"It's not my place to tell you how she feels or why she does what she does. I can tell you she is scared. She's away from her father for the first time, and no matter how bad of a person her husband was, she's on the run for his murder."

Dan took another sip of his coffee. He was hoping she would be a little more help than that. The camp had started to come to life. A few of the cowboys had gone to check on the herd. Ross and Charley were at the edge of the camp, joking and carrying on like a couple of schoolkids. The birds in the trees around the camp chirped their morning songs.

"Henry already told me the basics, but when I tried to talk to her, she rushed away again. It's become something of a regular occurrence when I try to speak with her. What do I do, Dorothy?"

"You give her time. She'll come around." She smiled. "Honey, it wasn't too long ago that you shut the world out, too. You became so difficult to talk to, and you didn't want help from anyone. Do you remember?"

"Of course, I remember. If it wasn't for you and Henry, I may have just lost myself forever. But with her–"

"See," she exclaimed. "You had us. All Pauline needs is the same thing. People to keep her spirits high, and when she is ready, she will know who to go to."

Dan knew she was right. They had been there for him since the passing of his family. Every drive he came on, Dorothy would take him under her wing. She and Henry had been the ones who would open him up and keep him laughing. They were always there when he needed a shoulder to lean on, and never complained when he went on his rants.

"I know you're right. I just feel like I keep saying or doing the wrong things. What if she doesn't come around to talking to me?"

"As I said, don't give up on her. The only thing you can do is to make sure she knows she has a friend in you. Everything else will come together when the time is right. Keep spending time with her. Keep being there."

"Thanks, Dorothy," he muttered. "I *have* been enjoying myself a lot more since we have been getting to know each other. There's something special about her."

"Oh, you know I'm here for you, Dan. There's something special about you, too. Just so you know, the loss of your family might make you the only one able to understand what she is going through. Relax, let her open up to you. I know in time she will, just like you finally did with us, and from what she has told me, how you opened to her."

"I don't know how you do it, Miss Dorothy. You always know just what to say and you're always right."

"Honey, I've known you for a while now. You're not that hard to figure out," she said. "Now, go talk to her. I'm going to make sure Henry is up and getting ready. Then I'll get breakfast started."

"Have you seen her this morning?" he asked.

"Not yet. I think she was already up and awake before me. After you find her and talk, come get some food. Maybe another cup of coffee would get you going for the day. Oh, and Dan..."

"Yes, ma'am?"

"Of course, I'm always right!"

He smiled, pouring the last of his coffee out and wiping his mug. He tucked it back into his sack. Dan watched as Dorothy headed back to the main tent, thinking about everything Dorothy said. It was a lot to digest. He knew what he needed to do. He had to find Pauline and make sure she was okay. He wanted to tell her everything would be okay.

It was still early as he glanced around the camp. He wasn't sure if Pauline was even still in the camp. He hadn't seen her anywhere yet. He decided to try and look for her. Walking over to her tent, he could tell she wasn't there. Dan walked over to the wagon and didn't see her there either. He glanced around the rest of the camp. She was nowhere to be found. Where could she have run off to?

As he surveyed the rest of the camp, he noticed Ross standing by himself. He was looking out toward the herd, likely checking on them himself. Charley no longer stood with him. Dan took his chance to talk to Ross alone. He figured if anyone knew where she might have gone, it would be Ross. He always had a way of knowing things he probably shouldn't.

"Hey, Ross," he said as he approached.

"Morning, Dan," he responded. "You're up early today."

"I'm usually the first one awake, I just had to get a good cup of coffee. Best way to start the day."

Ross took of his hat and wiped his brow. Beads of sweat were already building on his forehead.

"Feels like it is going to be a hot one today, better stay hydrated," Dan declared.

"I was planning on it already. Do you think it would be a good idea to get the cattle down to the river for a drink before we head out? Might put us behind this morning if we do, but I think it would be safer. What do you think?"

"I think you're onto something there, kid," Dan laughed. "Go ahead and get a few of the other men to help you get them down there. Dorothy is waking Henry now, and by the time you get back here, breakfast will be ready."

"Yes sir, boss man!" Ross joked.

It wasn't that Dan was trying to be in charge. He had been on enough drives to know Henry would have had him do the same thing. But he chuckled anyways, momentarily forgetting he was hunting for Pauline.

"Yeah, yeah. Don't you know to respect your elders?"

"You're not that much older than me, Dan."

"Maybe not, but there are times where I feel a lifetime older than you."

Ross shrugged and laughed. "Every day you are looking older than me, too!"

"Okay, okay," he teased. "Just remember you have all this glory to look forward to."

Ross burst out laughing. "Don't worry. At least you aren't as old as Henry. You'd still be asleep."

Dan laughed before suddenly remembering why he had gone over to talk to Ross in the first place. "Hey, have you seen Pauline this morning? I've been looking all over for her and can't seem to find her."

"Well, I think you were talking to Dorothy when she rushed past us toward that wooded area over there. She had a sack with her, it looked like it was full."

He pointed toward the trees on the other side of the field where the herd grazed. When he looked out over the landscape, he still didn't see any signs of her. A small panic overtook Dan. He hoped he wasn't the reason she had taken off. He thanked Ross and told him to get started on getting the herd down to the river.

"Will do, Dan," Ross replied.

Dan left his side and headed over to Jesse. He began to worry even more. Had she run away? It was a possibility, and he was concerned with her safety. He knew she was better off with the group; she had made friends with mostly everyone. He didn't know if he would find her and if she would even listen if he did, but he knew he had to try.

He quickly prepped Jesse and threw his saddle onto his back before mounting him and taking off in the direction Ross had pointed out. They rode past the herd as Dan continued to look all around, hoping to catch a glimpse of her somewhere.

The air pressing against his body as they rode through the field was hot and humid. It was surely about to be a hot day. To his left he caught a glimpse of Pauline sitting against a log, and he could tell she was sketching again. His heart relaxed. He had found her, and she hadn't run away. He brought

Jesse to a slow trot. He didn't want to startle her. He was just outside the row of pine trees on the edge of the woods when they came to a stop. He hopped down off Jesse and tied him to a small tree stump.

He fed Jesse a carrot from his bag and thanked him for a job well done. He was thankful he had found her so quickly. His worry faded as he walked toward her. Dan almost turned around and let her be, simply because of how content she looked. He wasn't going to force her to talk, though. They were getting close to Dodge City, and he knew their time together was running out. He just didn't want her to think she was alone.

Chapter Twenty

Pauline had fallen asleep waiting for Herschel to get home. The dinner had been prepared and was waiting on him. She awoke to plates crashing and Herschel yelling. As she got up, she became afraid. He had gotten angry with her before, but it never was this bad. Suddenly, the bedroom door flew open. Standing in the doorway was her enraged husband. He was drunk again. His face was red with rage, lit up only by the oil lamp she had left burning when she fell asleep.

"I told you I wanted dinner when I got home!" he screamed.

"I... I have it done," she stammered.

"You expect me to eat cold food? I suppose you got to eat your dinner when it was nice and hot, didn't you?"

She stood and approached him, trying to speak softly and calm him. "Honey, I can just heat it—"

His hand moved so fast that she didn't see it coming. The pain in her cheek and the heat that instantly came from his slap were excruciating. Pauline fell to the floor and the tears built in her eyes immediately. Before she had time to react, he grabbed her arm and threw her on the bed. In an instant, he was on top of her.

"Please... please just stop—"

His hand came out of nowhere as he backhanded the other side of her face. Everything became blurry. She continued to cry out, but nobody was coming. Even if someone heard her screams, they would be ignored, like they always had been before.

"Time and time again. I ask nicely for you to do something, simple tasks really. You can't even complete those. Can you do anything right?" he growled.

"Okay, you're right... I messed up. Just... just let me fix it."

"Just shut up!"

She was starting to catch her bearings again. The tears in her eyes only made it harder to see him. She was still confused; he had hit her before, but he had never held her down. Her heart was racing and the blood rushing to her face felt like embers on a fire. She had to get away from him. Without thinking, she pushed her body up and tried to maneuver out from under his weight, but he was too strong. He placed both hands on her shoulders and shoved her down hard.

"When I ask you to do something, I expect it done right. Do you understand me?"

"I'm sorr—"

He slapped her again, this time hard enough that she felt blood trickle from her nose. The throb of pain was intense. Through her tears and swelling, she saw he had lost his balance, and fell beside her on the bed. She jumped up, pushing through the pain in her face. Just as she stood to run toward the door, she felt the pressure of his hand on her ankle. He pulled her ankle hard, and she fell to the floor.

She began to crawl, aiming for the now-open door leading out of the bedroom. She didn't know what else to do. Even in his drunken state, she was no match for him. The only thing going through her mind was that he would kill her this time. She reached her hands and knees and tried to lunge from his grasp, momentarily breaking his grip. She took her chance and tried to stand up. Just as she reached her feet and made it to the doorway, the back of her head exploded with pain. The *force of the impact of his fist had caused her to fall into the wall. He gave her no chance to move from there.*

In an instant, he grabbed her shoulders and spun her around, her back slamming against the wall. Before she knew it, he had his hand wrapped around her throat. A trail of red seeped from her nose and above her eye. The grip he had on her throat made it impossible to speak. Although he only used one hand to choke her, the two of hers couldn't stop him. He smacked her again with his free hand.

"Your 'sorry' means nothing. I've given you chance after chance and all you do is mess things up. Sitting around here drawing all day! It's a waste of time, Pauline. You're mine and you need to do as your told. You made me do this to you. This is your fault!"

Pauline was losing consciousness. His grip never relaxing, everything went black.

She woke up afraid and alone. She was soaked in sweat, her heart still racing from the nightmare. She knew she had to get away from the camp; she just didn't feel like talking to anyone. All she wanted to do was to clear her mind.

The nightmare was just another reminder of how free she was now, but the realism of it left her shaking. She grabbed her bag that contained her sketch book and other drawing supplies. She just needed a few minutes to herself. She got up and headed in the direction of the cattle. She had walked in an area the night before that she knew was well-secluded.

It was a quiet morning around the camp when she scurried out, she saw Dan and Dorothy sitting by the fire having a conversation. She picked up her pace after that, trying not to let Dan see her. She didn't want to talk. She was afraid the effects of her nightmare would be written all over her face. She rounded a group of trees on the edge of the camp and nearly ran right into Ross. She quickly dropped her head and started walking faster.

She walked past the herd, her pace almost a jog. She made it to a small, forested area on the other side of the field. It was secluded, but close enough that she would be able to see if they were leaving without her.

She settled in under the old pine trees, pulling out her sketch book as she sat on a felled tree. Her thoughts were everywhere, and she was still reeling from the nightmare. She had been there for only a short time when she heard the trot of a horse. She wasn't able to see much past the trees and wasn't sure who could be riding up. The only person who had seen her head out was Ross. It quickly dawned on her that it was probably Dan, since she knew that Ross would tell him if her asked where she had gone. As she looked up from her sketch, she saw Dan walking her way, he had a relieved look on his face.

"Is everything okay, Dan?" she asked. "You look like something's worrying you."

"I'm sorry. I don't mean to startle you. I've been looking for you and Ross said you left the camp in a hurry. Until finding you, I thought maybe you had run away."

"No... I was just trying to clear my head. You caught me off-guard last night. I didn't expect you to know about me."

"Look, Pauline, I don't know everything," he admitted. "I only know the little Henry shared with me. The only things I know are that you have been abused, and you're on the run for the murder of your husband—I want you to know I am here for you if you want to talk."

"You have no idea how good it makes me feel that you believe me. I was surprised when you said you knew about me being on the run. I don't want to put you in danger, I've done that enough already."

A slight smile crossed his face. "Of course, I believe you. I only wanted to hear you say it. It's important that everything I hear comes from you. It's also important to me that I apologize for how I treated you when we first met. I'm still dealing with my own past. I wasn't sure what to think when I first saw you. The more I learned from other people only sent me further down the wrong path."

She hesitated for only a moment, collecting her thoughts before laying it all out for him. She wished she had talked to Dan already. He deserved that.

"I didn't kill my husband. I came home and found his body, though. I ran directly to my father, rather than the Sheriff, because I was scared. The whole town knew about Herschel's abusive ways. So, they all just assume I'm guilty. The Sheriff is lazy, too. He's probably just following everyone else's thoughts because he wants to stay in their good graces. I was scared to tell you, or anyone, really. Henry and Dorothy only knew because they have known my father for a long time."

He appeared to be deep in thought, and she wasn't certain as to what he could be thinking. For a moment, she thought maybe he was still wondering if she could have killed him, until he spoke again.

"Pauline, you know my story. You said Dorothy told you. I found my family dead, too. I know the trauma something like that can cause. The nightmares and dreams. The feeling of failure. Hate the man or not, he was someone you knew. Is there anything we can do to prove your innocence? Do you have anyone you think did it?"

"The only thing I know is his pocket watch is missing. Or at least I think it was. I don't remember seeing it when I found him. He never went anywhere without it. I know it has to be someone who had been to the house. Herschel never did business with people at our home unless he had dealt with them before."

She continued to tell Dan about the watch and everything else that had happened. She told him about her father setting her up with Henry and how her best friend, Lucy, had come and warned her they were going to arrest her. She tried not to leave any details out as she told Dan everything.

"Well, then we need to get the word out about his watch. We can tell everyone in our group and then make sure your uncle has the information as well. There's a good chance we can find this watch. Are there any markings on it that make it unique?"

"It has his initials etched into the back of it. He had it engraved after it was handed down to him by his father. It's a family heirloom."

"I'll do whatever I can to help you, Pauline. One day at a time. I'm glad you were able to talk to me. We'll get you through this. You deserve a life better than the one you've lived."

He gave her a slight smile, lifting her spirits. Dan had a way of making her feel at ease, giving her a bit of hope and strength. She had never had anyone willing to go as far as her new friends had gone for her. Now she had a group of people willing to protect and help her.

"I honestly believe finding that watch will lead to whoever killed Herschel. I just wish I had something more," she said.

Dan opened his mouth to respond but just as he did, a group of riders made their approach. Pauline wasn't able to make out who they were, until they came to a stop. The first man to jump down from his horse was the spitting image of her husband.

Pauline's heart dropped. The man who looked like Herschel, had to be none other than his older brother, Allen. She had never met him, but Herschel had talked about his older brother all the time. He didn't live near Windy Reach. From what he had told Pauline, Allen was a businessman and traveled all over, which was why they'd never met. He hadn't even made it to the wedding. This was working in her favor as he rode in with his posse.

Allen approached them, and already too close for her to give Dan a proper warning.

"Dan," she whispered while standing and taking his hand.

She couldn't find the words as fear gripped her body. Aside from taking his hand, she was frozen in place. All she could do was to keep her grip in his. She gave it a few more squeezes, hoping it would be enough to grab his attention. He looked over her, the confusion on his face evident, but her expression must have told him everything he needed to know. He tugged on her hand, pulling her closer to him.

The leader stomped over to them, not bothering to offer Dan a handshake as he squinted at them in the sunlight. "Name's Allen Hogan. I'm looking for my brother's murderer. One of her father's farmhands said she left Arizona several days ago, heading this way to Dodge City. She was his wife and she killed him in cold blood. I'm hoping to find her and hang her; she needs to pay for his death. Her name is Pauline. Have you seen or heard about any women trying to head out this way?"

Pauline began to shake, fear paralyzing her. Dan squeezed her hand; she knew he was trying to help her relax, but the words Allen said struck hard.

"My name's Dan, and this is my wife, Anne."

He let go of her hand and put his arm around her shoulders, pulling her in close to him. Without thinking, she put an arm around his waist. His words had surprised her. She hadn't expected him to be that protective. She could only hope the ploy would work. She was still scared, but somehow, even with everything going on, Dan managed to make her feel safe and sound within his arms.

Chapter Twenty-One

Dan wasn't entirely sure what was happening. He had felt her squeeze his hand several times. Assuming she knew who this man was, she was trying to warn him. His initial response was to call her his wife; he just hoped the ruse worked.

"You say you're looking for a killer? Do you know what she looks like?" Dan asked.

"Yes, she killed my brother. I don't know what she looks like; I haven't seen my brother in a few years. Business kept me away, and he married her shortly after I left for Europe. I tried to talk to the woman's father, but he wouldn't say a word. Just kept telling me he hadn't seen her. I knew he was lying."

He almost sighed out loud with relief. They didn't recognize her because they had never met. Dan knew he had to protect Pauline. He decided to keep the lie hidden with a mixture of the truth.

"That's just awful. We've been on the trail for just over a week. The only thing we've seen is cattle and trees. The occasional wild animal, maybe. We are headed to Dodge City with this herd, we make this trip a few times a year."

"You haven't seen a stray woman? I suppose she could have traveled with someone else, maybe they were out this way together," Allen said.

"The only women we have with us are my wife here, and Dorothy back at the camp. She takes care of the meals while we are out here," Dan answered. "The only stranger we have run into was a man with a dead horse."

"Seems to me that it's about breakfast time. Do you think they would mind if we grabbed a meal with you? We've been riding all night trying to reach Dodge City, and we're famished."

Dan knew that could be dangerous, especially with Charley. He glanced out toward the field where the herd had been, and he saw they were not there. After thinking about it for a moment, he realized most of the group should still be down at the river, getting the herd some water. He just hoped Allen and his group would be gone before they got back to the camp with the cattle.

"That shouldn't be a problem. Dorothy should have breakfast done right about now anyways. You're more than welcome to join us," Dan offered. "You can follow us up to the camp, it's not that far across the field."

"Thanks, that sounds good. It will give me a chance to ask them if they have seen or heard anything,"

Pauline squeezed his hand again. This time it was much harder. He knew she must be scared, but it was the fastest way to get rid of the group. Dan only hoped it would be enough to get rid of them for good. He quickly helped her get her things and walked her over to where Jesse had been tied up. He hopped up on his steed and held his hand out to Pauline. She grabbed it and he helped pull her onto the horse's back. Once she was in position, with her arms wrapped around his waist, they waited for Allen and his men to mount up.

"What are we going to do now? If they find out who I really am, they will have me hanged for sure," she whispered.

"We should be able to get them over to the camp, fed, and on their way before the rest of the group gets back. I sent Ross and the others down to the river to get the herd a drink.

I'm hoping that gives us enough time so Allen and his men don't get to ask too many questions. Trust me, I'm going to protect you."

"I'm trusting you with my life, Dan," she murmured.

"Did Herschel look like Allen? He said you two have never met, yet you knew he was here for you."

"He's never been around. From the time we married until now, he has been away on business. But yes, he looks just like Herschel. It's almost like seeing a ghost," she continued in a hushed voice.

At that point, Allen and his men were ready. They rode together and headed out across the field. Dan could see the flat spots in the grass where the cattle had been laying. The sun was a little higher in the sky and the temperature was slowly going up. He knew the day would be a long one. The group was about midway to the camp when Allen started talking.

"Looks like you are herding quite a big group."

"It's a little bit larger than we normally take with us, but not the biggest we have moved before," Dan responded.

"So how long have you two been married?" he asked.

"Oh, for about two years now," Dan said without hesitation. "Are you married?"

Allen scoffed. "I don't have time for a woman. Well, at least not one that would be waiting at home."

His laugh echoed through Dan's ears. He already couldn't stand the man, and it had nothing to do with him being the brother of Pauline's abuser. Businessmen in general were people Dan didn't like. They all acted like they were better than everyone else.

"My business takes me all over, sometimes even across the ocean. The only reason I came back this time was to visit my brother and meet his wife. Never thought I'd be out here hunting down his killer."

Dan remained quiet the rest of the short ride. As they reached the edge of the camp, Dan smelled the aroma of bacon and coffee filling the air. He knew Dorothy was just finishing up cooking. She looked up and smiled at him. He gave her a little smile and nodded his head toward Allen, quickly adding a wink in hopes she would understand what he was about to say next.

"Morning Dorothy, this here is Allen Hogan and his posse. I already introduced myself and Anne," he said.

Her smile faded and a concerned look took its place. He brought Jesse to a stop and helped Pauline down from the horse. She was still trembling and the look on her face told Dan she was still frightened. He needed to make the situation go as smoothly as he could.

"Howdy, Allen. What brings y'all out here?" Dorothy asked.

"I'm looking for a woman, her name is Pauline. She was married to my brother for the last few years, and now she's on the run for his murder," Allen announced.

"I don't know any Pauline. Heck, besides the one man we let join us along the way, we haven't run into anyone. His horse was lame, and we took him on with us because he was heading to Dodge City as well."

"That's all I needed to know. What about the others, where are they at?"

Just then, Henry came out from the tent. Dan was relieved he had been close enough to hear the conversation. Too many awkward looks could blow the whole thing. Henry stepped out and looked at the men.

"This is my husband, Henry. The other men took the herd down to the river for some water. It will be a spell before they get back, if you want to wait on them. Then we will head out for the day."

"There won't be any need to wait on them, but Dan here said you'd be okay if we joined you for breakfast. My men and I are hungry. Been riding all night trying to get to Dodge City," Allen declared.

"That won't be a problem. Hope you men like bacon, and you're more than welcome to get some coffee," Henry interjected. "Anne, why don't you help Dorothy get these gentlemen some food?"

Everything was working. Ross, Charley, and the rest of the group were at the river, and Dorothy and Henry were doing exactly what Dan hoped they would do. They fell right into the story and kept it going as if it were the truth. Pauline walked over to Dorothy and started helping her with the food.

Allen and his men took a seat around the fire pit. They were all talking to each other, and Henry joined them. Dan sat down in a spot where he could keep an eye on Pauline. He could see she and Dorothy were having a long conversation. He was fuming. Almost all of his worries came back. The fear of Pauline's situation putting them in danger. He couldn't blame her, though. It wasn't her fault everyone was against her. But the anger was still there.

"Do you think you'll be able to find this woman you're looking for?" Henry asked.

"I'm not going to stop looking until I do. I plan on having her hanged for killing my brother," Allen said sternly.

"Just being curious, but how do you know she killed him? You said you haven't been around. Did someone see her do it?"

"Not exactly. The Sheriff told me she was his only suspect. For family reasons I won't say much, but I believe she thinks she had good motive to do it. Once I find her and am able to recover the family watch our father gave him, that will be all the proof I need to have her hanged."

"So, she took his watch after she killed him?"

The mountain of a man, Allen, shifted in his seat. Dan could tell he was becoming was annoyed, and Dan was worried with the line of questions Henry was asking. The comment of the watch made him look toward Pauline, who glared at Allen. She had heard it too. It only made Dan believe her more. No way she would have killed him, even in self-defense, then steal the man's watch.

"I'm sorry to hear about the loss of your brother. I hope you find this woman," Henry added.

"It shouldn't be too difficult. As far as I've been told, her father has a brother in Dodge City. I'm sure, if she makes it there, asking around won't take long to find him and then we will find her."

A sudden crash made everyone turn. Pauline had dropped one of the coffee mugs and the sound echoed through the camp. She looked at Dan and he jumped up to help her.

"Honey, are you all right?"

"Yes. I... I just lost my grip," she mumbled.

"Here, let me help you," Dan said.

He helped Pauline distribute the coffee to each of the men and then took Allen's cup to him directly. He wanted to keep her as far from him as he could. After handing him his cup, Dan walked back over to the women; he knew he'd only have a moment to talk to them. He tried to keep his voice low as he spoke to them.

"Just keep doing what you're doing. Everything is going the way I planned. We just need to get them out of here before the rest of our group gets back," Dan whispered.

"Do you really think they are just going to leave right after eating? What if they decide to travel with us?" Pauline asked.

"Oh, honey," Dorothy cut in. "They're in a hurry to try and beat you to your destination. They know you are heading to Dodge City, they want to try and get there before you, or shortly after. Just play this little game, and we'll keep you safe."

"Okay, Dorothy."

"Listen, when you bring the food over, make sure to sit with me, Pauline. It will look off if you don't."

"That makes sense, I'd rather not be anywhere close to them, but I understand what they might think if I don't," Pauline agreed.

"I'll get them some plates, then maybe we can rush this along," Dorothy added.

Dan went back to the campfire and sat in the same place. He wanted to make sure Pauline was able to see him, and more importantly, that he could see her. Dan felt like she could bolt at any moment. She was much safer with him.

"I just don't get why a woman would put herself through all this trouble over a watch," Henry said as Dan sat down.

He couldn't believe Henry was still going on with the questions. He was starting to worry Allen would get angry with them and want to know more. Sometimes, curiosity could be a bad thing, and to Dan, this was one of those moments. Henry looked his way and Dan gave him a confused look.

"It wasn't all about a watch!" Allen exclaimed. "There's more to it than that. She probably thought she could get some money from it to help in her escape. But I promise you, I will find her."

"Sorry, Allen. I'm just naturally curious. I didn't mean to upset you; you just don't hear too many times where a woman commits murder and I wonder what she was thinking. That's all," Henry clarified.

Allen fell silent. Henry removed his hat and wiped his forehead. Everyone sat quietly, drinking their cups of coffee. Dan looked out toward the field; he wanted to be able to make a break for it if the others came back before Allen left. The field was still clear, meaning they had time. Just as he was about to get up and ask where the food was, Pauline and Dorothy came over with a pan of bacon. Pauline's hands shook when she let Henry grab some and then sat next to Dan. Dorothy handed out food to the others and took her seat next to Henry.

The silence was almost unbearable. Dan took a bite of his bacon, but the situation was keeping him from having much of an appetite, and when he looked at Pauline, she wasn't eating either.

"Where'd you two meet? Before y'all got married?" Allen asked.

Dan almost choked on his bacon. He wasn't sure if the man was just trying to make conversation, or if there was something he didn't believe about their story. One thing was for certain—they had to get these guys back on the road again, and fast. He also needed to choose his next words very carefully.

Chapter Twenty-Two

The question caught Pauline off-guard. She hadn't expected the personal question and was concerned how Dan would answer. She continued to pick at her food, not hungry at all since the arrival of Allen. Trying not to look nervous, she put one arm around Dan, and leaned on his shoulder.

"Well, I run my family's ranch in Windy Reach. My parents left it to me when they died. I met Anne shortly after that. She came to my ranch to have one of her horses broke. During that time, we just sort of fell in love with one another. The rest is history, so they say," Dan quipped.

The quickness with his answer surprised Pauline. It was working, though. Allen looked as if he believed every word Dan had said. She still couldn't bring herself to eat. Time was standing still, and all Pauline wanted was for them to leave. Her teeth were starting to hurt from gritting them so hard. She was worried about her safety, but also the safety of her new friends. She'd known the law would be looking for her, but it had never occurred to her anyone else would come for her.

"Would you like anymore bacon?" Dorothy asked. "Maybe a little more coffee?"

"No, ma'am. You have been very gracious, but we need to get going. Have to try and get to Dodge City by tonight. Thank you for everything. Best of luck getting the herd there," Allen said as he stood up.

The other men in his group stood with him. They dumped the rest of their coffee out and piled the cups next to the pit. Relief flooded through Pauline as the men stood. They'd be heading out soon and Ross and the others weren't back yet. Dan's plan had worked so far.

"Oh, you're very welcome. I hope you find this woman you are looking for," Dorothy said.

"Thank you, Dorothy. I know we will find her. It's just a matter of time."

The men mounted their horses. Allen gave Dan and Pauline a look before spinning his horse around and heading off into the open field. Nearly weak with relief, she watched as the men started to ride away, when suddenly she saw Ross and Charley. Her eyes darted between Allen and Charley. Charley tipped his hat to Allen and they both kept riding. She kept an eye on Charley as he reached toward his breast pocket, then dropped his hand back to the reins. Ross rode up to her and the others.

"What did those men want?" Ross asked.

Charley joined beside him and climbed down from his horse. His eyes gave a look of confusion, but he asked the same question.

"They were riding all night and were just looking for a warm meal," Henry said. "I wouldn't worry too much about them."

"Aw, man. Does that mean I'm gonna have to wait on my breakfast, Miss Dorothy?" Ross joked.

Dorothy smiled. "Well, now. You don't think I already have the next batch cooking? That's almost hurtful. It's almost done now."

"You can have mine, Ross. Not feeling very hungry, anyway," Pauline offered.

"Thanks," he said, smiling. "Can I still have some fresh bacon, Dorothy?"

"Of course, you can."

"That's why you're my favorite person. You really know the way to my heart," Ross laughed.

He took the food from Pauline and followed Dorothy over to where the fresh bacon was cooking. The lightness in the air since the men had left helped Pauline feel a little better. She still worried they were looking for her. She gave a smile and a nod to Ross when he glanced back at her. Dorothy was piling the fresh cooked meat onto his plate and the two of them were laughing hysterically at something he said. Her musing of the situation was interrupted by Charley.

"So, all they wanted was a meal? Does that happen a lot when you guys are on the trail?" Charley asked.

The man's nasally, soft voice was annoying. She didn't know how anyone could stand to listen to him speak. She still sat next to Dan, and Henry was across from the two of them. Charley attempted to tie off the horse he was riding but struggled to tie the knot around the tree. Pauline noticed him trembling as he tried to figure out the right combination of loops.

"Well, no, it doesn't happen that often. There's only been a few times in the years I've been herding that anyone has stopped for a meal," Henry answered.

Pauline followed the two back and forth. When she looked back to Charley, he was giving her a curious look. He watched her a moment longer before returning to the tying of his knot.

"You need some help with that, Charley? Looks like you're struggling a bit," Henry asked.

While Dan and Henry tried to help Charley tie up the horse, she took a moment to wander toward Dorothy, who was still at the main tent. Ross was walking back, and he stopped her about halfway.

"Thanks for the extra grub, Pauline. I woke up hungry today. I'm always okay with extra food."

"I think it will be better to eat more this morning, it feels like it will be getting hot today. Either way, you're welcome," she said.

He just nodded, his mouth already full of food. She gave him a kind smile and continued on her way to Dorothy. She smiled at Pauline when she approached. She was so thankful to have Dorothy in her life.

"Dorothy, I just wanted to thank you for that. I know you didn't have to lie for me, but you did. I don't think anyone has ever been that kind to me," Pauline said.

"You deserve a chance, my dear. We all know you didn't do anything wrong."

"Would you like some help cleaning up before we leave?"

"I would normally say yes, but it looks like someone else needs some of your time," she answered.

Dorothy nodded her head in the direction behind her. She turned to see Dan walking her way. Joy filled her heart. Dan had gone out of his way to protect her, and Henry and Dorothy had followed his lead. If it wasn't for the trio, she'd be on her way to her execution.

"Dan, thank you so much! You really did a great job of steering them away from me."

"Do you mind if we have a few minutes to talk, Pauline? If you're not too busy," he asked.

She told Dorothy she would be back to help and followed Dan to the edge of the camp. When they reached the edge, it looked as if he was checking all around to make sure no one was around to hear. When it looked like the coast was clear, he began to speak.

"Listen Pauline, I'll help you in any way I can. You don't deserve to be tracked down like some kind of animal. There are a few things I have to say."

"Okay... I just want you to know I appreciate your help. I know you didn't have to do any of that for me. So, thank you."

"You're very welcome, but why didn't you tell me your husband had a brother? That put us all in danger. Is there anyone else that will be out here looking for you? Anyone else we should be worried about?"

Dan's tone was angry, but he didn't act like he was mad at her. There was a look of concern on his face, a level of caring Pauline hadn't experienced before. She'd known from the beginning she was putting them in danger. Henry and Dorothy had signed up for the extra danger when they agreed to take her on. The only difference was Dan didn't get that chance. She felt guilty about not telling him sooner.

"I'm sorry, Dan. Like I said though, I had never met Allen. As far as I knew he was still on the other side of the world. I never would have imagined my husband would be killed just as he was coming for his first visit. The timing is just crazy. I'm sure they didn't come looking for a few days after we left. How'd they find us so quickly?"

"Well, we might have had a head start, but they aren't herding cattle. They are able to ride at night and at a much faster pace. It wouldn't take much to catch up to us like that."

"All I know is I am very grateful to you. I'm sorry I put you all in danger. I didn't kill my husband and I don't understand why all of this is happening to me," Pauline whispered.

Tears welled up in her eyes. She dropped her head and looked at the ground. Crying had become a normal thing for her, and she didn't like it. She couldn't believe Allen had come looking for her. Her heart ached with fear for her new friends. Dan reached out and touched her cheek, brushing her tears away with his thumb. For the first time since they met, she didn't flinch.

"Pauline, I'm so sorry all of this is happening. I don't know why bad things happen to good people. I know you have a good heart. I know you had nothing to do with the death of your husband. I really wish we could prove it, but I don't even know where to start."

As they continued to talk, Pauline noticed Henry walking their way. He looked worried, but he continued to smile. She could only wish to be that happy. Happy enough that everything going on around her, whether good or bad, would have no effect on her smile. The kind of happiness that made life worth living.

"Hey Henry, thank you for protecting me, I–"

"You're welcome, but there is no need to thank me. I made a promise to your father that I would get you to where you're going, and I will keep that promise," Henry declared. "I came over here to let you both know we are going to be leaving soon. We're already a little behind because of their arrival. It's going to be hot today, and I am worried about the cattle."

"The cattle are going to be slow today," Dan added. "We should be getting close to Dodge City by now."

Pauline's attention was interrupted while she looked around the camp. A few cowboys were still packing their gear. Dorothy was putting away the breakfast dishes and preparing for the day. As she looked out over the prairie, she felt the eyes of someone staring at her, but as she looked around, she didn't immediately see anyone watching. She saw movement from the corner of her eye, but when she turned fully around to look, the only thing she saw was Charley dumping out his coffee. She thought nothing more of it and turned back to the conversation Dan was having with Henry.

"So, how can we protect the cattle with the heat being so high?" Pauline asked.

"There is nothing we can do while on the trail, but Dorothy has a sister outside of Kingsley. It will be about half a day's travel with the heard. We will be able to stop there and let the herd rest before we leave for the last leg of the trail. They have a good general store where we can get a few supplies as well," Henry said.

The idea gave Pauline a pause. She had already put the rest of the group in danger. She didn't want to add any more names to that list. Being around more people who could recognize her and cause her more hassle wasn't high on her list of things she wanted to do.

"Are you sure it will be safe there?" Pauline asked. "I don't want anyone else to have consequences from meeting or hiding me. You all have done enough as it is."

"You let us worry about protecting you. We will get you to Dodge City, and to your uncle," Dan interjected.

"Dorothy's sister is just as caring as she is. There won't be any problems there and I don't think anyone will know to come looking for you. It will only be for one night, so there is nothing for you to worry about," Henry added.

They both were very convincing, but the fact Allen had found them when they were basically out in the middle of nowhere just added to her fears. She felt like she had to come up with her own plan. Not only to save her friends from anymore hassle, but to save herself as well.

"Dan, me and the boys will get the herd ready to go. My things are already packed, and Dorothy should be finishing up the chuck wagon now. I'll still need your help here and there, but if you want to ride with Pauline and keep her company, I completely understand," Henry assured.

"I would like that," Pauline said.

"Well, there you have it. I'm off to get the herd going. I'll let Dorothy know you're riding with Dan. Keep your head up, Pauline." Henry smiled.

"Thanks, Henry," Dan reiterated.

Henry walked back into the camp, Dan and Pauline following further behind. They stayed quiet for the short walk. Pauline couldn't keep her thoughts from running back to her friends being in danger. The man had already tracked down her father and gone out of his way to follow her this far. If her presence continued to put people's lives in danger, she would have to leave. It was as simple as that.

She continued to ponder her options as she cleaned up. She put everything in her bag and loaded it into the wagon with her tent. There wasn't much time before they would head out for the day. While she waited for Dan to finish, she looked out toward the west. She missed her father and Lucy.

Dan finished packing all his gear onto Jesse. As she watched him, she couldn't help but think about all the things the man had been through. She cared about him. She cared about all of her newfound family. Her fear grew as she thought about the dangers ahead. What would she do if Allen found her in Dodge City? She didn't know, but she couldn't run forever.

Suddenly, Dan appeared at her side riding Jesse. He reached his hand out and helped Pauline up onto the horse's back. She wrapped her arms around Dan, and they slowly trotted off to follow the group. As safe as she felt with Dan, her fear was stronger.

"Dan, I think I need to head out on my own. I can't put you all in danger anymore."

Chapter Twenty-Three

Dan wasn't sure he had even heard Pauline right. He didn't understand what would make her think she would be safer on her own. He brought Jesse to a stop and spun his upper body so he could look her in the eyes.

"Why would you do that? You're much better off with us. There's more of us to protect and watch over you."

"I'm scared for my own life, Dan. My fear of being hanged becomes more consuming every day. I don't want you, or anyone else, to have to worry about me, let alone put your lives in danger to try and protect me," Pauline said.

"Are you worried about Dorothy's sister, or more worried about the town?" he asked. "You can talk to me, Pauline."

"Both," she murmured. "I thought I would have more time. I never expected a posse to hunt me down. Now all I can think about is losing Dorothy, Henry, and you. When all these people really want is me."

"There is no way I am going to let you run away. We will figure this out together," he reasoned.

He watched as the fear in her eyes began to dissipate. At least for now he was able to calm her. He gently kicked his heels into Jesse and the majestic horse carried them onward toward the herd.

The group of cattle trudged along the path created by other drivers. They were moving slower than the days before, already feeling the heat. He could tell by the position of the sun that they would reach Kingsley not long past midday. The path they followed would lead them to a forested area. The thick foliage would keep the pace slow, but the continued shade allowed them a small amount of cool air.

Dan quickly rode up to Henry. "We aren't stopping until we get to Kingsley, right?"

"I think that would be for the best. If we ride through lunch, we should be able to get there with plenty of time to get settled in," he said. "If you have any better ideas, I'm all ears."

"None that will get us there any quicker," Dan said.

With that, Dan pulled the reins back and moved them back to the end of the herd. He knew the best place for them was at the back of the pack. They followed behind the cattle for several hours before Pauline broke the silence.

"What happens if Allen and his search party get to Dodge City and don't find me? They could come back this way, asking more questions."

"That's been on my mind too. I don't think they will; we really gave them no reason to doubt us," he reassured her. "Let's not worry about things we have no control over. I think that's just wasted effort."

"You're right. I just don't want to risk anything for you. I know you say you'll protect me, but it's really hard to see a positive ending to this mess."

"Pauline, you have to think of the positive. You're innocent!" Dan encouraged. "Look, I have been to this little town a few times. We'll reach Kingsley first. They have a store and a saloon. We can get some supplies and then be at Dorothy's sister's shortly after. You'll be safe there and then we can try and find a way out of this mess for you."

They had just reached the end of the wooded area they'd traveled through for the last couple of hours. Dan was relieved to not have to follow the cattle through the trees, but the heat that struck him in the face when they exited almost took his breath away. Sweat began to pour from under his hat. He had to keep using his shirtsleeve to wipe the salty liquid from his eyes. It was worth the long day without a stop. They were almost there and the tops of the buildings in the small town were peaking just over the hill they prepared to climb.

"There it is, Pauline. Can you see it?" Dan asked.

"Oh, thank God. I've never been on the back of a horse this long," she noted. "My legs are sore, and I can't wait to get a break."

Dan laughed. "It takes practice to be able to ride this long. I've been doing it for years. See that field over there? We'll drive the cattle there. We'll leave a few guys to watch the herd and we can check out the general store with Dorothy."

That brought a smile to her face, which made him smile too. They drove the herd to the field and met up with Dorothy. Henry, Charley, and the other cowboys stayed with the herd, as Pauline, Dan, and Dorothy all took the wagon into the town. Ross followed behind on horseback.

The town wasn't very big, although they had added a few buildings since the last time Dan had been there. He felt Pauline scoot over closer to him. He knew she was afraid, and he didn't blame her. Any time new people rode into any town, folks there would stare. It even made Dan uncomfortable. He knew they wouldn't be there long, but his own fear made him wonder if there would be trouble.

They slowly made their way through the town. Dan took in all the sights. They passed the saloon and the barber shop. Outside the saloon were several pretty girls. They weren't prostitutes—their only job was to get men inside the saloon, and then pay them enough attention so they would stay and buy more drinks. The girls smiled and waved for them to come in. Dan turned to see Ross' reaction and smiled when he saw him grinning ear to ear. Pauline nudged him.

"What are you smiling about?" she asked.

She sounded jealous and Dan couldn't help but chuckle. Dorothy answered before he had the chance to speak for himself.

"Don't you worry about ole' Dan here. I know he's not smiling at those girls," she laughed. "That's never been something Dan has given any thought to. Now, Ross on the other hand–"

"Ross is all smiles back there," Dan added.

He watched as Pauline turned and looked at Ross. Dan smiled again when she laughed at him. He guided the wagons to the front of the general store. He tied off the lead and watched as Ross jumped down and tied his horse off as well.

Pauline walked to one side of the shop with Dorothy, while Ross went to the other. Dan searched through the store alone, looking at different spices and tools. He never knew when he would run into a tool he would need for the ranch. He grabbed some crackers, hardtack, dried fruit, and coffee. He had to have his coffee. After getting everything, Dan walked up to the counter and waited for his total. Dorothy and Pauline walked up shortly after.

Dan glanced around the store another moment or so, before realizing Ross was nowhere to be seen. "Where'd Ross run off to now?"

"Oh Dan, you know as well as I do he's over at the saloon making friends with the ladies," Dorothy laughed. "He follows wherever attention is given."

Pauline giggled and Dan gave her a smile. He paid for his things and walked back to the wagon, carrying a few things for Dorothy along the way. She had gotten a big bag of flour, sugar, and a handful of other things for herself and Pauline.

After loading their things into the wagon, Dan headed toward the saloon. He knew he would find Ross mingled in with the rest of the crowd. He walked by a few of the girls as he headed through the gates of the saloon. He had barely made it through the entrance when he heard the familiar sound of Ross' laugh. Sure enough, Dan found him surrounded by women. He looked as if he was already had a few drinks, too. He couldn't help but smile to himself as he walked over to get Ross. The kid just had a way of making people laugh.

"Come on Ross, we have to get going."

"But all the beauty in the world is right here!" Ross objected.

"I understand that, but we have things to do. You know you can always come back later, right?

"Well, how do you do! I didn't think about that. You hear that, ladies? You will all see me later!" he shouted.

Dan walked to the bar and paid Ross' tab. After paying, he headed back over to Ross and practically had to pull him out of the saloon. He was already half-drunk. He couldn't blame him for wanting to have a little fun, but they still had work to do, and the herd was waiting. He finally got Ross back to his horse and he took his position back on the wagon. He turned them around and headed back for where Henry was waiting. As they passed the saloon on their way out, the smiles and waves came again.

"Bye, Ross," said three women who smiled and waved in unison.

"Ladies," Ross answered and tipped his hat.

Dorothy and Pauline nearly fell out of the wagon they were laughing so hard. Dan grinned and held back his own laughter. Ross just smiled and kept moving forward. It wasn't long before they reached Henry and the herd, and they headed back out on the road. The ranch Dorothy's sister lived on wasn't far from town. Within half an hour they were unpacked, and the cattle were led to a fenced-in area with a watering hole.

The women headed into the house to start dinner and everything else had been handled. There was still a nagging thought in the back of Dan's mind that Allen could come back and find them again, so he grabbed his bag and walked to the edge of the field where the fence stood. He leaned against the fence, surveying the property, hoping he wouldn't see any signs of trouble coming for them.

As he watched over the property, Dan's mind continued to race. He would do anything for Pauline to be safe. His worry over his friends and Pauline were one thing, but Allen could be a big problem. He knew the man wouldn't stop looking for her until she was hanged or proven innocent. The sweltering heat was getting to him. He found it harder to focus the longer he stayed out in the heat. He pulled out his canteen and took a drink. He grabbed a handful of crackers and tossed them in his mouth. Having something in his stomach helped and so did the water.

He was still looking out for Allen and his posse when the perfect silence he had enjoyed for the past hour was interrupted by a noise from behind him. He turned around and there was Charley, standing a few feet away.

"What do you want, Charley? Can't you see I'm out here trying to take some time for myself?"

"Dan, I'm not trying to bother you, but what did those men this morning really want?" he stammered. "I know there has to be more to it than what Henry said."

The question took Dan off-guard. He wasn't sure why the man would be concerned with Allen and his men. Charley looked worried, and while Dan thought about that, he realized he hadn't said much since they left that morning. Since they had let him join their group days ago, nobody could get the man to be quiet for longer than a meal.

"They had only been riding hard and were hoping for a quick meal, just like Henry said," Dan asserted. "Why are you all worked up, Charley?"

"Whoa, I'm just asking a question, Dan. I'm not worried about it or them. I just find it curious a group of random riders were only looking for a meal," he said nervously.

Charley started to reach for his breast pocket, and quickly dropped his hand into his pants pocket. Dan assumed he was looking for something to wipe the bead of sweat from his head, so he handed him his handkerchief. Charley took it from his hand and thanked him. After patting his head dry, he handed it back.

"You've been acting funny since this morning. Are you sure there isn't anything you want to tell me? It's been my experience that people only act like that when they are hiding something."

Charley's face went white. The expression he had was of confusion and fear. Dan didn't understand the man's reaction.

"Maybe you've just been in the heat too long today. Is that what it is? I'd recommend going inside and have a drink."

"I... I think you're right. I haven't eaten anything today either," he faltered. "I should just go lay down until dinner. That might be best."

"That's a good idea. If you happen to fall asleep, I'll make sure to get you for dinner. Drink some water, too. It will help," Dan said.

Charley turned and walked away without saying another word, leaving Dan to wonder about what had just transpired. The man was odd, that was certain. He still didn't understand why he would ask about the men from that morning. Dan shrugged it off and looked back toward the road. Allen could be coming, and he wasn't going to let them take her if they did.

He stood there for a few more hours before hunger and sheer exhaustion had him walking back to the ranch. The past few days had been tough emotionally, but the high heat and sun had taken its toll on him today. It was still a couple hours before the sun would go down; he hoped the coming nightfall would give them all a nice break from the heat. He continued to wonder what he could do to help Pauline. If only they could find the watch she had described to him. That would be enough to clear her name.

Dan suddenly understood he didn't want to be without Pauline. His feelings continued to grow, no matter how difficult her own fears had made it. His own fears were driving the wedge between them as well. The longer he thought about it though, the more he understood that he cared about her. He cared about her more than he had cared about anyone in years. He was determined to find a way to make this right. For her, and hopefully himself, too.

Chapter Twenty-Four

Pauline helped Dorothy make dinner, constantly distracted by the thoughts racing through her head. Tomorrow they would reach Dodge City and the idea of meeting her uncle for the first time, under these circumstances, worried her. She didn't know how he would react to meeting her, either. She had put so many people at risk already.

The men had already made a makeshift camp outside, but all the food was prepped in the house. It would be nice to have a real cooked meal again. Not that Dorothy was a bad cook, but there were so many more choices for dinner when cooking at home.

Darla and her husband had ridden into town. They liked to gamble at the saloon and probably wouldn't be back till late. That was fine with Pauline, as she couldn't handle putting anyone else in jeopardy. As she looked around the quaint little ranch, she didn't see Ross or Dan anywhere. She walked over to where Dorothy was serving the other cowboys' food.

"Have you seen Dan or Ross? I saw Ross shortly after we got here, but not since. Dan, I haven't seen since we unloaded the wagon."

"You know Ross probably went back to town to flirt with the girls at the saloon," she laughed. "He can be quite the hound dog, if you know what I mean."

Pauline smiled. "I can understand that. He seems like a fun person to invite to any party. What about Dan? Have you seen him anywhere?"

"The last time that I saw Dan, he was headed out toward the edge of the property. I think he is worried Allen and his men will come back for you. He cares about you. Did you know that? I haven't seen him worry about anything since his wife passed."

The thought of Dan worrying about her, after all that he had gone through, brought back all the fear she had from earlier in the day. She thought about Allen and her concern grew again. What if he did come back? The thought of running off on her own was becoming more of a possibility. Her presence there had not only put them in danger; it was almost like everyone's mood had changed.

"I think I can see he cares about me. With everything going on, it's hard to be sure what people are thinking or feeling around me. I don't like that I've put you all at risk."

"We made that decision ourselves when your father dropped you off with us. I'm a grown woman and can take care of myself. I love having you here, and I'm happy we got to meet. Don't regret any of it."

Dorothy always had a way of helping her see the bright side of things. Or, if not, at least making her smile. She had gone from feeling like no one had ever cared about her to having a whole group of people prove they would protect and care for her. The sensation was new to her, and Pauline was unsure how to feel. On one hand, she appreciated their warmth. At the same time, however, there was an overwhelming feeling of guilt. What if she let them down?

"I know you and Henry made the decision, but Dan and the rest didn't have much of a choice in the matter," Pauline said. "You all might be worried about me, but I worry about you all too."

"That's fair," Dorothy said. "Even with that, we're still going to be here for you. Anything we can do to help, just ask. Dinner is ready. I think I saw Charley go lay under his tent.

I'm going to make sure he is up. Don't need anyone skipping dinner after this hot day."

Pauline smiled and nodded. She decided to have a look around the ranch. Besides the quick view when they rode up in the wagon, she hadn't had a chance to look around. She could see fencing all around the property. The herd they had brought with them were locked up in a separate area. The makeshift camp was close to that fence line. The ranch was an off-yellow color, with a full wrap-around porch. The barn looked like it had been recently built, the obviously new red paint a giveaway.

Overall, it wasn't much different than other ranches she had visited. The land was green and plentiful, and a river about a mile from the ranch supplied all the water. There were a few mountain peaks off in the distance. If it hadn't been so terribly hot, she would have continued to explore, but she needed to get out of the heat. As she rounded the corner of the house, she saw Dan returning from his post. He staggered while he walked. It was noticeable to anyone who paid attention. The warm breeze blew the hair hanging from below his hat.

Dan saw her and began walking her way. Her heart skipped a beat as he grinned at her. His smile charmed her every time.

"How're you feeling?" he asked when he reached her.

"I feel okay. Can't wait to dig into dinner. One can survive on the trail meals, but nothing beats a homecooked meal," she said.

"I'm looking forward to dinner as well. Are you still feeling like you want to run away?"

"No, you're right. I'm a lot safer here with all of you than I would be on my own."

The lie escaped her mouth before she could stop it. It didn't matter—if the timing was ever right, she would take her leave. The thought of anything happening to her friends was driving her mad.

"You ready to eat, then?" he asked. "That's if you don't mind sitting next to me."

His tone was calming; he could say anything to her, and she would have agreed. They each grabbed a bowl and filled their cups with coffee. She followed Dan to the camp and sat on one of the logs set up around the fire. She noticed Charley was quieter than normal. She still didn't like the man, but it was strange not hearing him joke around or tell stories. Henry and Dorothy both sat quietly eating their dinner, worried looks on their faces. It felt as though all the joy had been sucked out of the group and she felt like she was the one to blame for everyone's change in attitude.

The group was enjoying their dinner, or at least everyone was eating. It was early evening, and still hot outside. Suddenly, Ross rode onto the ranch. After tying off his horse, he joined everyone for the meal. As he grabbed his food and a cup of coffee, Pauline noticed he was unsteady on his feet. He wasn't completely drunk, but he'd had more than a few drinks for sure. He walked over to the rest of the group and sat down near Pauline and Dan.

"Have yourself a good time, did ya?" Dan asked.

"I had a few drinks and then sang the girls a couple of songs. I got one of them to dance with me, too. So, yeah, I would venture to say it was a good time."

"I'm glad you enjoyed yourself, Ross. Surprised you got back here so early. I was beginning to think you wouldn't be back till morning."

"Aw, Dan, you know I wasn't going to miss Dorothy's cooking," he chuckled. "She'd have my hide if she knew I ate somewhere else before this job was done."

Dan and Pauline both laughed, but something was still off with his mood. Pauline couldn't put her finger on it, but she assumed it had something to do with Allen showing up early in the day. The way Dan had become so protective of her still surprised her.

"Dan, is everything all right?" she asked quietly. "You seem a little distracted tonight. Everyone does."

"It's not because of you, Pauline. I'm worried Allen will come back, that's all. I don't need you to go running off, either. We'll figure it out if it happens. Until that possibility actually happens, I just need you to stay calm, and trust me."

His confident tone helped her relax some, but she couldn't shake the feeling that everyone would be better off without her there.

***

They had all finished eating and now sat around the campfire. It was still warm, but the sun had gone down and the little change in temperature felt nice. As she surveyed the camp, everyone was quiet. There were still small conversations going on throughout the group, but the laughing and singing were nonexistent. She had started to think about ways she could get away from the group when Ross leaned over and whispered to her.

"Why's everyone seem to be in a bad mood? Did something happen while I was gone? And where is Charley at? I haven't seen him since dinner."

Pauline looked around the camp and realized she hadn't seen him either. It was another oddity for him—since joining them, he'd always wanted to be the center of attention.

"I'm not sure. As a matter of fact, I don't think I have seen him since dinner either. Maybe he just went out for a walk, but I think I'll be fine if we don't have to hear any of his stories tonight."

"Not a big fan either, I see," Ross snorted.

"Can't say that I am," Pauline said. "As for everyone's mood, I just think the heat has gotten to everyone."

Ross shrugged and continued to look around. Pauline wasn't sure what to feel. If even Ross was noticing, then it had to be bad. A sudden fear washed over her. She felt like everything was her fault, and she couldn't get past it. As she looked around the camp for another time, she watched Ross walk over and grab a guitar. She hadn't seen Ross play, but one of the other cowboys had brought one along and played several times throughout the drive.

"Do you think a song would cheer everyone up?" he asked as he started to pluck the instrument's strings.

"Couldn't hurt," she replied.

The crackle of the fire burning was then joined by the tones of the song Ross started to play. The music from the guitar caused everyone to turn and listen. He had a good technique, and the song had a melody everyone enjoyed. Dan came over to sit next to her again, grabbing her hand. Pauline tried to relax as his palm rested atop hers. It was no use. A few seconds later, Ross' singing took her by surprise.

"Alone I stumbled into a bar,

The maid I noticed from afar.

SALLY M. ROSS

Her body moved with an enticing sway

My eyes were locked, I couldn't look away.

She sauntered over and gave me a wink.

I fumbled through when she asked my drink.

We talked all night, my heart in her hands.

And when the pub did close, I took her to bed.

All night we frolicked in the dark of the night,

Until the sun did crest and brought its light.

To my horror I jumped from the bed,

A painful ringing in my head.

The haze lifted as my companion rose,

Between her legs a dangling hose.

I tried to flee but she held me tight,

I'll tell you that man put up one hell of a fight!"

As Ross finished the song, Pauline looked around. Dorothy was the first to burst into laughter. Everyone fell in line after her. Soon, the whole camp was laughing and joking.

"Did you write that song yourself?" Henry asked, still laughing.

"Well... I mean, yes," Ross murmured.

"Well, son, I think it's pretty good. I think we all needed to have a good laugh. I can't believe you can actually sing. That didn't sound half bad. You're just full of surprises, Ross."

"Yeah Ross, thank you," Dorothy said.

Everyone's mood was instantly better. Pauline couldn't help but to smile. Everything felt normal again. Well, normal for how everyone had been since her joining the group.

Ross gave a grand display of bows and sat back down. Pauline leaned over so he could hear her.

"That was great, Ross. I think you managed to get everyone smiling with your song. It's better when everyone is happy, you always get everyone laughing and that's a good thing."

"Mama always said laughter is the best medicine," he said.

"Mama was right," she said with a growing smile. "It's a good thing you listened to her as a kid."

"Strange enough, she's been right about many of the things she told me growing up."

Dan's hand slid from hers and she looked up at him as he stood. His stare was out in the direction of the dark. She didn't know why he had stood so quickly, but she found herself standing next to him.

"What are you–"

"Do you hear that?" he asked.

The camp grew quiet, trying to hear what Dan had heard. For a moment, Pauline didn't hear anything but the wood popping in the fire. Then, the sounds of an incoming horse. The galloping sound was distinct, and she could tell there was only one horse.

Pauline's heart started to race. The approaching horse and rider were unable to be seen in the darkness the night had become. She didn't see who the rider was until the man jumped down off his horse and began walking toward the fire. It was none other than Allen. Anger was evident by the look on his face. Standing tall, he glared at Pauline as he looked over the camp.

Henry was the first to say anything. "Where's the rest of your men? I thought you had a few more men last time we saw you?"

"They were too drunk to come with me, but I'm here to take that woman with me!" he snarled. "I know you all lied to me. She is not who you said she was, and she knows why I'm here!"

He pointed right at Pauline as he yelled. The color in her face drained and her body went numb. Somehow, he had figured out who she really was. All her fears and worries were coming true in that moment. The full realization of everything struck her in an instant. He was there to take her, and there was nowhere for her to hide.

Chapter Twenty-Five

Dan wasn't surprised Allen had returned. After all, he had been looking out for them all day. He was, however, shocked to see him alone. He knew he had to defend Pauline, or else she would be taken and hanged by the next day.

"I'm not really sure where you got your information from, but this is my wife and I'd take kindly to you moving along." Dan could tell from his expression he didn't believe a word he just said.

"Let me put it clearer to you," Allen said. "I know that's Pauline. Your own man Ross there was just at the saloon, bragging about being on the road with a pretty woman heading to Dodge City. You calling him a liar, too?"

The comment shook Dan to his core. He knew Ross could let things slip from time to time, but he never thought he would go as far as to tell everyone about Pauline. He gave Ross a look of disappointment, and shame filled the young man's face. He knew he had done wrong, but there wasn't time to deal with it. He had to deal with Allen and protect Pauline. He moved to stand between her and Allen. He wasn't going to let her be taken by this man, or anyone for that matter.

"Well, that's all fine and dandy, but if you want to get to her, you'll have to go through me," Dan asserted.

Time stood still. Each second that passed only made Dan stand more firm. He wasn't a fighting man, but when it came to the people he cared about most, he was willing to sacrifice everything. Which was how he knew, in that moment, that he loved Pauline.

Allen only stared at Dan. He glanced past him several times, glaring at Pauline. Dan could tell he was sizing up the situation and trying to come up with a plan. He knew as a last-case scenario he could pull his gun on the man, but he was trying not to get himself shot. The situation became more dire when he noticed Allen look down at his revolver several times.

"I'm not here to start trouble for the rest of you. I just want Pauline, and I'll leave all of you out of it," Allen said. "She murdered my brother in cold blood, and she deserves what's coming to her."

"You weren't there, none of us were. How do you know she did it? How do you know she isn't telling the truth about everything?" Henry asked.

As Allen turned to look at Henry, Dan looked back at Pauline. He could see from the look on her face that she was terrified. He wanted to reach out and grab her, pull her close to him, and promise everything was going to be okay. There just wasn't time, and he had no idea if everything was going to be okay. While the man was still looking the other way, Dan moved his hand into a better position to pull out his six-shooter, a Colt Single Action Army revolver with a polished steel barrel and wood grip. The revolver had been a gift from his father. He wasn't the fastest draw, but he had practiced enough growing up that he could be lethal if needed.

"She's a liar. I might not have been there, but the way everyone sees it in Windy Reach is she just snapped and killed him. He might not have been no angel, but he didn't deserve to die like that. I just want justice for his death. I have no quarrel with the rest of you. At least not yet," Allen threatened.

"Then why don't you just let the law handle this? Let them come and get her, because I promise you, you're not getting her tonight!" Dan roared.

Allen looked like he was weighing his options. He was outnumbered at this point two to one. He didn't have his posse, and Henry had Dan's back.

Ross had stood as soon as the man arrived. He had put the guitar down and stood a few feet from Pauline. Dan assumed he had hung his head when he realized what he had done, but now, he walked over and put himself between Pauline and the angry man.

"You'll have to go through me, too. If you knew Pauline at all, you'd know she couldn't have killed her husband. She just isn't that kind of person," Ross defended.

Dorothy had been cleaning up after dinner when Allen arrived. Now, she stood next to her husband, silently nodding in agreement. She had a concerned look in her eyes, but her face hadn't given her away. Finally, it looked as though she'd had enough.

"Let's just get straight to the point," Dorothy said as she walked over and took Pauline's hand. "You're going to have to get through us all. We aren't going to just let you walk in here and take our friend."

Dan was amazed with how quickly everyone came together to protect Pauline. He knew what he was willing to do to keep her safe, but he hadn't realized everyone else would do the same. By the time Allen looked around the camp and then back to Dan, his face grew red with anger.

"I might not get her tonight, but you all won't be around to save her forever."

The man turned and walked back to his horse. Dan let out a sigh of relief as he turned and looked at Pauline. He could see she was still afraid. Dorothy still held her hand and rubbed her arm, trying to calm her.

"I will be back, and the next time I won't be alone!" Allen yelled as he mounted his horse.

He kicked his heels into the side of his horse, and the horse took off into the night. For a few moments, the only thing Dan could hear was the pounding of the horse's gallop, until they were too far to hear. He turned to Pauline, placing his hand on her shoulder.

"I told you we are all here for you. We will protect you and you are safe with us," Dan told her. "Thanks for having our backs, Henry. I'd have gladly taken him on myself, but it's always nice to have backup."

"We are all family here, we protect each other. Anybody comes for her, and we'll set them in their place," he said. "Once you are part of our family, you'll never be alone again."

"Thank you… thank you all," Pauline piped up. "I'm really grateful to have met you all. I never thought people would care about me the way you all do."

Dorothy gave her a great big hug. The tears started rolling down Pauline's face, and in that moment, Dan could see she had never felt real love before. His connection to her grew immensely. All he wanted to do was save her from all her pain.

This was the reason Dan enjoyed being on the trail as much as he did. He loved the family setting and knowing each person would protect the other. While Dorothy continued to console Pauline, Henry waved his hand to catch Dan's attention, then nodded his head in the direction of the main tent. He knew Henry wanted to talk.

"Pauline, I'll be right over here if you need me for anything," Dan said.

"Okay, Dan. Thank you."

Dan followed Henry to the tent, his heart still racing from the events that had just taken place.

"Dan, I hate to say it, but Allen is right. We won't be able to protect her forever and we surely can't always be with her. We will make it to Dodge City by midday tomorrow. I'll go into town and find out about her uncle, then I will have her ride with you to wherever his home is."

"I know he will be back. I'm only hoping it isn't tonight. Maybe we could have someone stay on guard and keep an ear out for riders tonight. We could do it in shifts and change out every couple of hours. I'll take the first shift," Dan volunteered.

"That's a good idea. Have Ross take the second shift and I will take the third. Then I'll get you up for the last one. That should cover us for the night."

"I agree. That will work best, and hopefully Pauline is able to get some rest. I'll let her know what we're going to do," Dan declared.

"All right, I'm going to go lay down and try to get a few hours of shut eye."

Henry turned and stared to walk into the tent. The emotions in Dan were running high.

"Hey, Henry. Thanks again for backing me up."

Henry turned. "Anytime, Dan. The whole thing took me back to the war. I didn't want to draw my gun, but if that's what it would have taken, I wouldn't hesitate."

Henry smiled, then disappeared into his tent. Dan couldn't help but think about all the things that could have happened. The thoughts sent a chill through his body. He shook off the feeling and headed back over to where Pauline waited. She was still visibly shaken, but the crying had stopped, and she was listening to Dorothy. Just as he reached her, Dorothy gave her a final hug and looked at Dan.

"We're all worried about her, Dan," she whispered. "But are you doin' okay?"

"I'm all right, I just want to check in on her and then we're going to take turns keeping watch tonight," he answered. "I don't want to be taken by surprise. Henry already laid down. I'll wake him in a few hours to take the next shift."

"That's a great idea," Dorothy said. "I'll go check on Henry. Make sure she lies down before you go on watch."

Dorothy gave him a quick hug and walked back to her tent, leaving Dan for a few minutes alone with Pauline. He was trying to formulate the words to help Pauline feel better, but he hadn't quite figured out what he was going to say, when she talked first.

"What if he comes back, Dan?" she asked. "I don't want you to be in danger because of me."

"You're not putting me, or anyone else here, in danger. As you can see, we all made our own choice to stand with you. We're not going to let anything happen. We care about you... *I* care about you."

Pauline just looked at him. He couldn't tell whether she was thinking or concerned that he had admitted he cared. After a few moments of silence, he spoke again.

"I'm going to take the first watch. If anyone comes tonight, we'll be ready and get you moved quickly out of sight. Just trust me, Pauline. I know I haven't given you many reasons to, but I promise I will protect you from him."

She stood up and approached Dan. Before he knew what was happening, she reached out and put her arms around him, squeezing slightly.

"It's going to be okay," he promised. "We'll figure this out, okay?"

"I know," she choked.

The embrace was short, but Dan felt his heart melt. All the walls he had built to keep people from getting too close were crumbling in her embrace.

"Why don't you try and get some rest? I know you might not feel like sleeping, but it will help," Dan said.

"Okay. Thank you, Dan. For everything."

As she turned and walked toward her tent, Dan couldn't help but wonder why she had said it that way. Surely, she wouldn't run off on her own after tonight? He had no idea what would happen the next day, or if he would ever see her after that.

Dan marched to his tent. He was on a mission to keep Pauline safe. He had placed Jesse's saddle next to his tent, and he reached down and pulled his Enfield rifle from the scabbard. The scabbard was nothing more than a sheepskin sheath that held his rifle. It was the rifle his father had used when he was a child, and on his twelfth birthday, given to him.

"Watch out around here, Jesse," Dan said to his steed. "I'm going to need you to have my back tonight."

He fed the mighty horse a few carrots and headed out toward the fence line, closest to the road to the ranch. The sunset and night had done little to cool the temperature. Although the sky was clear, and all the stars were out, there was still a gloom in the air.

He reached the fence line and found a comfortable spot where he could sit with his back to the ranch. He wanted to stay vigilant, so he brought along his cup that he had filled with coffee. The field in front of him had nothing to block his view. It was the perfect spot.

As watched over the property, his mind wandered to Pauline. She was innocent, and after seeing the way she reacted to Allen, it only secured his belief in her. He continued to survey the field, every noise causing him to jump. He wasn't afraid of what would come, but he wanted to be ready. Dan watched as a group of deer ran across the field. On another night, he could have taken a shot, and taken the meat and the animal's hide. But this was no average night, and there would be no time for hunting.

Chapter Twenty-Six

Pauline sat at the front of her tent, heart still pounding. When Allen had first appeared out of the darkness of the night, fear had shot through her, and she knew her days were numbered. Her fear was quickly quelled by the defense of her new friends. They had stood up for her and literally put their own lives in danger, but she knew they wouldn't be around to protect her much longer. She would have to rely on her uncle, whom she had never met. There was no guarantee he would protect her.

She had watched Dan take his rifle and walk out into the night. He would be watching over the camp for the first few hours, and she knew if she was going to make a run for it to protect her friends, she would have to wait until he came back. She'd never make it off the ranch with him watching. He would be the hardest to get around. She had to wait for Ross to take watch, only because he was younger and would be paying less attention.

Time dragged as she watched and waited for him to return. She had a plan, but until she knew everyone was asleep, she couldn't do anything. She thought about her father, hoping he was okay without her. She loved her father; through everything, he had shown he loved her.

Pauline began to pack her things, making sure all her drawings and pencils were in her bag. She hadn't brought many things with her, but she wanted to make sure she had everything. Just as she finished loading the items into her satchel, Dorothy appeared.

"I was just laying there next to Henry... it always amazes me how fast that man can fall asleep, but I was worried you couldn't sleep either. I just wanted to make sure you were okay."

"I'm okay, Dorothy. I was just getting ready to lay down."

"I see you have all your things packed up. Are you planning on taking off, dear?" Dorothy asked.

"No," she stammered. "I was just making sure I had everything ready for us to leave tomorrow. You know, one less thing to worry about."

"Honey, I know you are scared. I can't imagine what you are going through right now, but we all are here for you. I wouldn't worry about them coming back. Even if they do, we won't let them have you. Henry and Dan will make sure of that."

"I feel like everyone will be safer without me here, but I don't want anything to happen to Dan. Well, not any of you. I feel like we have gotten really close. You've become my family."

Dorothy laughed. "That man can take care of himself. Tonight should prove to you that he cares about you. It's obvious you care about him too. Just have faith, my dear. This will all pass, and you'll have a chance to be happy again. By the way, I know I have said it before, but you are family to us too. Don't go forgetting that now."

"I know, but what if it's not okay? What if they come back and try again? I couldn't handle if anyone got hurt because of me," she said, trembling.

Pauline started to tear up. The thought of her being the reason for anything happening was consuming her. The fire continued to crackle, and she looked over into the flames. She felt the pain of wood screaming out not to be burned. It felt like her life right then. All that had burned to the ground after she found Herschel's body.

"Honey, it will all work out. I promise you that. God doesn't want you to worry. He has a plan for us all," Dorothy said. "Just promise me you'll stay here tonight. We can figure anything else out in the morning. We don't need you running off and leaving us all to worry about you. Try to get some sleep."

Pauline wiped the tears from her face. She knew she was safer with them, but she couldn't take that chance any longer. She was planning on running, but she knew if she said anything to Dorothy, she would tell Henry or Dan and they would try and stop her. There was no question in her mind. They were men, rugged and domineering; their instinct would be to keep her safe, but she didn't deserve it. Pauline had caused nothing but trouble for them. So, she lied.

"Okay, I promise I am not going anywhere tonight. I only wanted to make sure I had everything ready. I have thought about it, but I think it would be best to stay here with you."

It hurt her to lie to Dorothy like that, but it would hurt more if something happened to her. She forced a smile as she'd done for most of her marriage. Despite feeling like second nature to her, she couldn't help the sickening feeling it created in the pit of her stomach.

"I'm going to take you for your word. I hope you don't go anywhere. I love having you around and am very thankful to have met a sweet girl such as yourself."

"I'm so glad we met; I just wish it was under better circumstances. It's been so wonderful to meet all of you."

"We're always here for you, Pauline."

Dorothy leaned over and gave her another hug. The warmth of her embrace made Pauline feel bad for lying, but she had no other choice. They said their goodnights and she watched Dorothy walked back to the main tent. After waiting a few minutes, she laid down in her tent. She left herself in position to see the whole camp, without letting on that she was awake.

Shortly after that, she watched as Dan strolled back into camp and walk over to Ross' tent. They spoke for a moment, then he went and laid down. She laid there quietly, pretending to sleep, patiently waiting for Ross to leave. Finally, he gathered his things and walked out of sight, into the direction Dan had returned from.

She still had to wait until she thought Dan was asleep. While she waited, she thought about Dan more. They had grown close after a shaky start and Pauline knew she would miss him the most. The way he made her smile and laugh. He had a presence about him that made her feel safe and brave at the same time. The bravery she was summoning now was entirely because of him.

After a short period of time, Pauline hoped Dan would be asleep. She hadn't heard any other noises around the camp and assumed everyone was asleep. Very quietly, she grabbed her bag and crept toward Dan's tent. Though she had only ridden Jesse a couple of times, she knew he offered her the best chance of getting to her uncle, and she trusted him.

Suddenly, she heard a twig break under her feet, and it stopped her in her tracks. Her fear grew with every passing second. The hair on the back of her neck stood on end; the pounding in her chest sent blood rushing through her ears, a steady rhythm growing as she held her breath. She had thought for sure she had just woken someone with the noise. Yet cowboys were a hearty breed and the chorus of snores continued. After a few minutes, she realized no one had moved. She continued toward Jesse.

Slowly, she reached into his bag and pulled out a carrot. Feeding it to Jesse, she whispered to him.

"I know you don't know me all that well, but you can trust me. Can I trust you? I need your help," Pauline whispered. "Great, now I'm talking to a horse..."

As she looked around, she spotted his saddle, just a few feet away from Dan's tent. She was nervous as she tiptoed toward its resting place. She started to pick up the saddle when she saw Dan rolling over from the corner of her eye. She paused, waiting a few seconds for him to adjust and fall back asleep before she carried it back over to Jesse. She was careful to watch for any branches or twigs so she wouldn't step on another one.

She carefully placed the saddle onto Jesse's back, constantly reassuring the animal everything was okay. After tightening everything down, she grabbed ahold of his reins and began to lead him away from the camp. There was a trail not far from the ranch that she was sure would lead her down to the river. She had seen it earlier in the day when roaming the ranch. It helped it was the opposite direction from where Ross would be standing guard. She only hoped it would lead her in the right direction.

When she was far enough from the camp, she mounted Jesse the way Dan had showed her. Pleased with her newfound ability to ride, she leaned over into Jesse's ear.

"I promise to get you back to him after I get to where I am going. You won't be away long," she said softly.

Pauline kicked her heels in, and Jesse began to trot in the direction of the trail. She could only hope Dan would forgive her. The trail led through a small, wooded area. The branches and leaves blocked out any of the light that shone down from the moon. It quickly became pitch-black and she left her trust in Jesse to lead the way down the path.

Without warning, Jesse began to become antsy, breathing heavily, and she grew concerned. She brought him to a stop and tried to soothe him.

"Jesse, it's okay. There's nothing out here. Nothing to be afraid of, okay," she said calmly. "Just you, me, and the darkness. We've got to work together now. We have to stay strong, and we'll make it through. One step at a time, friend. Nice and easy."

Her words appeared to go unnoticed, as Jesse still breathed heavily. He began to prance. Trotting in place, the horse was obviously spooked. It was common knowledge that horses were prey animals, but more so, she'd learned over the years of their ability to pick up on their rider's emotions. The more she felt fear creeping in, the better her chances were of scaring them both and ending up lost in the wilderness. Taking a deep breath, she tried to soothe Jesse and herself, despite the lingering fear.

"It's all right, Jesse. There's nothing–"

From off in the distance, a loud howl broke through the dense trees.

"Coyotes," she whispered. "All right, buddy, don't worry. There's nothing to be scared of. You're twice the size of them. Walk easy, friend."

A branch made cracked nearby and, entirely out of fear, she dug her heels into Jesse's side, causing him to break out into a full run. Pauline held on tightly to the reins as the horse led her through the woods. Dan hadn't yet had the chance to teach her how to slow a frightened horse. All she could do was grip the reins and hold on with her thighs the best she could.

Through bushes and around trees, Jesse kept sprinting. She leaned as far forward as she could, trying to dodge the onslaught of incoming branches. She tried to 'whoa' him and tug at his reins, but to no avail. He wasn't going to stop until he became less scared or hurt himself. They continued on for several minutes, not knowing if they were even on the path.

It wasn't until the edge of the trees, where the moonlight started to shine again, that she could see the river's edge. There was a sudden splash, and cool water hit her legs. Jesse had run straight into the water. The rush of water, along with the mud below, caused Jesse to stumble. Pauline fell off his back. She panicked. In a flash, her back hit the water. Somehow, she was able to keep ahold of his reins as she resurfaced.

As she tried to catch her footing, he spun around and headed in the direction they came. He trudged along the edge of the river as she tried to make her way to the bank. The howling had stopped, but the water kept the horse afraid, and he continued to fight her. Just when she thought she would have to let go of the reins, he stumbled, pulling her under the water. Fighting against the rushing water, she was able to use the horse reins and reel herself back to his side.

Jesse neighed and thrashed in the water. The way he was moving around, Pauline could tell he was stuck. She pulled and pushed but couldn't get the horse to move. She became afraid, worried she would lose him. She'd never be able to look at Dan again if something happened to Jesse.

"Jesse, it's going to be okay," she said. "Calm down. We are going to figure this out, I promise you. I'm not going to let anything happen... I can't... not to you."

She spoke softly, trying to settle the horse's spirit. Slowly, his fear subsided, and he settled down. He was still stuck, but without his constant thrashing, she could find a way to free him from the sinking mud. The glow from the sky allowed her to see very little. She couldn't immediately find anything that would help. She thought about it a little longer before she spotted a nearby tree. She realized she had Dan's rope, which hung from the saddle.

She grabbed it, trying to remember how to tie the knot Dan had taught her how to make. After a couple of attempts, she got it right. She tied one end to the saddle horn.

"All right, boy. I have to leave you for just a minute. I'll be right back."

She pet his mane for a while, keeping him calm. Then she slowly backed away and moved toward the tree. It wasn't a thick tree, but if something happened, it would be strong enough to keep Jesse from being swept away by the river. She knew she had to keep that from happening, even if she wasn't able to get him free.

Pauline climbed the bank and tied the other end of the rope to the tree and slowly made her way back to Jesse, getting herself stuck a couple of times on the way. Using the rope she had tied to the tree as leverage, she pulled as hard as she could. All at once she lost her footing and Jesse lunged, causing her to slip under the water. Pulling the rope, she was able to get back to her feet. Gasping for air, she started to cry.

"Somebody, help!" she screamed. "Help!"

It didn't feel like there was any use; no one would hear her from this far away. She cried and continued to yell. She screamed until her voice cracked. She was sore and tired. Her body ached from the ride and her attempts to pull Jesse free. Pauline was afraid and alone. She didn't want to leave him alone to get help, not with the sounds of wild animals off in the distance.

She wiped her tears and mustered enough strength to try one more time. As she yanked on the rope as hard as she could, she fell again into the water. Pulling herself back to her feet, she made her way back to the bank. She cried uncontrollably. Unless someone found her, Jesse would never get out of the water. She collapsed on the muddy ground, her cries for help going unheard and becoming softer with each breath.

Chapter Twenty-Seven

Dan awoke to stirring around the campsite. People were up and moving despite it being early in the morning. He and Dorothy were usually the first two people to get out of their tents and begin making coffee. Something was not right. He could sense it.

He climbed out of his tent and surveyed the area. Ross was up talking with Charley about something that seemed urgent. Dan made his way over as the two of them wrapped up their conversation. Charley gave Dan a look of concern but walked away. Before he could ask Ross what that look was all about, he noticed something peculiar—the place where he had tied Jesse up for the night. His horse was gone. All of the others were accounted for, meaning it wasn't bandits.

"Where's Jesse?" he asked Ross in a state of panic.

"Your guess is as good as mine. She must've took off with him in the middle of the night while we were all sleeping."

"She?"

Then it hit Dan. Pauline had run away. Allen scared her off. He also realized the way he treated her certainly had not helped the situation. As a result, she was on the run with his trusted steed. While traveling was inevitably dangerous, the risk multiplied when somebody set out on their own. Pauline, likewise, was wanted for murder and most likely did not have the skillset to survive on her own. The two of them out there together was a disaster waiting to happen. Dan could not risk losing anyone else, not if he could stop it. His hands trembled as he nervously surveyed the campsite in the hopes he was wrong.

"Dan, you okay?" Ross asked.

"We need to get her," Dan said with a firm tone.

"I don't know that she wants to be found," Ross quipped in response.

Dan clenched his fist in anger.

"You think it's funny if that poor woman dies out there?"

He pressed a finger into Ross's chest and watched his expression shift.

"I'm sorry Dan, I was, I just—"

"Enough of that. You, Charley, and the others just hold down camp for the day. I'll go find her myself if that's how it's going to be."

Dan turned around and started to walk toward the other horses.

"But Dan," Charley pleaded in a desperate tone as he held out his hands and looked around. "We can't lose a day of travel. Let her go if that's what she wants. I'm sorry about the horse, but we can get you another one when we get to Dodge."

Dan froze in his tracks before turning to give Charley a hard glare.

"You don't get it, do you? There is no getting to Dodge City without Pauline. That's the whole reason why we're doing this. And besides, I've got to get Jesse back. Neither one of them can be replaced. I suggest you wait for me to come back or leave without me. Those are the options. Got it?"

The men said nothing. Dan walked over to the other horses and untied one of them, mounting himself as he rode off. The rest of the camp stood in disbelief as he departed. Beneath the clattering of hooves, he could hear them talking to each other about what was going on. None of it mattered to him. The only thing that mattered was making sure Pauline was safe. Even Jesse, God forbid anything happened to him, felt like less of a priority. The idea of her being in danger made him ride faster until he found himself out in the open prairie, unsure of where to even begin looking.

Dan had been an excellent tracker before settling down with a family. His skills came from early days on the trails, and it had become a service people sought him out for. The first thing to look for was tracks. Jesse's hooves left a special mark, something only he could notice. There was an array of tracks and footprints that had indented themselves into the lone pathway away from camp toward the city. The trail extended past the horizon, with two mountains to the west. Had she and Jesse stayed on the road, there was a good chance they were too weary to go on. Save for the distant mountains, it was open for miles around them.

As he searched the landscape, Dan looked for additional clues. The first one being any signs of struggle. Maybe someone had robbed her and Jesse, leaving her stranded. The idea made Dan's blood boil. He couldn't stand the thought of her being attacked again, this time out in the middle of nowhere. In that sense, the fact that there were no stranded items, like women's clothing, gave him a wave of relieve. If she was out there, Jesse was with her.

Dan traversed the area until he came upon a set of tracks that bore similar resemblance to Jesse's. There was one hoof, on the back right leg, that had the slightest crack along the bottom. It made the curvature of the footprint somewhat crooked, barely noticeable to the untrained eye. The ground was soft enough that the tracks extended out beyond the horizon. The mud was drying out from the morning sun. He needed to move to get to Pauline before someone else on the road did first.

He made the horse gallop at breakneck speed, following Jesse's tracks as he pushed on. This trail was makeshift, going off in a direction that would have taken Pauline away from Dodge City to parts unknown. Perhaps it was a camp that did not wish to be found. Dan's heart raced. What if she stumbled upon a camp of wayward criminals? He had to shake the thought out of his mind.

"Pauline!" he yelled.

Silence.

Dan sped the horse up, who let out a noise of dissatisfaction. The tracks moved deeper into the ground as the trail rounded a corner. This was a small pass between two mountains. Somewhere bandits liked to hide. He could not waste any more time. Another hour passed as the sun began to reach its midday point. If Pauline didn't have any water, neither she nor Jesse would be able to make it through the day.

As Dan rounded the corner into the mountain pass, he heard water flowing in the distance. The horse was beginning to make tired sounds and they would need to take a break. He wanted to shout her name once again but could not be certain he was alone. That would only bring more danger. As he got closer, he noticed the trail was submerged by a river with a strong current. White caps of water splashed up against half-submerged rocks. Jesse's tracks had walked right up to it, but he could not see them on the other side. A woman's figure was sitting by the riverbank. Dan's heart raced as he sped up.

Her clothes were tattered as she sat there, sobbing, with streaks of mud running down her arms and legs. Dan hitched his horse and jumped down, running to her aid. It was Pauline. Although he wanted to feel relieved, seeing her cry triggered an immediate urgency; it was a problem he had to solve before doing anything else.

"Pauline!" Dan yelled as he ran to her. "Pauline! Are you okay?"

Pauline continued to sob. She looked up at him with tears streaming down her face.

"Dan?! How did you…"

She stopped and let out a sigh of relief.

"Are you okay, Pauline? Are you hurt?"

He kneeled and put a hand on her as she cried more. Dan began to caress her gently with one hand before she pulled away.

"No," she sputtered, "I'm not hurt. It's… Jesse…"

She broke down again and continued to sob.

"It's okay, Pauline. Just tell me. What happened?"

"I tried to cross the river," she began to say between tears, "I don't know why. I just had to go. And I tried to get Jesse across with me. He started to float away. I jumped off and made it back, but he's downstream, stuck in the mud. I tried to get him out, but after struggling all morning I almost drowned myself. So, I waited here, but no one came until you did. And I haven't heard him in so long. I'm… so… Dan," she stopped and caught her breath, "I'm so sorry, Dan."

"It's okay," Dan said, "I'll get him, I just need to know you're okay."

He looked at her. Pauline's lips trembled as more tears welled up.

"I'll be all right," she assured him, "better once I know Jesse's safe."

"You said he's downstream? I can find him, just wait right here. I'll come back."

Dan ran down the riverbank and saw Jesse struggling, his legs half-submerged in the thick wet mud. He was alive and unharmed but could not move. He ran toward him and could see his beloved steed nearing circulatory shock, where the horse's cardiovascular system would not provide enough oxygen to the horse's organs and would lead to its death.

"Jesse!" he called out as he trudged through the shin-deep mud. "Jesse! I got you, buddy!"

Jesse struggled upon contact, letting out a noise indicating his fear. It was obvious the horse was in a state of exhaustion. Dan used his foot to clear the mud around his front left leg. If he could get the first two out, Jesse would be able to get the back ones on his own. Dan found his front left leg was too deep to be moved. He struggled for several minutes before he retreated to the dry land so he could catch his breath.

Pauline came up behind him, still sobbing.

"Will you be able to save him?" she asked in a shaky tone.

Dan was upset but needed to keep himself calm in order to save Jesse in time. "It's going to take some extra help."

"What do we do then?"

"We need to get you back to camp," Dan said as he caught his breath, "that's the most important thing. After that I'll run back out here with some help and hopefully be able to save him." He was beginning to feel a rushed sense of urgency. There was no time to be wasted.

"Get me back? Dan, they won't take me back. Not after I ran away."

Dan paused to look at her. She had spent the day trying to save his horse. Although it was her fault Jesse was in the situation, it was obvious she cared. Whatever reason it was she had for running, they would need to talk about it later, once Jesse was free.

"You're family now. We took the day off just so we could find you."

Pauline said nothing, but Dan noticed the tears streaming down her face even more after what he said. He reached out a hand to help her. She refused to touch him but still followed back to the horse.

"I'm going to drop you off, Dorothy can take care of you from there, and then me and the boys will come rescue Jesse."

"Thank you, Dan," she said as she climbed up on to the horse. Dan flinched at first when she touched him, but something about it felt right. He had not yet forgiven her, but in the moment it did not matter. All he could focus on was the way her arms slipped softly around his waist, clasping her hands together where they met on his front side and resting there. His heart began to race as her chest pressed against his back. It felt so natural and safe to have her sitting so close.

"Jesse! We're coming back!" he yelled to the horse.

Jesse neighed desperately as they sped off. Dan and Pauline rode with haste, paying no mind to the horse beginning to wear down. The trail seemed much closer now that he knew where they were going. He could not help but wonder what she was thinking. At the same time, it was dark out when she left. She probably had no idea where the horse was going.

Why did she do this?

Dan reached the makeshift camp Henry and Ross had set up for the cattle they'd recollected from the fields. Dan rounded the two men up, along with two of their best bulls, and made their way back to the river. It was nearly nightfall when they got back to his horse. They needed to move quickly before it was pitch black between the two mountains.

Dan splashed into the shallow water and tied ropes around Jesse's barrel and rear end. The horse began to panic again as Dan tried to calm him.

"On my count, one, two, PULL!"

The men had their bulls begin to move. Jesse let out a noise of pain. Dan wasn't happy seeing the horse struggle. The two bulls continued to move. He was budging, but it would take more work.

"Keep going!" Dan yelled, "Don't let up!"

Jesse thrashed as he began to reach circulatory shock. There wasn't much time to go. Dan continued yelling to Ross and Henry. He watched as one of Jesse's legs began to surface.

"That's it!"

Jesse started to seize up. Soon his body would shut down if they didn't move quick enough. The bulls were pulling with all their strength. Suddenly, the rope loosened as Jesse fell forward onto the dry land. Dan ran over to see his horse hyperventilating. It had been a close call, but his beloved horse was going to be all right after all, barring no permanent injuries had occurred from the fall.

"It's okay buddy, you're free now."

Dan inspected the horse and was relieved to find there was no long-term physical damage. Psychologically, Jesse would need to recover for a while. They walked back at a slow pace so Jesse would not overwork himself. As he approached the camp Henry and Ross had set up, he saw Pauline sitting there. She smiled at him and suddenly Dan experienced a sudden burst of rage coupled with fear. He jumped down from his horse and ran up to her. Before she could talk, he pulled her away from the rest of the camp. When they were far enough away, he turned around and the look on his face made her pull back.

"What were you thinking?" he yelled with his finger pointed at her, "Or *were* you thinking, I guess I should ask? You know you could have gotten yourself killed out there."

Pauline's face dropped and she turned away, walking silently back to the camp. After saving her, she was probably ready to talk and open up about her past, but Dan was too mad and had too much on his mind for a normal conversation. Stopping in her tracks, she turned around once again, looking as if she wanted to try and talk things out.

"I thought you were—"

"Spare me that," he spat, "what you did was—"

"Dan! Cut that out," Henry yelled as he ran toward them. "You know better than to yell at a woman, especially when she's been in distress."

"I don't care. What she did could've cost all of us our lives."

"But it didn't."

"You can't be serious right now."

Henry sighed. "Listen, Dan. We all make mistakes. Things happen out here too. Sometimes caused by people, sometimes not. It doesn't mean you can talk like that, though."

Dan watched Pauline walk back to camp as he took Henry's words in. He was right. It was never okay to talk to a woman like he did. He wanted to catch up to her and apologize, though he knew she probably needed some space to be alone, probably to draw.

It wasn't even about Jesse, he realized. It was the idea of Pauline getting hurt or killed that made him feel so angry. When he saw the tracks disappear into the water, Dan had thought he'd lost another person he cared about. It was fear that had driven him to act out of line, driving her away. Now Pauline was back, safe and sound. He didn't want to risk losing her again.

He sat down by the fire and contemplated. Dan had lost so much; the mere idea of losing anyone, or anything, else set off something inside of him. It had allowed Dan to track her down, but what would be the point if that was how he was going to respond once she was safe? He went to his tent and laid there. Without realizing it, Dan felt the tears streaming down from his eyes, dripping to the ground on which he slept.

Chapter Twenty-Eight

The next morning, all was silent. Pauline slept later than normal, having needed to catch up on rest from the night before. After being confronted by Dan, she had retreated to a place where she could be alone to draw. She did not cry. Instead, she drew a detailed sketch of Jesse, highlighting his strong features to make the portrait even more flattering. It would be a peace offering, so long as Dan apologized for his behavior too.

She had come back to the campsite relieved to find that Dan had gone to bed and spent some time by the fire as Henry and Ross drifted off to sleep next to the cattle. It was nice to be back around people, even if she did not wish to see Dan right away.

When she got out of her tent, Pauline was surprised to find that nobody else was awake yet. Everyone needed the additional rest after their long night rescuing Jesse. Was that her fault? Did she cause additional stress on this group of people? The burden of guilt would be too much for her to bear, regardless of whether Dan would point it out to her later. Deep down, she hoped he would wake up in a better mood. It still made her wonder: how often did he lose his temper? Would she always have to be wary of this? Or was she still recovering from her husband's abuse?

These thoughts swirled through Pauline's mind as Henry stirred in his sleeping mat. He had gone to sleep by the campfire opposite from Ross, and now the morning dew was collecting in particles on their faces and clothing. Henry opened his eyes to see Pauline standing there and smiled.

"Hey there," his voice uttered, raspy and half-awake.

"Hey," Pauline said shyly. She was relieved that at least one of the men was not angry with her. Henry looked around without getting up and gave her a look of confusion.

"Where are we again?" he asked. "What happened last night?"

Pauline said nothing. She was afraid he would realize why they had to come out there and then take his anger out on her, just as Dan had done. Henry had been the one to stop Dan, though it was the morning now. They had no food, a long ride back to the ranch, and who knew what else. To Pauline, men could get mad about anything. Sometimes it was obvious, sometimes it was not. Henry waited before lifting himself so that he sat up in his bed.

"Ross!" he yelled in a half-whisper. "Hey, Ross! Get up, lazy."

Ross let out a moan from the other side of the campfire. He rolled over onto his stomach and put his hands over his ears.

"Ross, I know you hear me," Henry said in a confrontational manner.

"What do you want?" Ross replied as he kept his face buried.

"What are we doing out here? Why aren't we at the ranch?"

Oh no, Pauline thought to herself, *he is going to realize why we are here and then they are all going to be angry with me.*

"Dan lost his horse," Ross said, still half-awake, "we had to go get it."

Henry let out a chuckle.

"Oh yeah, good old Dan lost his horse in the river."

Ross returned it.

"Oh, I bet Dan is going to be saltier than a bucket of beef when he gets up," Henry quipped. Then he looked over at Pauline. "Best recommend that you don't say nothing to him about it whenever he gets up. You are still in good standing with him. Don't want to be like Ross over there." He laughed.

Oh, do not worry, Pauline thought to herself as she stood over them, *I will not be bringing any of this up for a while*. It was still nice to see that Henry had a sense of humor about the situation. things. Ross did not seem to be too upset about it either. He rolled over, eyes still groggy, as he looked at Pauline and smiled. She was relieved that they were so casual about what had happened. She could not help but smile at their playful bantering.

"Don't believe what this man says," Ross looked back and forth at them, "Dan loves me."

"Why don't you ask him that when he gets up then?" Henry said with a smile as he stood up and stretched, letting out a contagious yawn.

"*You* ask him." Ross laughed. "I know I'm right, so I don't need to."

Pauline let out a laugh. It was nice to know that even if Dan never spoke to her again, the rest of the guys from the caravan still seemed to like her. Maybe they were right. Maybe she was family now. Family members made mistakes sometimes. That did not mean they were exiled. It was what support systems were made for.

Pauline heard another stirring noise—Dan, who had awoken while they were all talking. Not only that, but they were talking about him. Suddenly, Pauline began to feel nervous. Even if the other two men at the camp had her back, she did not wish to be accosted again. Especially not from somebody she had begun to have feelings for. She did not like that feeling of unease. It reminded her of those nights when her husband came home late from the saloons. She knew what it was: unpredictability. When Pauline heard Dan begin to undo the flaps of his tent, she began to feel a sickness in her knotted stomach.

"Hey Dan," Ross began as he winked at Pauline, "Henry wants to know if you love me."

Dan looked at him and grunted. He did not seem angry. Pauline had seen what he looked like when angry just the night before. In fact, he did not seem to be wearing any sort of emotion. He was tired, like he had not slept well. Was he up because of her? There came that rush of guilt again. Although she was intimidated by his presence, Pauline wanted Dan to talk so that she could better gauge who she would be dealing with for the rest of the day, if not longer.

"Well," Ross began impatiently, "do you?"

"I love everyone," Dan said gruffly, as if he were being sarcastic.

Henry let out a laugh and pointed at Ross.

"I told you!" he yelled to him.

"Wait—no, that counts!" Ross shouted. "Dan said everyone. I'm a person too!"

"Are you sure about that?" Dan looked up at him with a smile.

Henry and Ross began to laugh hysterically.

There it is, Pauline thought to herself. He may not have given her any attention yet, but at least he was in a better mood. Ross was a good buffer for that. If he were still in a rotten mood, Dan would not have had the patience for someone like him. Instead, he was able to joke back. She shared in their laughter. It came as a relief.

The rest of the morning was silent again. Dan took care of Jesse and ignored everyone else as they packed up their gear. Pauline tried to help as best she could, but Henry and Ross were too prepared and knew exactly what had to be done. She didn't like being useless standing there, though she knew they were trying to leave as quickly as possible and did not want to explain nor instruct. Before she knew it, everything had been packed up and the men were ready to head back to the ranch.

Pauline looked over at Dan, who seemed to be focused entirely on Jesse. Dan sat on the saddle, stroking Jesse's head as he talked to him sweetly. She wished he would do that with her at some point, but only if he was truly sorry for the night before.

"Give him some time," a voice said behind her, "I think he's embarrassed for how he was talking to you."

She turned to see Ross looking at her. The expression on his face let her know that he knew exactly what was going on. She looked back over at Dan, and he was looking at her too now. There was something on his face that she could not readily identify. It could have been guilt, frustration, or even fear. Whatever it was, she still felt safe around him. That was the difference between Dan and her husband. She had never been safe with Herschel; not until he was dead.

"Pauline," Henry began, "you good to ride this horse by your lonesome?"

"Ain't she been doing that this whole time?" Ross said with a laugh.

"I'm just asking!" Henry said defensively.

"What do you have to ask for?" Ross laughed again.

"She's a lady, you're supposed to ask!" Henry yelled.

Dan came forward as Jesse let out a noise.

"That's enough from you two." He looked at Pauline and flashed a grin. "Let's get back to the ranch and see if we can get some breakfast before it's too late."

"Breakfast? Well, you don't have to tell me twice!" Ross hopped onto his horse. "Let's go, buddy!"

He began to ride off. The rest of them got on their horses and tried to catch up. The cattle trailed slowly behind them. Dan stayed behind to herd them. Pauline knew she was not ready to go as fast as Henry and Ross, though she also enjoyed the freedom. The sky was open and blue, with a few scattered clouds. She had been stuck in that mountain pass for so long that she'd forgotten how lovely the landscape had been.

* * *

When they arrived back to the ranch, the other members of their party had been waiting for them. Nobody seemed upset to see her, though she was still too embarrassed and ashamed to notice.

"Dorothy!" Ross yelled. "Dorothy! We are back and we are hungry!"

"Settle down," Henry instructed him. "Sorry, Dorothy, he got too excited about breakfast."

"Oh, that's all right," she said to them, "I'll make something for you all."

Dorothy bent around past Henry and smiled at Pauline. It warmed her heart to see her reaction. The elderly woman came forward and put her hands around Pauline's and let out a deep exhale.

"Pauline," Dorothy began, "I am so glad you are safe."

When Pauline saw her eyes, she felt a surge of emotions. "I'm... so sorry. I don't know what I—"

Dorothy held out her hand, a serious look in her eyes. Pauline went silent.

"Listen, whatever reason you had, that is yours to keep. We cannot always have good reasons for doing what we do. I am sure it felt right, whatever it was. I'm just glad you are not in any danger."

Dorothy gave Pauline a hug. It was good to have somebody out there who understood. Pauline was angry any man could treat such a kind person that way. Dorothy brought her arms back to her sides and placed a hand on Pauline's shoulder.

"If you want to talk about it more later, you know where to find me. Right now, I need to make some food before Ross eats one of our horses." She let out a soft laugh.

As they sat there eating, Dan came riding in from the distance with the two bulls in tow. Charley went over and spoke to him as he dismounted. He did not seem angry anymore. Pauline watched as the two of them spoke casually. She finished up her meal and stood up. Reluctantly, Pauline made her way toward Dan. Her legs grew weaker with each step, her body telling her to stop and turn around. Dan was taking the two bulls back to their pen. Was he too busy to talk? She could not wait any longer to clear things up, but also feared he was still upset. They were next to the pen now, with no one else around. Pauline knew there would not be another chance to get him away from everyone. It was now or never.

"Dan," she began softly as she came up behind him. "Dan, I'm so sorry for putting Jesse in danger. You're right. I wasn't thinking. I don't know why I did what I did. But if you know I'm sorry, that's all that matters to me."

Dan led the bulls into their confinement. There was no one else around. If he wanted to yell at her again, he could have done it. In the distance, Pauline heard Ross telling the story of their morning to the rest of the caravan. After closing the gate, Dan turned back to look at her.

"It wasn't about Jesse," he said as he looked down and shook his head.

What was he thinking? What was he trying to say? Pauline worried he was going to go on a tangent about something else. She tried to gauge his face for a reaction. His eyes stared ahead at her in the sunshine. It was scary, although in a way, the fear excited her. Finally, she realized Dan was waiting for her to say something.

"But... I put his life in danger," she reiterated. "Shouldn't you be mad at me for that?"

He pulled his head back, like he had just realized the punchline to a good joke.

"Pauline," he began, "I wasn't mad about Jesse getting put in harm's way. I was mad about *you*. If something happened to you out there, I don't... I..."

Dan froze as he looked away at the camp. A warmth spread inside Pauline. Beautiful as they were, his words had taken her by surprise. *He was worried about me.* That was why he had gotten so upset. Nobody had ever cared for her like that. When her ex-husband was upset, it was always over other things. Dinner, guests, gambling losses. It was never out of concern for her well-being. She did not know how to respond.

She noticed Dan looking at her now and knew she had to respond.

"Dan, I didn't know you cared so much about me."

"We all do!" Henry shouted from behind them. He was still sitting at the circle where the rest of their group had been eating. Pauline entered a state of shock. Did they all hear their conversation? Were they listening in?

"Yeah, Pauline," Ross chimed in from next to him, "You're one of us now. We have to take care of you whether we want to or not!"

"Oh, stop it!" Dorothy said as she gave a friendly slap to his knee. "He is right, though. You are a part of our family now."

The rest of them nodded in agreement. Everyone except Charley, who kept his head bent over the food he had been eating. Although she could sense their warmth and acceptance, there was still a part of her unsure what to do. These were good people, and if she stayed with them, she would continue to put them in danger. Taking her in meant they were accomplices to the murder she was wanted for. It was guilt by association in the eyes of the law. They all said they would protect her, but Pauline was not sure if she was worthy of them making that sacrifice. No matter what they said, she would never allow any of them to get hurt because of her.

Henry stepped around Pauline and walked back up to the group.

"All right, everybody," he began, "we've already lost a morning's worth of work. The good news is we're in the final stretch to Dodge City. If we start getting ready now, we might be able to get there before sundown today. That's a big 'if' though, so let's start making moves."

The rest of the men got up from their seats. Pauline looked around at them and became envious of their sense of urgency, knowing exactly what to always do. She started to collect items to clean when Dorothy came up and put a soft hand on her back.

"Pauline, dear, he wasn't speaking to you."

"I want to help though," she said in a pleading manner, "it'll make me feel useful."

Dorothy sized her up and down with her eyes for a moment. "You need rest. If you want to help, the best way would be to take a nap. None of these men are going to think twice of it now. But on the road, if you slow them down..."

Dorothy shook her head and gave a light chuckle.

"You're right. I'll try my best to nap."

She walked over to a well-shaded tree and laid down. In the distance she listened to the men shout back and forth to each other. Dorothy was right. There was not much for her to do. She tried to make herself sleep, but instead she kept thinking back to her conversation with Dan. He did care about her. Not in the way the others did. He really cared about her, enough to be that upset about her running away. Did it excuse the way he spoke to her? No. Was it something they could eventually work through? Hopefully.

As she thought about these things, Pauline was unable to sleep. The setting was tranquil, with birds chirping in the branches overhead. The silence made Pauline's thoughts swirl loudly within her head. What if Allen was on his way back to the ranch with his men? She kept thinking of Dan and wished he was there with her. Maybe then she could sleep. Suddenly, she heard footsteps behind her. Was it him? Did he somehow hear her wish?

When she opened her eyes, she saw Charley standing over her. "What is it?" she asked nervously. "Is everything okay?"

"You tell me," he said to her coldly. "Is everything okay?"

"I'm still a little shocked from it all, if that's what you mean."

"I mean Allen," he clarified. "I know you're still worried about him. Aren't you?"

Pauline was scared. She nodded in agreement anyway. "I'm not worried about what they will do to me. I am worried about what they'll do if they find out I was with you."

Charley nodded his head. "That's why I'm here. I don't want anybody else to get hurt. Last night was enough of a close call. You want to turn yourself in, don't you?"

Pauline nodded.

"I figured that's why you ran off. Now Dan and the others, they won't understand. Me, on the other hand, I get it. That's why I'm offering to take you to Allen myself. We can slip out now without anyone noticing, but that's only if we go now."

She was not sure what to say. It was a generous offer, though Pauline did not know why Charley was so willing to help her. What if they arrested him too?

Charley stood there waiting for Pauline to respond.

"Well, listen here: I am going to go wait by my horse. If you decide to go ahead and do the right thing, come find me. Just don't take too long. Every second you spend here puts us all in danger."

Pauline hesitated. Before she had the chance to respond, Charley turned and walked away. Could she make it work with the caravan? Would Dan be able to truly forgive her for leaving? Or should she just leave and get it all over with?

Chapter Twenty-Nine

Dan apologized to the bulls as he re-hitched them to the wagon. They had just returned and had barely any time to rest. The long part of the day was just around the corner too. The creatures were strong and agile, though everything needed a break here and there. He knew the road ahead would be long and arduous, so he gave them some extra food to compensate.

He was also relieved, having had a better conversation with Pauline. There was still much to be discussed, and he needed to apologize for the way he spoke. It was nice to know they *could* talk about it, though. Once they were settled for the night, whether it was Dodge City or camp along the way, he would have a more in-depth conversation with Pauline. Now that she had returned, they could take their time to become more comfortable with one another. Dan was just happy he had not yet ruined things with her.

He heard the clattering of hooves and panicked for a moment, thinking the rest of the caravan had started to leave without him. When Dan looked up, he only saw one horse riding off with two people in the distance. *Strange*, he thought to himself, *what are two people doing out there by themselves with no supplies?* They were riding away and doing so rather quickly.

Dan turned away, thinking it was just somebody passing through. Half a second later, he turned back around. One of them had a feminine physique. That was when he recognized her—Pauline. She was riding off with someone. But why?

Dan wondered if it was because of him. Something he had done or said must have scared her off. Without hesitating, he ran to the first horse he could find and jumped into the saddle.

"Hey! Wrong horse!" Ross quipped. "Unless you're giving me Jesse, I suppose."

Dan said nothing. He untied Ross' horse from the station and immediately galloped after them. Pauline and whomever she was with were mere dots on the horizon. *Not again*, Dan thought to himself as he made the horse go faster. *I am not going to lose you again, Pauline.*

The open plains raced past Dan's field of vision. It was a lovely summer's day, not too hot nor humid. Any other time in his life, Dan would have stopped to appreciate the cool breeze. But now it only seemed to push him further along as he exhausted Ross' horse. This was not Jesse. This horse was younger and more fragile. Dan could not worry about that now, though. It would be good training for this horse. Ross would thank him later.

The two of them had rode past where Pauline turned the other night. He could see the beginning of that mountain pass in the distance. His stomach quivered at the sight. He had hoped by the time they saw that road again, he and Pauline would be back on good terms. Now he was out here chasing after her once more. It was beginning to frustrate him, leaving Dan with more questions and fewer answers each time. The sense of dread had been building inside of him. Would she keep trying to run away? Or would he be able to convince her not to? And why was he so concerned? Dan knew there was only one possible answer: he was falling in love with Pauline.

Pauline and her ride began to slow down. Dan pushed Ross' horse to the brink. The steed was beginning to slow down despite his commands, taking long breaths and showing signs of exhaustion. They were too close to let up, though. Dan continued to make the horse gallop. When they got closer, he finally let up. They had stopped to take a break next to the river crossing. It was as if they had no idea they were being followed. When Dan got close enough to be in earshot, they turned to see him riding up. That was when Dan saw who Pauline had left with and his blood boiled with anger.

"Charley!" he yelled. "What do you think you're doing?"

The man looked back and said nothing as Dan slowed to a stop. He jumped down and ran toward him, ready to give the man a beating. Pauline jumped in front of him.

"Dan!" she yelled as she put her hands on his chest. "Dan, don't hurt him!"

The way her hands pressed soft on his skin made him stop to take a deep breath. They had not touched like that since he yelled at her the night before. He thought she would never touch him again. It sent a coolness through his system immediately. After he took a few deep breaths, he looked down at Pauline. She seemed even more worried than him. Something was not right. He knew Charley would never kidnap somebody. What were they doing out here?

"Why?" he pleaded to her. "Why do you keep leaving?"

Pauline said nothing. Her face dropped with sadness.

"I have to." She spoke with a somber tone. "I will not let anyone from your group get hurt because of me. This is my problem to deal with and nobody else's."

After saying her piece, she turned back to Charley. He had already gotten back up on the horse and was waiting for her. Pauline climbed up as Charley took the reins. Dan charged around to the front of them and grabbed the reins himself so the horse could not leave.

"Pauline, don't go! We can make this work. I don't care what they think you did. What do you think is going to happen anyway?"

Pauline shook her head. "I have to turn myself in," she said in a matter-of-fact tone. "I can't let you, or Dorothy, or Henry, even Ross or any of the others get hurt for something *I* did."

Pauline looked at Dan with pity in her eyes. It was as if she felt sorry for him.

"You didn't do anything though. All of us believe you."

"The law does not care at all about that," Charley interrupted. "Come on Dan, you know that just as well as I do. This is the best thing for everyone."

"You shut your mouth!" Dan yelled. He could have hurt Charley for what he was doing to Pauline. She was innocent. He knew it now within his heart of hearts. If he had to spend his life protecting a woman from the law, so be it. He turned back to Pauline.

"Pauline," he began, "you can't just hand yourself over like that. They are going to kill you for a crime you did not commit." Dan was pleading her now. His voice had grown shaky as he kept the horse from moving forward.

"It's better than the rest of you getting killed too," she reminded him, "I don't want to live the rest of my years in hiding, putting other people at risk. It's not fair to anyone."

Tears ran down his face again. He was choking on his words. There were too many emotions surging through him. The only thing left to do was be honest with her. He was losing someone he loved again, but at least this time he had a chance to say how he felt before it was too late.

"But Pauline," he said again, "I love you. I know this feeling. And I also know," he paused to collect himself, "I can't lose another love."

"Dan," she replied, looking down at him with adoration beneath her sadness, "even if I stay, they will find me. I know you do not want to lose me, but I am afraid I am already gone. At least that's how it seems. I'm sorry Dan, this is how it has to be."

"No, it doesn't!" he pleaded desperately. "I will protect you. I will do so until we find the real killer and then we clear your name. We can do this Pauline, just don't go. Please don't go."

Dan turned his face away. He was beginning to feel the same way he did when his family was killed. All she had to do was get down from the horse and leave with him. When he looked back up at her, tears were welling up in her eyes as she looked out over the horizon.

"I have spent too much time running," she said as she shook her head. "I can't do it forever. I don't want to spend my life looking over one shoulder, always wondering which day will be my last. I've been scared long enough. It's time for me to handle things once and for all."

Dan felt the weight of her words bearing down on him. He knew why she felt that way. It made complete sense to him. If Dan were put on trial for the murder of his family, he would not have wanted to live his life on the run either. Fortunately, he had the burden of proof in his corner. As for Pauline, their situation could be salvageable. All she had to do was get down from the horse. If he could change her mind, he would be able to make this all work out. It would become a distant memory one day. They would sit back and tell everyone the story when they were older. All he had to do was convince her to get down.

"Pauline," Dan said, "I'm begging you. Do not go." He let go of the reins and put his hands around hers. They were still to him, almost lifeless. "I have not felt this way for anyone in such a long time. I've fallen in love with you. We have a connection. You and me. It's worth saving, isn't it?"

Charley sat in silence. From the corner of his eye, Dan could see him shaking his head. He couldn't help but wonder why Charley was doing this. He wanted to ask. Instead, Dan kept his focus on Pauline. He waited for a reaction that never came. She took another deep breath and shook her head as she stared down at him. His hands were trembling around hers.

"Don't you love me too?" he asked her.

Pauline paused again and looked out at the horizon. He waited with bated breath as she stared at the road ahead. The only sound between Dan's heavy breathing was the chirping of birds overhead. Finally, she turned back to him. She stared directly into his eyes and Dan felt a combination of fear and excitement as she opened her lips.

"No, Dan," she said, "I don't love you."

Dan let go of her hands. Something inside him collapsed in on itself. It was as if his entire world had crashed in that moment. Pauline had given him a renewed purpose in life and now she was leaving. He dropped to his knees as Charley kicked the horse. It let out a noise and began to canter away from him.

Pauline did not look back at Dan. He waited there to see if she turned her head, though she never did. Instead, they became dots on the horizon. This time, however, there was no chasing after them. She was not going to return to camp. Even if she did, Dan knew it would only be a matter of time before she ran away again. There would be no convincing her. He had given her enough chances.

Dan ran through every possible reason why she did not love him. Every idea that passed through his mind filled him with more regret. He regretted how he'd treated her those first few days, finding her bathing, and especially yelling at her. But none of those moments were what he regretted the most.

The worst of it all was that Dan had opened up to someone. Something he swore to never do again after what he had been through. Now he was not only regretful, but there was also a sense of embarrassment in their final encounter. Dan knew they could have made it work. The two of them together would have been able to overcome anything. That was only worthwhile for them if they loved each other though, and now he knew his love for her was not shared.

Dan waited until he could no longer hear nor see them. The silence of the landscape bore down on him. The pain of loss had overtaken him once again. It was an illness to which there was no cure. Dan knew the feeling well enough to recognize it inside of him. He was suffering from a broken heart.

Chapter Thirty

The ride with Charley had been uneventful, at best. He barely spoke to her as they traveled across the open plain. Pauline had not even bothered to ask where they were going. It did not matter to her anymore. Her fate would be the same no matter where Allen and his crew caught up to them. It was only a matter of time before she would be executed for a crime she did not commit.

She could not bring herself to think about Dan. Even though she had to leave, for the sake of the caravan, she had still managed to hurt someone before she left. Pauline wanted to say she loved him but knew it would have ruined everything for them. She still felt terrible for how she had to be. It reminded her of Herschel, when he said after beating her that it was for her own good. That she needed to learn and would come out on the other side a stronger person. Was that her now? Had she become the person she feared the most?

Every time Pauline closed her eyes, she saw that look of defeat on Dan's face once again. She saw the way he collapsed as she lied, saying she did not love him back. It had to be said. Dan may not have understood, but she was doing it for his own good.

Charley was attentive to her needs. He would slow down when the horse needed to and ask if she needed water, or was hungry, or just needed to stretch her legs. It was not like Dan, who always kept a watch on her. This was more formal, as if he was doing so out of obligation. Charley did not actually seem to care about how she was doing. He just wanted to make sure she stayed alive out there. But why?

Why was she worth this risk? Why was he breaking away from the camp to help Pauline turn herself in? Surely, she thought, Charley had to know the dangers of traveling with a wanted woman. There were so many things that could go wrong. Charley did not seem wary about any of it. He barely spoke even when they stopped to rest. His eyes remained fixated on the road ahead of them. Pauline tried to read his face to see what he was thinking, but there was no expression. It was as if he had no soul behind his eyes.

"Charley," she said at one point during a break, "thank you for doing this."

Charley turned and looked at her with his empty gaze. "Sure thing," he said apathetically.

Pauline waited for him to say something else, but Charley had gone mute. In her mind, Pauline began to make sense of it. Charley must have known she would be hung as soon as she was in custody. There was no point in the two of them forming a relationship. He was helping her protect the rest of their caravan, and she just had to stay alive and breathing for their trip to town. It confused Pauline to some extent. Charley was a stranger they had picked up along the way. What did he care? Either way, they had no reason to talk about feelings, beliefs, or anything else beyond "let's go" or "time for a break." It was pointless for them to get close.

She began to miss Dan. She missed the way he watched to make sure she had what was needed. She missed the way he chased after her, even when she was doing something wrong. There were times along the journey when she listened for the clattering of hooves behind them, when her name would be called out hastily, and she would turn around to see him riding up. That never came. Dan had learned his lesson. She fought off her emotions at the idea. Charley did not need to be put through that. He was fulfilling her wish to be turned in to Allen. She agreed to going. There was no room for tears, and Pauline had none left to cry.

When they saw the town on the horizon, Pauline's heart sank into her chest. This was it. They had arrived at Dodge City. She would be face to face with her destiny soon enough. Allen and his crew were waiting for them here. The sense of unease grew as the sight of town drew nearer.

At the front of the town, she could see the saloon. The sign had been painted so travelers could see it from far away. Behind it was an array of wooden buildings and homes scattered about the dirt roads, with several ranches fenced off in the distance. Pauline had hoped Dodge City would resemble the promise for a better future. Now her fate was uncertain. Charley slowed the horse to a canter and time began to move at half-speed.

They approached the front of the town as Charley studied the area.

"We'll start at the general store," he said to her. Pauline felt like she had not heard his voice in hours. It gave her no comfort. He moved the horse around to the other side of town. There was a large wooden structure people were moving in and out of. Every time somebody looked at them, Pauline grew more uncomfortable. It was as if the whole town knew she was wanted and was ready to shoot her themselves. Pauline trembled with fear.

Charley approached the front of the store and dismounted. As he hitched his horse, he looked up at her with his expressionless gaze. She felt uneasy at his lack of emotion. When she stared in his eyes, it was as if he did not care at all what happened to her. So why did he agree to help her like this? Things were not adding up.

"I'll be right back," he said coldly. "Don't you go anywhere."

Pauline nodded as he walked up the wooden steps. She got down and stood, stretching her legs as she considered running on foot. She looked out at the empty horizon. Surely, she would die out there. That was obvious. But it would be better than her fate with Allen, who was a relative of her dead husband. There was no telling how alike they could be. Perhaps Allen was even worse.

"All right," Charley said as he came up behind her.

"What did you find out?" she asked nervously. Part of her hoped they were in another town. That she would have a day or so to rest before her execution. She was desperate for some shred of hope.

"They're staying above the saloon," Charley explained to her. "Let's head over."

That was it. The men were here and so was she. Charley untied the horse and hopped up onto the saddle. He held out a hand and waited for Pauline to accept. She hesitated, her hands and legs beginning to tremble. It felt as if she were being led to her own death, and her survival instinct now told her to run away as fast as she could.

"I know this can't be easy," he said, "just know you're doing the right thing."

Pauline let out a sigh and took his hand as he helped her up. She knew he was right. This was no longer about her. It was about everyone involved. They may have considered her family, but they would move on. Even Dan would be able to get over her and fall in love with somebody else. He was still young and had plenty of life ahead of him. He could meet someone who was not wanted for murder, who could take care of him and not spend life on the run.

They circled back to the saloon. Pauline could hear the music playing inside over the clanking of bottles and shouting. This would be it. The last thing she would remember. Charley brought his horse to the hitch and started to get down. As he did so, Pauline watched his foot slip, getting caught in the bridle as he started to fall.

She tried not to laugh. If it weren't for her situation, maybe she would have. She thought it would be difficult to conceal until something distracted her. As Charley fell, something came out of his left breast pocket. It looked familiar. She got down to help him and noticed it on the ground—a pocket watch.

This was no regular pocket watch. There was something engraved on it. She stuck out a hand to help him as she directed her gaze to the pocket watch on the ground. When she looked closer, Pauline nearly screamed out loud. The engraving had the initials "H.H." across the face that shone back at her. She knew that watch and would have recognized it anywhere. This watch belonged to her late husband: Herschel Hogan.

Pauline could feel her face turn white. All the blood began to pump inside her pounding heart. Deep in shock at the revelation, Pauline found herself unable to move, until Charley reached up for her hand still stretched toward him.

Pauline pulled her hand away as she stared down at Charley. There was still no emotion in his eyes. He looked at her coldly, with an expression that said, *yes, I did it, and there's nothing you can do about it.*

In a flash, Pauline jumped for the watch. The ground was muddy and wet from the endless number of horses stationed there. Pauline did not care. To her, it meant life or death. If she had the pocket watch, she could prove she found it on Charley. Likewise, if he continued to hold on to it, he could lie and say he had found it on her. Right as she leapt toward the accessory, Charley lunged for it as well.

She landed on top of him. People gathered around, watching the two of them wrestle for it. Charley touched the watch with his fingertips when Pauline hit it further away. He tried to crawl for it, his hands sinking into the wet terrain, as she did her best to hold him down. She pressed his face into the mud as he struggled for air. The crowd was yelling at them now. People wondered what was going on, who was trying to kill who, and more. They called them lovers, enemies, and more. Pauline ignored them as she kept her eyes fixated on the watch.

In a moment of brute strength, Charley pushed himself up from the ground as Pauline slid off him. His clothes were too muddy for her to hang on. When she hit the ground, Pauline shot back up and lunged for the watch, but it was too late. Charley stood there holding it, looking down at her. Only now he did not wear a blank expression on his face. Instead, he smiled at her.

"You weren't supposed to see this, you know."

Pauline's lips trembled. He knew that watch belonged to her husband—Charley had probably been the one to kill him. He was going to let Pauline take the blame so he would never face the consequences.

"You killed him!" she said angrily as she stood up.

"From the looks of it," he said as he glanced at the watch then back at her, "I found this on you after you killed him."

Pauline lunged for it again. Charley lifted the watch over her as she flew forward and landed on the ground again. She laid on her back with the sun in her eyes. Nothing mattered anymore. She had gotten her answer about the murder, only now it was no use. *If only Dan was here*, she thought. *Dan or any of the others.* If they knew who they were traveling with, everything would be right. Instead, she was left with a cold-blooded killer who was going to let her take the fall for his crimes.

Charley crouched down and looked her in the eyes. There was something new about him. Now that Pauline knew who he really was, she could not see anything else. He was a killer. The kind that felt no remorse for his actions. He lied and said he was going to help her. In the end, she was the one doing him a favor. And now he would live to kill other people too. Perhaps he would take somebody innocent next, maybe even someone from the caravan. Pauline felt herself begin to break into tears.

"Now, now," Charley said, "I suggest we both just pretend this never happened."

"How could you do this?" she asked.

Charley ignored her. He grabbed her arm and stood up, bringing her with him. The crowd that had gathered was gone now that the scuffle was over. It was just entertainment for them. They would probably be the same people that watched her get executed too.

Dodge City had once represented the promise for a new future. Now, she realized, it was where things came to an end.

Chapter Thirty-One

The racing of hooves sounded, coming closer, distracting her and allowing hope to spring anew in her chest. She waited to hear his voice calling out to them. She hoped somehow, deep down, Dan had come for her anyway. As Pauline waited for that clattering sound to stop behind them, it instead grew distant once more. It was somebody passing through. Someone completely unaware of her situation. It had been a brief glimmer of hope for Pauline, but now it was gone.

She looked up and Charley was still standing there. A flash of evil glimmered in his eyes. She could see it now. Had it been there before? It probably had been, she was just unable to see it in him. Charley had offered to help. He had gone against the wishes of the rest of the caravan for her. Now she knew why. The sight of him now made Pauline sick to her stomach. And the worst part of it all was that it made complete sense. Charley cleared his throat and made a step toward her.

"Now listen," he began, "we both know how this is going to end."

His eyes became colder, somehow, as he zeroed in on her. Pauline began to shiver. Chills ran down her spine.

"I understand if you need a second, but I've got to get back to camp before anyone notices how long we—I mean, *I* have been gone."

He studied her some more. Leaning in, she and Charley were face to face. His hot breath brushed upon her face. It made Pauline even more disgusted with him. She began to breathe in jagged bursts. There was no remorse in his eyes. Not for the murder nor for what he was about to do. His face was blank, until he noticed the fear in her eyes, and then he raised his mouth into that grin Pauline had grown to hate.

"Sorry you had to see it fall out of my shirt," he whispered to her gently before tapping on his breast pocket haphazardly. His face dropped back to that empty expression. "Best you just pretend that never happened so we can be on our way."

Pauline wanted to scream, to run, to do anything. But she knew it was useless. She'd had her chance to get away, in one final moment with Dan. That was her chance to avoid her fate. But then she remembered what would have happened if she stayed. It would not have been fair to the others, like Dorothy, Henry, or Ross. They did not deserve to suffer for her crimes, only now, maybe they could have figured it out somehow. Henry and Dorothy's team was resourceful and had devoted themselves to helping her. *If only I had gone with Dan*, she thought.

Charley reached out his hand and nodded, signaling for them to get on with their agenda. She had come so close. Her mind could not stop bringing Pauline back to that thought. If only she had just gone with Dan, maybe some how it could have worked out. And yet again, as she snapped back into focus, Charley's glare reminded her it was too late to get away.

"I do not think you understood me, so I'll say it again: let's go."

Charley grabbed her hand and yanked her forward. Pauline's legs gave out for a moment, but he would not let up and drug her along as he made his way to the doors of the saloon. People stirred inside, turning to look as the doors swung open. Charley walked ahead and gave an uneasy tug. When she stumbled forward Charley shoved her into the barroom.

People stopped what they were doing and turned to look at her. Pauline looked up and saw the splintered wooden walls. In the corner, the piano player had stopped to see what was going on. Everyone formed a small crowd around them. Bottles clanked in the background as they stared down at her. *This is it,* she thought to herself, *this is how it all ends for me.*

"What's going on with the girl?" the bartender asked, polishing a glass as he stared at her. There was something uneasy in his gaze. To him, Pauline's struggle was just another day on the job.

Charley stepped forward and grabbed the men's attention.

"This right here is a wanted woman," he quipped with a disturbing sense of cheer. The man had taken on an entirely new persona now they were around new people. Charley was using a fake charm at her expense. It reminded Pauline of the friendliness he had conveyed to the caravan. That was how he tricked people into believing he was good.

"I believe one of you has been looking for her, and I found her for you."

Of course, Charley was talking like that, Pauline thought angrily as she took deep breaths. Just get this over with, she wanted to yell at him. This was never part of the deal. Pauline flashed him one nasty glare and saw his smile staring back at her.

"I'll have you know, sir," the bartender began, "you are going to have to go more into detail if you think I will let that fly. Otherwise, this place would be full of people like you."

Pauline saw Charley's face turn. He was angry at having been insulted. None of the other men in the room noticed. Instead, they got riled up, making comments mostly against the bartender's strict adherence to decency. Charley saw that as he scanned the crowd and brought his grin back.

"You wish to know what this woman has done?" he began. Charley was starting to walk slowly around the group with his artificial charm. "Well, I say that's more like it. I would love to fill you all in on what—"

"That's enough," a voice commanded from the other room attached to the main part of the saloon. From the opening, she could now see someone had been sitting at a table reading as the scene in the barroom had ensued. The sun shone through the window behind him. Pauline could not make out his face. The silhouette put the book down and stood up as the men parted. As he stepped forward, Pauline felt her stomach drop.

Allen Hodge stood there in front of her. As he looked down, Pauline felt the blood drain from her face. He stared at her with eyes of fire. This was not the icy expressionless gaze Charley had given. There was feeling in Allen's face. The rage there made Pauline even more afraid than she had ever felt with Charley. Allen looked like the devil himself, full of malice. He looked around at the group with a similar sense of disdain.

"While my men may be content to drink all day and night and get a show out of you and your sales pitch," he shot an unsatisfied glance at Charley and turned away, "I would prefer to wrap things up so I can move on with my evening."

Pauline shuddered. Beneath his calm words she could sense his longing for revenge. She suddenly wished for things to slow down. Let Charley entertain them. Do whatever had to be done to stay alive longer. The rage in Allen's eyes had triggered Pauline's survival instinct.

"Hey, Allen," one of the men said half-drunkenly, "what if it isn't her, though? This guy seems like he might be full of it."

Another one chimed in, "Yeah, you know I think I saw him at the camp she was at. You came back all mad that night and said they were protecting her, remember? Well, that got me thinking now. What if they found someone to replace her and he's trying to pull a fast one?"

"It's her." Allen said, shaking his head in annoyance. "We've spoken. I don't know why he decided to bring her, but I know this woman. She murdered my brother in cold blood."

Allen glared at the two of them. Pauline looked over and saw Charley was uneasy. Her gut instinct suddenly pulled for her attention. *Wait a second,* she thought to herself, *maybe this could be my chance.* She waited for the men to quiet down and took a deep breath. Her whole body shook as she yelled.

"It was him!" she screamed frantically. "*He* is the one who did it!"

She pointed a shaky hand at Charley. Some of the men turned to look at him. She knew it was now or never and continued: "He's got the watch on him right now! Let him show you! He killed my husband and stole that watch."

Some of the men gasped. Others laughed. Charley shook his head in disbelief with his confident grin. It had been a noble effort on her end, but Pauline already knew the men were going to take his word over hers. He reached a hand up to his breast pocket and flashed his eyes back at her in a way that said, *nice try.*

"She's talking about this," Charley pulled the watch from his pocket and held it out so everyone could see. "I found it on her and figured it meant something to someone. Didn't expect her to use it against me though." He let out a chuckle.

Pauline resented the way he could lie so casually in a pinch. She began to hyperventilate. Behind her, Allen made his steps forward. He was closer now than he had ever been before. She could feel his hatred, misguided as it was, resonating toward her. Allen leaned in and looked at the watch, then back at her.

He shook his head and glared at Pauline like a disappointed parent.

"You know, I asked for this back in Windy Reach. Believe it or not, this is a family heirloom. It's been passed down for three generations now. That is, until you cut one of those generations off." His eyes sharpened toward her. Allen's voice was calm and devastating in the same capacity.

"When the Sheriff told me they never recovered it, I figured you must have taken it. Herschel loved that watch. He probably told you that and you figured it was worth some money as you ran off."

Allen studied her reaction after each sentence. Pauline could hardly stand. Things had become so hopeless. Her body had no strength remaining. How could this be? Why did Allen trust Charley all the sudden? It was not Charley, she realized, but his total disdain for her. Herschel's brother had made up his mind a long time ago: Pauline was guilty.

He turned from Pauline and looked at Charley.

"Thank you for bringing her to me. Now I never set a bounty. But I suppose not killing you for protecting this little lawbreaker the first two times is a fair settlement."

"That's it? After bringing her to you…" Charley said through gritted teeth. A rage simmered beneath his exterior. Pauline could see it quickly manifesting. This had been all about the money to him. Never mind getting away with murder. Charley was only turning her in so he could collect the money he thought was due.

"Get out of here before he changes his mind," one of the men said.

The others began to chime in.

"Some of us wouldn't have a problem roughing you up anyway," another one said.

The men began to move in on Charley. They had been drinking and were looking for entertainment. Pauline silently hoped he would stick around and fight. The odds would not have been in his favor. At least she would get to see the person who ruined her life get what he deserved. She stood there watching as the men gave Charley the chance to reciprocate.

Instead, Charley cursed them all and left the saloon. The men yelled curses back at him and laughed as he unhitched his horse and rode off. He was riding back to camp, Pauline thought. She wondered what he would say to them when they asked, knowing it would be another lie. What would Dorothy say? She could not help but wonder, even though it made her sad to think about.

The men stopped hollering and resumed their respective areas of the saloon. The piano player picked up from where he had stopped before as the men pretended like nothing had ever happened. Pauline looked around and startled when a hand grasped her arm tightly and pulled her in.

"You're coming with me," Allen growled in a low voice. "We're going to make sure you don't run off again."

Allen pulled her to the other room. There was a set of French doors she had not noticed before. He swung the doors and threw Pauline inside. She stumbled in as he pulled the door shut. It was a smaller bedroom along the back end of the building. Pauline saw a tattered twin bed nestled in one corner. The setting sun shone in through the windows. She looked around for another door. Then she heard the clicking noise behind her.

Pauline ran to the door handles. She tried to twist, but they had been locked from the outside. Allen was keeping her captive. Even if someone came looking, they would never find her. She began to panic. Her palms grew sweaty. Pauline felt her heart pound. Her mind raced, telling her to do something, anything, that could buy her some time. She was not ready to come face to face with death. Not yet.

"Help!" she yelled as she struggled with the door handles. "Someone help me!"

Footsteps approached from the other side.

"Listen to me," Allen's voice said from behind the doors, "it's getting late, so we are going to post up for the night. We will be heading back to Windy Reach first thing in the morning so you can get your trial."

Pauline let out a scream as she pounded on the door. She did not want to be on the road with them for several days. She would rather be killed in that room. Allen would have several days to torture her. It was a fate worse than death. *Why is he doing this?* She had to try and convince him. It was her only hope, she began to tell herself.

"He's lying!" she yelled frantically. "I'm innocent! He killed your brother! Not me!"

The footsteps walked away. She heard him sit down at the chair he had been at before. Allen was not going to be convinced of her innocence. In a sense of defeat, Pauline turned to look at the room. The men in the main area had grown louder. If there were a way out, she had their noise as coverage. At the same time, however, she knew Allen was likely sitting there on the other side of the doors, reading among the chaos.

She screamed some more, pounding on the door. Eventually, she thought. Eventually he would listen. Suddenly the doors swung open. Pauline fell forward. Allen took her back into the room and threw her onto the mattress. She felt a rush of fear, uncertain of what he would do.

"I don't want to hear another sound from this room," he told her.

"Just..." She began to sob. "Just kill me already."

Allen shook his head. "Oh no. You're getting a trial back in Windy Reach. Unlike you, my family prefers to do things by the book."

Allen turned and stepped out of the room. He closed the doors, and she heard the click of the lock once again. *I have to get out of there*, Pauline thought. The look in Allen's eyes reminded her too much of Herschel. Now that she was facing him, Pauline realized the grave mistake she had made.

Pauline made her way to the windows. She tried to push up on one of them. Her fingers struggled against the panes of glass. It would not budge. She moved to the other. Nothing happened. Both windows, it appeared, had been sealed. She could break the glass, but Allen would surely hear and run inside to catch her. Pauline remembered his eyes. No, she thought to herself, his retribution was not worth the narrow chance of escaping.

She gave up and moved to the wooden bed frame. The mattress creaked beneath her body as she sat down. This was it. The men in the saloon sounded as if they were celebrating Pauline's defeat. That was why Allen had trapped her for the night. He wanted Pauline to suffer as she listened to his men celebrate her death sentence.

Pauline shuddered. She could not even cry. Her entire marriage, from beginning to end, had been a cruel injustice. The man she married for love had turned out to be a monster. And once he died, society believed she was the monster instead. It did not take long for them to accuse her. The fact Herschel beat her without mercy only added fuel to the fire. Nobody but her father believed she was innocent; that was, until she joined the caravan.

They had shown her kindness when nobody else would. Dan, Dorothy, Henry, and Ross had given her a sense of belonging. It was unfair she had to leave them, though Pauline supposed it was concurrent with life. Being a young woman was to suffer. Because all that time, under her nose, the real killer had been in their midst. Charley was a snake in the grass, waiting, curled and ready to strike on unsuspecting prey. Pauline laid herself back onto the bed as the room begin to spin. *If only I had gone with Dan,* Pauline told herself. *He would have saved me somehow.*

Chapter Thirty-Two

Dan stared into the campfire. He took in every detail. The heat radiating against his face. The different shades of orange and red overtaking everything it touched. Even more specifically, he noticed the crackling of the branches. Each one withstood the fire for as long as it could. Eventually, however, even the strongest of them would succumb to the extreme heat and pressure.

He thought about that in grave detail. Without realizing it, Dan became so lost in his mind, it was as if he himself burned in the fire. Sitting inside patiently, he was doing his best to hang on. The other members of the caravan, the ones who stayed, still needed him. But it also felt as if he were burning alive on the inside, and he would not be able to hold on forever.

A shared feeling of loss surrounding him. Dorothy and Henry sat to his left. Henry had been comforting his wife, who was doing her best not to burst into tears as she knitted something half-heartedly. On his right, Ross sat on the ground and hummed a soft melody. Nobody dared speak to Dan. It had been that way since he had arrived back at camp.

The entire group had gathered when Dan first reappeared on the horizon. Dan saw them gather excitedly from a distance. Knowing they would be let down only made him hurt more. He got closer and watched them dissipate, shaking their heads in sadness, when they realized Pauline was not with him. Dan wanted to explain what happened, but in that moment all he could focus on was his broken heart. Instead, he got off Ross' horse and said nothing.

After that, everyone had given Dan space. The caravan went through their daily routines without discussing what had happened. Henry and Dorothy made the call to stay put for another night. Nobody put up a fuss. Even the ones who wanted to get a move on knew not to challenge them. Dan knew Dorothy was still not yet ready to accept the fact Pauline was gone.

Dan had no choice but to accept it. He stared into the fire and reflected on their last conversation. He had emptied himself out for her, bearing the part of his soul he expected to keep hidden. Maybe he waited too long. If he had opened to Pauline sooner, maybe she never would have left the camp. He thought about the way she looked at him when he confessed his love. She looked at him with disappointment in her eyes. There was no love in them. His feelings were not shared.

Then he remembered how he let her go after that. Dan had been so hurt by her rejection that he had only thought of himself. *What of her safety?* He questioned this to himself. *You forgot about all that just because she made you feel bad. That's why you don't deserve to be with anyone. People get hurt because of you.* To him, it was the truth. Even though she said she did not love him, she was still in danger with Charley. Whatever happened to her in Dodge City was Dan's fault.

And maybe that was okay after all. Dan had had his chance at true love. He failed to keep it the first time, heaven forbid he fail a second time. It was better to be alone. He did not deserve love, nor did he deserve to be loved. Instead, he could stay on the road and never talk to another woman again. But then he thought about Pauline again. He could not help but ask himself: *what if he had not let her go?*

He should have said it did not matter and it was a matter of protection. She deserved that. She just did not know it. Pauline had lost all hope. How could he have expected her to love someone? With her gone for good, he became reminded of how that felt. It was empty. Feelings such as comfort and joy were unattainable. A voice in his ear whispered: *But what if you did all of that and she still did not want to go?* The idea made Dan shudder. He wondered if he would be doomed to ask himself these questions for the rest of his life.

Such was life now, Dan told himself. He would be forced to always ask himself, *what if?* The possibilities would forever haunt him. This was his punishment for not protecting others. He did not feel good or bad about it. There was nothing left for him to feel. Even his stomach had forgotten to be hungry that day. All he could do was sit by the fire and stare, wondering what would happen next, or if it really mattered.

A few horses passed by on the road. None of them stopped that he noticed. Earlier in the day, Dan had wondered if Charley would come back. People were upset with him, even if he was "looking out for the group." Dan had his doubts regarding Charley, although he had been too focused on Pauline to bring it up. When the sun went down, Dan figured the old man was gone. *Good,* he thought to himself. Dan did not need anything to remind him of Pauline. It allowed him to continue focusing on the campfire's warmth.

But the familiar voice nearby made Dan finally snap out of his trance. Charley had returned to camp without making much of a fuss. It was smart. He had waited until nightfall when people were going to sleep. Dan got up and looked in the direction he'd heard the voice. His feeling of emptiness was immediately displaced by the rage of seeing Charley. In the flickering firelight, he caught a glimpse of Dan's face and stopped talking to the other silhouette.

"Hold on," Charley said to the other, "We can talk later, okay?"

Dan marched toward him. His blood had turned to boiling water. This man had no business doing what he did. Charley had known about him and Pauline's developing relationship. Everyone in the caravan did. From one man to another, interfering like he did was completely uncalled for. Dan had a lot to say. Each statement raced through his brain so quickly Dan began to worry he would not be able remember everything he needed to express.

When the distance between them faded, Dan could see Charley was scared. He clutched onto his shirt with both hands balled into fists and pulled him into his face.

"What were you thinking, sending an innocent woman to her death like that? You're the the murderer, not her," he growled.

"Whoa, whoa now," Charley pleaded between gasps, "Dan, don't do this."

Dan squeezed his shirt even tighter. "I'll do what I want. You know you crossed a line today."

Charley continued to breathe faster, clearly scared. "I did what the lady wanted. I didn't make her do anything."

Dan shook his head in disbelief. He let go of Charley's shirt and pushed him backward. He stumbled over a tree stump and nearly fell over. Charley let out a cry and then looked back at Dan. He was trembling now and could not hide the worry on his face. Dan spit at the ground near his feet.

"Of course, only a coward like you wouldn't own up. Why on earth did you ever think it was okay to come back here, anyway?"

"I am only here to get my things." Charley still spoke soft and innocent. "Then I will never be around you guys again. I know you don't trust me anymore, but that's a promise."

Dan sized him up again. It would not be hard to beat him in a fight. What would that accomplish though? Pauline still would not be coming back. The man was already scared to death. He let out a grunt and shook his head. Charley was pathetic. Whatever reasoning he had, the man was never going to admit it. Every second Dan spent with Charley was an utter waste of time, and that included getting revenge.

"Get your things and learn to disappear."

Dan turned and walked away. He heard Charley muttering to himself. None of it mattered. Charley had a point anyway. Pauline wanted to leave. He just decided to help her. But what did he get out of it? How did he benefit? *Never mind that*, Dan thought to himself. No revelation would fulfill his needs.

When he started on his way back to the fire, Ross came out of the shadows and pulled him aside.

"I know you're mad," he began in a half-whisper, "but all of us were hoping you were going to pound him into the dirt."

Dan let out a soft sigh. "It wouldn't do a thing though, would it?"

"Sure, it would!" Ross gave a friendly nudge and smiled.

Dan said nothing. Looking up, Ross saw his face and his turned somber.

"I was just..." he paused. "Look, I know it isn't easy for you right now. Just... Tell me if you need anything, okay? We could hogtie him until the morning just for coming back. You think that might be fun?"

"No, no," Dan shook his head, "I appreciate it, but I don't need cheering up, Ross. Sometimes a man just needs to be sad. And I think that's what I'm going to be for a while."

Ross nodded his head. "I get that. You guys may not see it, but I get sad, too."

They stood there in silence for a moment. Dan looked and saw Ross thinking about something. His face contorted. Something unpleasant was on Ross' mind. Dan decided to distract him.

"I've got to say, though—why the hell did he come back?"

He gave a fake laugh in hope Ross would join in. That never happened. Instead, Ross continued staring off into the darkness. Dan was about to ask if he was okay when Ross finally spoke up.

"It was probably for that pocket watch," he answered.

Dan tilted his head in confusion. "What watch?"

"You know that nice one he kept showing off? It had the initials H.H. engraved on it. I don't know how you forgot. He wouldn't shut up about it on the first night."

All of the details suddenly connected. Dan felt a jolt of energy as he left Ross behind and made another run for Charley. This time, he was on the other side of camp gathering his belongings. He didn't notice Dan until the last second, when he gasped, dropping his things and made a run toward his horse.

"I don't think so!" Dan yelled as he sped up. He leapt into the air and took the man down with a tackle. Charley struggled as Dan pinned him to the ground.

"You said you would let me go!" Charley yelled, his voice full of fear. "You lied to me, boy! Let me out of here right now!"

"And *you* said you were just helping a lady do what she wanted! You didn't mention that *you* were the one who killed her husband when you helped her turn herself in!"

Charley let out a gasp as he realized Dan knew the truth. Beneath his calm exterior, Dan could see a flash of fear. Just looking at him made Dan angrier. Charley was the last person he would've expected to be a cold-blooded killer.

"Tell me. What was the point of getting Pauline to turn herself in?"

"She wanted to save the caravan," Charley answered. "She told you herself, remember?"

Those words made Dan even angrier. He shook Charley violently for a moment, cursing his name and saying unspeakable things he would do in return.

"Wait!" Charley cried out. "Just stop! I'll talk."

Dan froze in place, with eyes that told him to get on with it.

"I..." he hesitated. "I..."

Dan knew it for certain now: Charley was a coward. Out of the corner of his eye, Dan noticed something gleam beneath the starlight. It was a small, round piece of gold. He reached and grabbed it, holding it up to his eyes and reading it closely as Charley hyperventilated beneath him.

"H.H." he said aloud to Charley. "Why don't you tell me what you think that stands for?"

Charley began to weep. He sputtered nonsense as Dan shook his head in disgust.

"I can't understand you, old man," he growled. "Answer me straight."

"I don't know what you're talking about!" he screamed.

Dan used his other hand to punch him in the face as hard as he could. Charley shrieked as blood trickled down the side of his cheek. He thought to do it again, but realized it was better to hear it from the source. Besides, sticking around beating him would not bring back Pauline. Dan had to go and do that himself.

"Where'd you find this pocket watch, old man?" Dan asked as he glanced back and forth from Charley to the tiny gold medallion. "Wait, let me guess: you found it back in Windy Reach, didn't you?"

Charley's stuttering grew worse. Dan saw the look in his eyes. It reminded him of an animal caught in a trap. He knew he was cornered. Would he strike? Or would he tell the truth? Dan needed to hurry things up so he could go save Pauline. People in the camp began to take note of the struggle, moving out of their tents into the firelight behind them.

"I'm waiting," Dan said with an artificial calm. "You don't leave until you talk."

"O-okay!" Charley yelled with tears in his eyes. "I confess! I killed Herschel Hogan. Before I found you guys, I-I was in a bit of a bind. Money problems. Y-you know how it is, don't you? He owed me!" He paused and took a several deep breaths.

"You mean he gambled at your seedy little spot and lost a bunch of money?" Dan said with a darkness in his tone. "Don't act like you don't know what I'm talking about."

Charley stuttered some more. Dan stared into his eyes and saw pure fear. He went silent as Dan stared, unable to get the words out. Dan shook his head at the old man. Anyone who was innocent would have been shouting it.

"Go on," Dan growled. "I'm waiting."

"He told me how much the watch was worth and I," he paused as he sobbed, "I thought if I followed him home and took it, it would cover his debt. But h-h-h-h... he put up a fight. I wasn't expecting that. I freaked out and shot him, okay? I told you so let me go!"

Rage coursed through Dan's bloodstream. Charley could see the hate in his eyes and whimpered. It told Dan everything he needed to know. Charley's facial reactions spoke for him. Dan decided to press him further and see what else he could divulge.

"So, you decided to let an innocent woman take the fall? Real heroic of you."

"I didn't know he had a wife! Well, I did. But he was bragging about how he treated her, and I thought I'd be doing her a favor. I didn't think his brother would get involved. Swear!"

Dan wanted to get revenge. He did not care if it did nothing to get Pauline back. He wanted to pound the old coward into the dirt. It would not have been hard. The man was a puddle of tears beneath him. He almost felt sorry for Charley, until he remembered that he was willing to let a sweet young lady be hanged for his crimes.

"I ought to kill you right now," Dan growled.

"Dan! Wait!" a voice yelled from behind. Footsteps made their way up. Before he knew it, two pairs of hands had gotten ahold of Dan and lifted him off the man exposed as a killer. Looking at him now, no one would have suspected him to be anything other than a pathetic old fool. The entire time, Dan kept his eyes on Charley, giving him a look that said, *you got lucky.*

"Thank you, boys! Just in time!" Charley cried, as if he had been rescued from a burning stable. He stood up and pointed a shaky finger at Dan. "You all need to do something about him. He's gone mad!"

"We aren't doing anything to Dan," Henry declared. He turned his head to Dan and gave him a nod. "See if you can get to Dodge City. We'll sit here with Charley and talk it out, won't we?" Henry turned and looked at the old man, who stood there shaking.

Dan moved in a hurry over to Jesse and unhitched him. The horse had been half-asleep and was startled at the sudden movement.

"All right buddy," Dan said in a friendly tone, "one last adventure for the day. When we get to the city, I'll give you all the snacks they've got for sale."

The horse made a snorting noise. Dan mounted himself. In the distance, he heard Ross and Henry yelling.

"Dan!" Ross yelled. "Dan! He's making a run for it!"

Dan looked out and saw Charley had hopped on his horse and was heading back toward Dodge City. He was going to try and beat them there to double down on his lies. Dan clutched the rope he kept on the saddle. It was tied into a lasso already, waiting to be used.

"The hell he is!" Dan yelled. "Jesse! Let's go!"

The horse made a noise and began to gallop. Jesse could hear the clattering of Charley's horse and followed the noise. Dan thought about Pauline, and how much trouble she was in. He did not care if she loved him. He was not going to let an innocent woman be hanged for a crime she did not commit. The wind whipped his face as he continued to speed up.

The head start had given Charley a considerable amount of distance. Dan could still see them going toward the mountain pass in the moonlight. If he caught up in time, Charley would be easy to spot. His horse was going fast though, and Dan did not want to make the same mistake and wear Jesse out too soon.

Charley could hear Dan and Jesse gaining from behind him. He let out a nervous yell for the horse to speed up. Dan continued his steady escalation of speed with Jesse. The gap between them closed inch by inch. Darkness was growing around them. As they made their way in on Charley, Dan lifted his rope. Jesse was going fast, and he risked falling off, letting go with one hand, but it was his best chance at catching the coward.

Charley cursed his horse to keep going faster. It had started to slow down, but soon they would reach the mountains and become shrouded in darkness. Dan knew he did not have much time to throw his lasso once the gap between them had closed. He would not let him get away again, though. The fool had made the mistake of coming back.

Charley continued yelling to his horse, refusing to look back. "Let's go! Come on!" he yelled angrily.

Dan could hear the shakiness in his voice. He gave the rope some slack. Just enough to cover the distance between them. Jesse sped up as the pair grew closer.

"Come on boy! Git!" Charley shouted with a growing hoarseness.

Dan felt the gap begin to grow again. He threw the rope and pulled back, unable to fully see whether it had gotten around the old man. Then he felt the swing of the old man's weight coming off the other horse. Charley let out a scream of pain. He had hit the ground hard. His horse continued to run. Charley had put too much fear into the poor creature. *Now it's free*, Dan thought.

Charley cursed as he struggled on the ground. Dan hopped off Jesse and made his approach, tightening the rope with both hands as he stepped closer.

"What the heck do you think you're doing, boy?" he said to Dan between gritted teeth. Charley rolled from side to side as Dan wrapped the remainder of the rope around his body. "You know they killed her already? She's dead! Get over it."

Dan let out a hearty laugh. "Sure thing, Charley. But you and I are going to go there first to make sure of it."

"Well, that don't even matter now, do it? She doesn't love you, boy. She said so herself."

"I don't care if she hates my guts," Dan said to him plainly. "She doesn't deserve to die on account of your cowardice, does she?"

Charley let out a cry of defeat. Dan had successfully tied the rope so he could no longer move. He pulled him onto his feet and called Jesse over. The footsteps clattered to them as Dan stood up, hitching Charley to the mount of his horse.

Dan hopped up onto the saddle.

"What's your plan now anyway?" Charley looked up and asked.

"Walk," Dan said with a commanding voice.

Charley stumbled forward. "Wh-Where are we going?"

"We're taking a trip to Dodge City."

Dan pulled the rope as Jesse trotted ahead. Charley had two options: walk or be dragged. He started to make an appeal for forgiveness until he looked and saw Dan's glare. Letting out a deep sigh, Charley walked alongside Dan and Jesse beneath a sea of stars. Neither of them said a word to each other for the remainder of the trail.

In the silence, Dan thought about Pauline. He pondered whether Charley had lied just a few moments earlier. Was he too late? Or could Pauline still be saved? There was only one way for them to find out.

Chapter Thirty-Three

Pauline sat up on the broken bed. If these were truly her last hours, she did not want to spend them sulking. She decided to move to the window and watch what remained of the sunset in the western sky. Despite her situation, she was able to appreciate the textured clouds beneath the pink and purple canvas, slowly growing darker with each passing moment. The men in the saloon were starting to quiet down as well.

"Busy day tomorrow," one of them said.

Some of them agreed, others protested.

"Allen's going to want to get an early start back to Windy."

The men groaned and reluctantly made their way to the rooms they had purchased. Pauline shuddered at the way they spoke. Her death meant a 'busy day' and nothing more.

She knew she would not sleep. It would be better to sit and watch the horizon, waiting for the sun to rise where she could not see. Perhaps it would be beautiful, just as the sunset in her window had been. The light was fading now. It would return in a few short hours. For now, she allowed the darkness to swell around her. The moonlight grew more apparent. For her art, nightfall was always when she felt the most inspired. The absence of light functioned as a blank canvas for her thoughts and feelings. Only now, it felt more like a burden than anything else.

She let out a deep sigh. Regret underscored every passing thought. Pauline had given up on her last chance at life. Not just life, but also love. She remembered the way Dan looked at her when she said she did not love him. She knew it was a lie. Unfortunately, Dan had believed her.

But I had to do it, she thought to herself. Dan was not going to let her go, and it would have gotten the entire caravan killed. Little did any of them know, the real murderer had been under their nose the entire time. Nobody would believe her, though. She'd tried to tell Allen and his men, but they would not listen. All of them fell for Charley's cover-up.

The neighboring buildings turned on their lanterns for the night. In the window next door, Pauline could see a reflection in the window of the dirt road they had come in on. It looked empty. Nobody was going to come for her. Not after what she had said to Dan. If only she could see him again, she thought. She would tell him the truth about how she felt. A voice in the back of her head mocked her. *Why would he ever come back? You had your chance, and you blew it.*

Pauline let out another sigh. There were too many emotions going through her now. Her stomach was empty, but too knotted for her to eat anything even if she could. The reality of her situation had set in. She made the choice and had to pay the price. Nobody would be coming in on that road. At the same time, however, she could not help but stare out the window at it. There was something about that last shred of hope keeping her gaze captivated.

In the distance, she could see two tall figures. She cursed herself, thinking it was her mind playing games with her heart. One stood shorter than the other and staggered as they both grew more visible. As their reflection grew, Pauline could see it was a man on a horse. Her heart began to race. She told herself it was not what she thought.

Moments later, Pauline noticed the man on the horse had a rope attached to the one stumbling. *It's not him*, she thought. It was probably some bounty hunter coming to collect a reward. Someone who had no idea she was being held hostage. *Don't be ridiculous*, that voice said to her, *no one is coming for you.*

Then Pauline heard his voice. *It's not him,* the voice hissed. She stopped listening to it. She would have known that voice from a mile away. Dan and Jesse had come back. And he had a rope tied around Charley.

"Where'd you say they were?" she heard him ask in his gruff voice.

Pauline could see them standing in front of the saloon now. Her heart leapt with joy. For a second, she thought maybe she had fallen asleep, and it was all a dream. But it felt so real. She knew it was him. The voice in her head disappeared. Instead, all she could feel was love when she saw him get off his horse.

"I bet I can find out *real* quick in here."

Dan was going into the saloon. He had left Charley bound and gagged to Jesse. She heard him yell at the piano player to stop.

"Okay, friends," he said from the other side of the wall, "I need help looking for someone. She's young and pretty, I mean really pretty, and I think—"

The French doors swung open. Allen glared at her and put a finger to his lips. He stared at Pauline with a burning rage. Without saying a word, he grabbed Pauline by the wrist and took her into the hallway. She saw the back of Dan's head as he spoke to the men. It gave her a sense of urgency. Allen was dragging her to the back door and had it cracked open. She needed to do something quick.

"Dan!" she screamed out. "Dan! Help me!"

Allen pulled her outside and slammed the door. Pauline began to sob, continuing to scream out for Dan. He had come so close. She knew it was meant to be. Allen moved through the darkness as he pulled her along.

269

"I told you already," he growled, "you ain't getting away this time."

Pauline shrieked. "Let me go!"

It was no use. Allen tightened his grasp and drug her along the road toward his horse. "Say one more word and I'll kill you right here."

Pauline tried to break free, but Allen was too strong. He was determined, had pinned her as the killer, and nothing could change his mind. They were almost to the horse when a familiar pair of hooves came around to the side of the building.

"Now where do you think you're going this late at night?"

Pauline's heart fluttered. Allen froze in his place and made a slow turn back. He looked at Pauline with that rage in his glare, then to Dan.

"I don't know who it is you think you're looking for," he said with his soft anger, "but I promise you it ain't this husband-murderer!" He yelled the last two words as he pulled on Pauline's wrist. She let out a cry of distress. Jesse made a noise in response. Even he was upset.

Dan let out a hearty chuckle. It was his confidence. She loved the familiarity.

"I think I got someone you need to talk to again about that." Dan nodded to the front of the saloon. "Come with me and we can all talk this out... together."

Allen gave him a sour look. "Why the heck should I listen to you anyway?" he said with disdain. "As far as I know, you could just be the next man to fall under this woman's spell."

Dan hopped down from his horse. The entire time, he kept his eyes on Pauline. She felt weak at the knees seeing him again, hoping he had forgiven her for all the trouble she had caused him. The way he looked at her now, it seemed none of it mattered to him.

"Well, that there isn't entirely wrong," Dan winked to her and continued, "I don't want to waste your time, or mine. That's why we need to talk to Charley over there. I think it'll clear the air up."

Allen froze for a moment, thinking it over. His face dropped back into a frown as he shook his head in disgust. Pauline trembled underneath his grip. If Dan could feel how tight he was squeezing, she thought, then even he would realize the situation was hopeless.

"I don't think so," he said, pulling Pauline closer to him, "we're going back *now*."

This is it, she thought. They had come close, but Allen was a man with his mind made up. They got closer to his horse. People around ignored them as she called out for help. Dan continued walking behind, doing his best to get Allen's attention.

"You know what I think?" Dan began as Allen ignored him. "I think you're afraid of being wrong. You'd rather go about your life thinking you caught the killer instead of second-guessing what could have been."

Pauline stood there watching him. It seemed Allen was listening but did not want either of them to notice. Dan continued talking. *Keep going*, she thought, *keep going and you might get him to listen.*

"I know what that's like, trust me. When you lose someone," Dan paused, "you always wonder what if. And it eats you up inside. That's why I came out here. I couldn't let myself live with what I had learned. And I want you to hear it from the man himself."

Allen let out a sigh. His hand eased itself on Pauline's wrist. Cold air brushed upon where he'd clamped down. What was happening? What was he going to do? Allen pulled her with him as he walked up to Dan. There was something he was going to say. She had no idea what to expect. Allen stared at him long, trying to see if Dan was worth his time.

"I'll tell you what," he began, "if she gets away, or if you try to fleece me over with some tall tale, know this: I will find out. And I will come back to your caravan with my men and have every one of your people hanged." He spoke in a voice so sharp it made Pauline shudder.

She was not sure about Allen's offer. What if he was not convinced of the truth? She looked at Dan, who stood tall and proud before them. No matter the result, Pauline knew her truth then and there—Dan was the love of her life.

He led them around the corner to Charley, who had been standing there with the rope in his mouth the entire time, moaning for somebody to help. Pauline saw the glare of concern in Charley's face. That should have been all the evidence Allen needed.

Dan walked up and nodded to him as the old man cowered in fear. Pauline could not help but notice his trembling. *Good*, she thought. Allen would see the real Charley now. Not the fictitious salesman he had tried to be earlier in the day.

"I'm going to let Charley speak for himself. And trust me, he's very sorry about everything. He told me so much that I had to put this around his mouth."

Pauline felt herself becoming cautiously optimistic. The rope fell out of Charley's mouth, and he took in a gulp of air. Allen stood there looking at all of them with contempt. It was all a show to him. He had little patience for anyone.

"Charley," Dan nudged him, "we're all waiting. Tell them about what happened back in Windy Reach."

"I-I..." Charley paused. "It's... You see..."

Allen rolled his eyes, growing impatient. Pauline began to worry as he looked back at her. She could see in his glare that he still considered her the killer. Allen turned back to Dan, giving him a look of disdain.

"You think this is going to convince me of anything?" He gestured to Charley. "Look at this pitiful old fool. I'm supposed to believe he killed my brother? He's just another low-down businessman."

Allen began to walk away. Pauline looked at Dan worriedly. Confident as ever, Dan let out a laugh. One that lasted so long, Allen had no choice but to turn around again and face Dan. *Just like Herschel*, she thought to herself, *every action driven by his ego.*

"Is there a reason why that's so funny to you?" Allen asked angrily.

Dan stopped and cleared his throat, giving a polite gesture that said, *excuse me.*

"Well, it's just that 'businessman' is a bit of a stretch. Charley over here, he ran a gambling business back in Windy Reach. Your brother knew him well, didn't he, Charley?"

Dan shook his head as Charley continued to stutter. Pauline felt like a fly on the wall. But Dan's words flipped a switch in Allen. He was now listening. His grimace had flattened, shifting to a look of intrigue. At the same time, however, she knew not to run. Otherwise, it could get everyone she cared about in trouble. Dan stepped forward. She felt his presence and shook with nervous excitement.

"Is that true?" Allen asked, tilting his head with intrigue. "You should have told me that sooner."

He walked over and crouched down to get a closer look at Charley. "I'm talking to you," he growled, "is this man over here telling the truth?"

Charley nodded pathetically as he stared at the mud surrounding Jesse's hooves. People from the saloon had gathered in the window to watch the conversation. Pauline saw their faces as they pointed with curiosity and amazement.

"Hey, that's the guy from earlier."

"Why's he tied up?"

"All of you shut up! They're talking!"

Dan put a hand on Charley's shoulder. "Now what he told me, after I beat it out of him, was that he had some money problems with your late brother, may his soul be at peace."

Allen gave a look of annoyance. His lip quivered for a moment as he pondered, eventually letting out a deep sigh. Pauline had seen the flares of temper within Herschel and his brother. Both, she presumed, were ticking timebombs. *If Dan came all this way just to get himself killed...* she worried to herself. *Please don't let this be how it ends.*

But Allen's demeanor shifted some more. He was no longer angry, or annoyed. Pauline saw in his eyes now, a sense of sadness. That was when she saw him in a different light for the first time. Beneath his anger, the man was still grieving.

"Though I do not like hearing about it," he tilted his head down, "I know my brother had his struggles." He paused for a moment and let out a sigh. "Although it upsets me to hear these things you speak of, I understand it is, most likely, rooted in truth."

Dan gave a look of empathy and nodded in understanding. Pauline was practically swooning with a sense of relief as he stepped forward and put a hand on Allen's shoulder.

"Be that as it may," Dan began, "it does not excuse Charley for what he decided to do about it. Why don't you tell them yourself what you did to get back at him?"

Charley hesitated and fell to his knees.

"I-I..." Charley stuttered.

"Go on now," Dan nodded, sounding less patient.

"I..." Charley stuttered some more.

"Come on and say it already!" Dan shouted. Charley whimpered in fear.

"That's enough," Allen said angrily. He held out a hand for them to stop and made his way forward. "I came here for justice to be served, not to witness a theatre performance."

Pauline heard the men inside moan in disappointment. All of them had been watching things unfold. It made her sick to think this was how they would have acted at her trial.

"But I do have one question for you both: how is it this man ended up traveling alongside the accused? It seems rather suspicious to me for him to appear by chance."

Allen looked at them with suspicious eyes and Pauline's stomach dropped in fear. On one hand, Allen was not denying what he had been told. On the other hand, he had questions, which meant doubt. She glanced over at Dan, who was nodding. He looked at her and grinned, filling her body with warmth.

"That's what I wondered myself," Dan said with certainty. "We found him on our way out of town with Pauline. No hard feelings, but her dad maintained her innocence, and a job's a job."

Allen glared at Dan now. He did not like being reminded of that detail, though he clearly understood. That was how the world worked. And it wasn't like the men inside were any better. They would have all done the same. People had to go where the money was. Dan redirected his gaze to Charley, who kneeled there in terror. Dan spit at the ground next to him.

"He left town not long before us. Unfortunately for him, his horse went lame, and we picked him up along the way. I think he recognized Pauline, decided to hang around, and then when you came along, he thought he could collect the bounty and come out on top."

"I see." Allen nodded.

Pauline waited for Allen to say something more. His eyes hardened, only now they were looking at Charley. She suddenly felt a surge of empathy for her ex-brother-in-law. He had come to the city in hopes of finding justice. Now here he was, unsure of what to believe. Though she felt relief he had eased off on her, she knew it was not over yet. Allen had a choice to make.

He stood there silently, staring at Charley some more. His eyes softened after a while and he looked up, shaking his head in disbelief.

"I don't want to believe it, that is the honest truth." He looked at Dan. "You hit the nail on the head when you said I wanted it to be Pauline. Truth be told, I wanted this nightmare to be over as soon as it could."

Allen paused and took a deep breath. He moved over, closer to Jesse, and put a hand on the horse's saddle. Jesse let out an empathetic neigh upon making contact.

"You see, when I went to Windy Reach, I made the grave mistake of going through Herschel's accounting books. There were large sums of money that seemed to have disappeared. In my grief, I took it out on you." He looked at Pauline apologetically, making her unsure how to respond.

"But in the back of my mind," he continued, "I knew if you had taken that much money, I certainly would not have found you so easily. I just... I wanted to believe Herschel had overcome his vices before he left this earth."

Dan put a hand on Allen's shoulder. Pauline saw now Allen had suffered a similar loss in Herschel. The conditions were different, though grief always reared its ugly head no matter the circumstance.

"Let me see the watch," Allen said as he stuck his hand out.

Dan reached in Charley's shirt pocket and pulled it out. Allen looked at it and began to shake. A sadness in his eyes had replaced the anger there before.

"You tried to use this against her," Allen said to Charley, "I knew there was something off about you when you rolled in here earlier. Lucky for you, I was ready to be done with this. But I don't have any respect for a man who uses grief against someone else."

Pauline saw the rage returning to Allen, only this time it was redirected. He stopped for a moment and looked up at Dan and Pauline. The hatred was gone from his face. She could see he was not the same man as Herschel. He was a grieving brother, who only wanted justice to be served. They had both misjudged one another in a catastrophic way.

"Ma'am," he nodded at her, "I'm very sorry for everything. You two can be on your way. I'm going to take him back to Windy Reach and try him. If other people can back up your claims, or they vouch for you as honest individuals, you won't ever hear from me again."

Allen undid the rope on the saddle and pulled Charley inside. The men in the barroom began to cheer. The doors swung shut. Pauline stared for a moment before turning back to Dan. Why was he here? What made him come back after everything she had said? She needed answers.

"You came back for me," she said to him in a wondrous half-whisper. "Why?"

"I had to," Dan said to her with a serious look on his face.

She kept staring at him, unsure what to say. Her body began to tremble. A whirlwind of emotions brewed inside of her.

"You're a good person, Pauline. And good people are worth saving."

Chapter Thirty-Four

Pauline looked at Dan and collapsed inside as she threw herself into his arms, burying her face in his chest. She breathed in, experiencing an unprecedented amount of relief as she curled up within his embrace. After everything she had said to him, Dan had still come back for her.

"I'm..." she began in a muffled voice, "I'm so sorry, Dan."

Dan said nothing as he held her tightly, rocking from side to side.

"I didn't mean—"

"It's okay if you did," he interrupted, "I still shouldn't have let you go."

Pauline heard the sadness in his voice. She had to make things right between them before anything else happened. She pushed herself out of his hug and looked him in the eyes. A single tear came down as she looked up and smiled at him.

"Dan," she began, "I didn't mean any of what I said."

His eyes lit up in response. "So, you do...?"

She felt his body tremble. Dan was nervous.

"Of course, I do," she said as if it were plainly obvious and smiled up at him. "I've known it since we first met. I love you, Dan."

"I love you too, Pauline."

They stared into each other's eyes. For Pauline, it was as if the world had stopped turning. The glow in Dan's eyes made her even more certain. Then, for a moment, she could not help but let out a laugh. She leaned forward with an uncontrollable giggle that echoed off the walls into the darkness.

"What?" Dan asked playfully with a hint of concern. "You change your mind or something?"

"No!" Pauline giggled, still in his arms. "It's just..."

Pauline hesitated. She was trying not to let the tears of joy take over and confuse him even more. The relief was overwhelming.

"I just didn't think... I guess I'm realizing... I thought this was it."

She tried her best not to break down. Dan held Pauline up to his chest and took deep breaths as he caressed her back.

"Come on now," he said with a warm cadence, "I don't think there was any way I could have let that happen."

"But why?" she asked, staring at the dirt road he rode in on with Charley. "Why did you still come back for me? What I said was so cruel. Your eyes..."

Dan separated himself so he could say it to her face. It was as if he was staring into her soul. She waited as he took a deep breath.

"I knew you were innocent. You're not a killer, Pauline. You left because you wanted to make sure the rest of us were safe. Criminals don't think like that."

She let out a sigh. Dan was right. Charley had proven criminals had no morals. He was willing to let Pauline die for something he had done. She could not do that, never in a million years. And Dan did not care whether she loved him or not. He believed in her all along, just as he'd said. It had been so long since she felt like somebody trusted her, that *she* had someone to trust. Having been on the run, even she'd begun to see herself as a criminal.

Pauline looked up at Dan. She loved the way he leaned against the pole as he asked: "What do you say we get going?"

She hesitated, leaning against the rail next to him as she shook her head. "I don't know, it's awfully late."

She tilted her head and looked in the window of the saloon. The men were kicking Charley from one side of the bar to the other, laughing with drinks in hand as he cursed them all. She gave a look of indifference then turned back to Dan.

"Not that I want to stick around here."

They both laughed for a moment. Finally, Dan cleared his throat. "Well, I know some people who will be mighty excited to see you've come back. Besides, I never liked it much around here anyway."

Pauline glanced around. The road back to the ranch was dark and treacherous. But with Dan and Jesse, Pauline knew she would be safe.

"Okay then," Pauline tilted her head and gave him a look of adoration, "if you say so."

They unhitched Jesse and hopped on as he groaned. Dan helped her up and she put her arms around his waist. It felt better than any time before. The voice in Pauline's mind, which had told her not to let herself enjoy her time with Dan, had disappeared. It had been replaced with a soft, warm one that told her to appreciate every second the two of them spent together.

Jesse galloped at a moderate pace. They even passed a few travelers along the way. Nightlife made their delicate sounds around them. Pauline listened to the nocturnal insects buzzing beneath the clatter of Jesse's galloping. Looking up in the darkness, she saw the moon and stars swirling overhead.

Though she had grown tired of travel by night, there was a sense of completion to this ride. It allowed her to appreciate the beauty of the valley. When they reached the mountain pass, Pauline no longer feared the dark. Instead, she tightened her arms around Dan as he and Jesse navigated the invisible path. Before she knew it, they were back beneath the moonlight, and the ranch appeared on the horizon.

From a distance, Pauline could see a campfire still ablaze. As they made their way closer, Pauline felt a surge of emotion as she saw the crowd begin to gather. Familiar voices hollered to one another, and they sounded excited as they rallied the others awake. By the time they reached the rest of the team, most of them were awake, celebrating Dan's return with Pauline. The warm reception was beyond anything she could've expected.

In the darkness, as the two of them dismounted, Pauline saw the glow of Dorothy's face in the firelight. She ran toward the old lady and threw her arms around her.

"Oh, my goodness, sweetheart Pauline, you came back!"

Pauline heard and felt the tears of relief as Dorothy spoke.

"Dan saved me. You owe it all to him."

"I owe it to the both of you," Dorothy said as she sniffled. "I'm just glad you came back."

Pauline closed her eyes and held Dorothy in her arms. She thought about Allen and his men. Had it not been for Dan's last-ditch effort, Pauline never would have been able to see them again. She knew exactly why she had to go. It would not have been fair for them to suffer on her behalf. She told herself to explain her reasoning. Moments later, she realized she did not have to.

"I had to come back," she said with her eyes closed, "you all are my family now."

Dorothy squeezed her even tighter. "It is so good to hear you say that."

Pauline opened her eyes when she heard footsteps coming toward them. She looked and saw Ross, standing awkwardly as he waited for the two of them to finish.

"I, uh, hope I'm not interrupting anything private over here."

Pauline gave him a weird glance, to which Ross winked playfully. Dorothy let go and put a hand on Pauline's shoulder before walking off.

"Pauline," he began, "I just wanted to tell you I am sorry. This whole thing never would have happened if I hadn't been yapping at the saloon before Allen came around."

He looked at the ground. Pauline was seeing a different side of Ross. There was a seriousness in the way he stood there, ashamed of what he believed to be his fault. Pauline put her hand on his arm and gave a warm smile.

"You didn't know," she assured him. "How could you?"

Ross gave a nervous smile and waited for her to continue.

"Besides," she nudged him, "I would have just had to keep running. Thanks to you, we got to figure out who really did it."

Ross's eyes lit up at the revelation.

"Well, I'll be..." he paused and looked around with a victorious expression before turning back at her with his mouth agape.

"Ain't that the dang truth! Hey Dan!"

Ross grabbed Pauline by the hand and pulled her behind as he made his way to Dan. He continued yelling his name as Pauline couldn't help but laugh. They found him talking to some of the other men when Ross broke up the conversation.

"Dan! Pauline made the best point." He looked at her and smiled. "Tell him what you told me!" He nodded, waiting for her to continue.

Dan let out a laugh. "What's this all about?" he asked, looking back and forth at them.

"Oh," Pauline laughed as well, "Ross got happy when I pointed out that if it weren't for him talking at the saloon, we may have never figured out about Charley."

Dan looked at Ross with one raised eyebrow.

"And also, you would have had to keep running from Allen!" Ross reminded her. "That was what you said!"

Dan smiled in a way Pauline had never seen before. His eyes gleamed in the darkness as they looked back at her.

"Well, I suppose that's true." He nodded. "Thank you, Ross. Your big mouth may have saved the whole dang caravan."

"You bet your bottom dollar it did!" Ross pointed at him. "I'm not going to sleep until everybody knows it too!" He did a dance that made Dan and Pauline laugh some more.

Finally, Ross walked away from them, trying his best to talk to the others as they ignored his story. Dan and Pauline stood there together now, with no one else around. They heard Ross' voice trailing off into the distance as they looked at each other.

"Hey," Pauline greeted.

"Hey," Dan replied.

The two of them stood there, unsure what to say next.

"It's, uh, getting pretty late," Dan said as he scratched his neck. "I had the boys make you a sleeping arrangement here next to mine. I hope that's okay."

Pauline let out a laugh. "Of course, it is."

They said good night to each other. She waited for a kiss that never came. That was okay, she thought. The two of them had the rest of their lives now. As she laid in her cot, Pauline thought about her future with Dan. It gave her a feeling of peace; one she had never experienced before. Moments later, she drifted off to sleep.

Pauline woke up the next morning at the sound of Dan stirring awake. *It was real*, she thought to herself. She had not woken up back in the saloon on the broken twin bedframe. The mere idea jolted her out of bed. By the time she got out of her tent, Dan was sitting outside with two fresh mugs of coffee.

"Morning," he nodded and handed her a cup. Pauline took the coffee and held it up to her nose. She took a deep breath and looked at him with glowing eyes.

"Good morning," she replied.

The sunlight peaked out from behind the mountains. Dodge City was now a distant memory. She stared at the horizon and let out a sigh of relief. The clouds had been brushed onto the sky. It was beautiful. Dan cleared his throat and got her attention.

"I was thinking we could start our way back to Windy Reach. We could leave right away or wait 'til later in the day if you need to. Whatever you're most comfortable with."

Pauline was taken aback. The idea had not yet crossed her mind. She sat down on the log next to him and stared off as she shook her head. Windy Reach. The place where she had been married to Herschel and accused of murder. Pauline had long since accepted that she would never be able to go back there.

"I... I don't know. Do you think it's too soon for me?"

"Too soon for what?" Dan asked as he sat across from her on the other log.

"I mean, everyone thinks I'm a murderer, remember?" She spoke as if it were plainly obvious to everyone but Dan.

"Not anymore," he said. "Allen caught the real killer."

Pauline put her head in the hand not holding her coffee. It was too much for her to think about. She feared they all saw her as a murderer. What would they say if she came back to town with a new man? How would they react to Dan? She knew how the people in town talked and it scared her.

"That don't matter to everyone. I ran. People are always going to say it was really me. And they're going to think you're the next man I want to kill."

She started to feel hopeless again, as if it would never get resolved. It was almost as if Herschel was haunting her from beyond the grave. First there was Allen; next, the town of Windy Reach. She continued shaking her head.

"That's why I say we go back," Dan said.

Pauline looked up at him. He had a face of determination. It gave her a sense of confidence as she waited for him to continue.

"If you never show your face again, yes, there is always going to be that chatter. And going back now, they will all get the chance to see how amazing you really are, Pauline. Now that Herschel isn't there, it won't be like that. I won't let anyone give you any problems."

As Dan spoke, a weight lifted off her chest. Dan was promising things would be better. She knew he would make sure of it.

"You're right." She looked at him and smiled. "Let's go."

Deep down, Pauline still felt uneasy about going back so soon. At the same time, however, Allen was on the way back with the real murderer. She knew Dan would protect her from the gossip of the townspeople. Things would be different. She was willing to face her fears as long as Dan was there to back her up.

He stood up and took her hand. Dan had already gotten the rest of the team to help them pack their belongings. Jesse was cleaned up and ready for them to go. Pauline made eye contact with the horse and saw he had forgiven her.

People gathered around to say goodbye to Pauline. It was bittersweet. Dorothy, Henry, and Ross were the hardest for her. She promised each one of them they would see each other again as soon as they could. When they began to ride off, she watched as the group waved. Most of them stood there until she could no longer see them. The caravan had shown her that good people were still out there.

Her arms around Dan also reminded her of that. In the daylight, she felt no fear of being seen. In the afterlife, Herschel had continued to cast a shadow over her existence.

As she rode back to her home with Dan and Jesse, Pauline smiled. She had cast that shadow away for good. She was free.

***

One week later, Dan and Pauline saw Windy Reach appear on the horizon. It was early in the morning and the sun had just finished rising from behind it. By the time they made their way into town, people were out and about. Familiar faces hardly noticed as she rode past them. She looked out from behind Dan.

"Where are we headed?" she asked him nervously.

"I thought we could see your father," he told her as he stared ahead. "Does that work?"

"Absolutely," she told him and hugged his torso tight for a moment. Pauline gave him directions and they arrived at his home. Pauline dismounted and ran toward the doors. By the time she reached the porch, her father had swung the door open. She threw her arms around him as he began to cry.

"My Pauline. I heard about Allen and I..." He turned to Dan who stood behind her. "Thank you so much, sir, I was worried sick this whole time."

Dan stepped forward and greeted Pauline's father. They went inside and talked some more. It was therapeutic, telling her dad about Charley. He had heard rumors about it around the town after the team had left. The Sheriff had admitted to finding new evidence but declared the case a lost cause after Allen and his men took off. He had been angry at the town, though there was nothing any of them could do. That had only made his frustration worse.

Pauline's father fought back tears as he spoke. He had been completely isolated among the rest of Windy Reach.

Nobody had thought Pauline to be the killer, he knew it, though they did not wish to interfere with Allen. All he could do was wait and hope justice would be served.

"And then I hoped," he stuttered, "maybe, just maybe, you'd come back, Pauline. No one would have told Allen. His men nearly drank the town dry."

"The good news is they have Charley," Dan informed him, "I bet they get things over with quick though. Allen was ready to go home when we last saw him. I don't think they'll be around long, not after the whole mix-up."

Pauline saw tears on her father's face. He was still in disbelief Pauline was back. She could tell as she looked around the house that he had been grieving. That was when Pauline realized her father had felt just as hopeless as she did.

"Daddy," she said, "if it weren't for Dan over here, no one would have believed me." She put her hand on top of Dan's. Pauline's father looked at Dan with a warm glow on his face.

"Well then, Dan, thank you for believing in my Pauline. It means the world to me you would go such great lengths to protect her. If there's ever anything you need, please, don't hesitate to ask."

Dan nodded and looked around at them. "It's been my pleasure to get to know her."

Dan paused and looked around for a second. Pauline could sense he was nervous as his body shook beneath her palm. What was going on with him?

"Say, Pauline," he looked over at her, "would you mind letting us talk for a moment, man to man?"

The question caught her off guard. She looked and saw some sort of insistence in his eyes. What was this for? Did he want to collect reward money? Pauline began to worry. Could she be wrong? Was Dan lying about who he was? She tried not to let her mind wander too far.

"It'll just be a moment," Dan said, "nothing bad, I promise."

The words gave her a sense of relief.

"I suppose I can do that," she said, still not wholly sure what was happening. She stepped out on the front porch and looked around. Jesse stood there waiting. She stepped over to him and brushed his face.

"You know, Jesse, I don't think I ever truly thanked you for saving me."

Jesse let out a neigh of approval. She stared into his eyes and felt a bond. Just as she pulled away, the door swung open, and Dan stepped outside.

"You ready?" he asked.

"Ready for what?"

Pauline looked inside and saw her father standing there. He looked sad, maybe. She could not tell for certain. What was going on? Where was he going to take her?

"Dan, what's going on?" She began to tremble. Questions ran through her mind so quickly she could not get them out. Dan walked up to her and looked down. Pauline's stomach was turning inside.

"I was going to do this someplace else, but I guess now is as good a time as any."

He got down on one knee and looked up at her, taking her hand in his.

"Pauline," he paused.

She saw the look in his eyes and twitched. Was this really happening?

"I just spoke with your father. I told him I love you. And after that, he gave me permission to ask for your hand in marriage. So, I'm asking now, Pauline, will you marry me?"

"Oh my..." She wanted to scream. Her heart fluttered in her chest.

"Dan," her voice was weak, "Dan, yes!"

He stood up and smiled, putting his hands on her arms. "You're going to make me the happiest man alive."

She looked up and parted her lips. Dan leaned in toward her. Pauline closed her eyes. When their lips finally touched, Dan was warm and tasted sweet. Dan's stubble brushed against her cheek. It felt so natural to her. They kissed a few more times before she pulled away.

"I still just can't believe this is how things turned out for me."

She looked inside and saw her father crying tears of happiness. He already approved of Dan, knowing everything he had done to save his daughter. Dan looked at him and nodded, then back at Pauline.

"If you want, we could stay here in Windy Reach. I still got my ranch. If you need to start over someplace else though, we could sell it. I'll be happy anywhere if I'm there with you."

"Oh Dan," she shook her head, "you're the sweetest."

She looked around her at her father's property. As much as she loved the idea of starting someplace fresh, Pauline could not leave him there. He deserved to see his daughter happy.

"I want to stay," she declared.

They looked at each other and smiled before kissing one more time. Pauline thought about her life in Windy Reach. She never hated living here. She hated living with Herschel. Now that he was gone, Pauline could let go of her fear. Instead of dreading the future, she looked forward to being with Dan and beginning their life together. All was bright on the new horizon.

Pauline let out a deep sigh of relief. It was the start of a new chapter. She was home.

Epilogue

Dan woke up at sunrise to tend the livestock. The sun had not yet risen in the sky. This was his best chance to get the work done. It was another day on their ranch. He had gotten the farm up and running after a long period of trial and error. He stepped outside and saw the first touch of light on the eastern skyline. There was little time to be wasted.

Today was a special day. It marked the one-year anniversary of marriage with Pauline. He wanted to do something special for her. Dan had not said a word about it, hoping she would think he had forgotten. He knew he had to be quick. Soon, their newborn daughter would be waking up, hungry and ready to be changed. They had named her Dorothy. She was only two months old but was already smiling and laughing.

The two of them had replaced the ghosts Dan had known. Instead of hearing his trauma repeated in the silence of the empty rooms, the house became filled with life once again. Pauline loved to sing. Sometimes he would stop what he was doing just to listen. Her voice was soft and delicate with perfect pitch. She and Dorothy would play, their laughter echoing throughout the property. Right now, however, things were silent.

It no longer bothered Dan. There were times when he appreciated it now that it was a rarity. The lack of noise gave him the space to meditate and process everything. He fed the cows and gave them water before checking in on the chicken coop. The smell was rotten. It was one of Pauline's least favorite things to do. That was why he had gotten up early. He wanted her to have the perfect day, just as their wedding had been. They'd had a small ceremony on the property and fell asleep that night as soon as they laid down. Everybody from the caravan traveled to Arizona to celebrate.

Dan thought back to that day as the sun continued to rise in the sky, illuminating everything around him. The chirping of the birds interrupted his thoughts until he went over and saw Jesse. As he fed the horse, Dan remembered getting back from their journey. He had almost lost both Jesse and Pauline. The entire experience had changed him for the better. Thanks to his determination, and Jesse being the trustworthy steed he was, things had ended as they should have.

He shook his head in disbelief. He had never expected to find love again. He was not sure if he had wanted to, either. That was what made him so conflicted over Pauline to begin with. He had been so transformed by his grief that it seemed unattainable for him. It took everything that happened for him to be able to open back up to someone. Sometimes he could feel Martha and Johnny in spirit. It gave him comfort to know they were watching over him. There was no regret anymore, only a sense of closure.

Suddenly, Dan heard the baby crying inside. Dorothy had woken up earlier than normal. If he wanted to give Pauline the day she deserved, he had to run in and pick her up before she cried too long. By the time he made it inside, her bedroom door was open. Dan could hear the chair creaking. He walked up and saw Pauline sitting there, just as beautiful as she had ever been, with baby Dorothy in her arms. Dan stopped in the doorway and smiled at her as she rocked. Dorothy smiled up at him and made a happy noise.

"I tried to beat you here," he said to her warmly. "You were too quick for me."

"Well, if that's the case, why'd you go outside and give me a head start?" she quipped playfully as baby Dorothy giggled.

Dan let out a laugh. She had a point. Pauline was good at keeping him on his toes. She gave Dan a challenge he loved.

Over the last year, Dan had seen her personality blossom now that she was no longer on the run or a victim. He had loved her as she was then, but it made him so happy to see who Pauline had become. Her natural wit allowed Pauline to always be one step ahead of him. He looked up and saw she was waiting for his response.

"I did all the work outside. Fed the animals, cleaned the coop, and got them all fresh water. After that I was going to get her up so you could sleep a little longer," he said with a laugh, "and after *that* I was hoping to make breakfast."

Pauline gave a hearty laugh and looked at him with a glowing admiration. "Why on earth did you think you could do all that?"

Dan shrugged. "I wanted today to be special. You know what it is, right?"

Pauline nodded. "It's our one-year anniversary. You know I would never forget."

"Me either," he said.

They looked at each other for a moment. Dan took in her loving gaze. He knew he did not have to do anything. It was that he wanted to. Then Dorothy made a noise.

"Are we not paying enough attention to you?" Dan said in his sweet voice.

Dorothy smiled at him and stuck out her arms. He came over and picked her up. She ran her hands in his beard and giggled.

"She's becoming a daddy's girl," Pauline said as she stood up. She put her face in Dorothy's. The baby made a noise and pushed her away.

"See what I mean?" she yelled playfully.

"That's why I can't go on any more drives, isn't it?" Dan said to her in his baby voice. "Dorothy would scream the whole time I'm away. Wouldn't you?"

She let out another giggle. Dan stared into her eyes. They looked just like Pauline's, though she insisted the baby looked more like him.

"You know you can go," Pauline reminded him, "I can handle her, and you know the money would help."

"I know," Dan said as he kept staring at Dorothy, "but how could I leave? Look at her!"

Pauline rolled her eyes. "Oh yes, you say that every time Henry, Dorothy, and the boys come by. You should go, Dan. You always love catching up with them whenever they come around."

"That's because we sit by the fire and talk about life on the road. That doesn't mean I want to do it again." He turned back to baby Dorothy, and she smiled.

"Maybe when you're older," he said to her.

Dan was in no rush to leave. He had been lucky to get a second chance at happiness with Pauline and their daughter. That was more important to him than work. The three of them had everything they needed in each other.

THE END

Also by Sally M. Ross

Thank you for reading "**A Hunted Bride for the Suspicious Cowboy**"!

I hope you enjoyed it! If you did, here are some of my other books!

Also, if you liked this book, you can also check out **my full Amazon Book Catalogue at:**
https://go.sallymross.com/bc-authorpage

Thank you for allowing me to keep doing what I love! ❤

Printed in Great Britain
by Amazon